D0397463

ALLAN, BURNING

Also by Donald Everett Axinn

poetry

Sliding Down the Wind
The Hawk's Dream and Other Poems
Against Gravity
The Colors of Infinity
Dawn Patrol
The Latest Illusion
Change as a Curved Equation
El sueño del halcón
Walking Through the Night
Caminando a través de la noche
Travel in My Borrowed Lives

fiction

Spin
The Ego Makers

ALLAN, BURNING

A Novel

DONALD EVERETT AXINN

Arcade Publishing • New York

Copyright © 2009 by Donald Everett Axinn

All rights reserved. No part of this book may be reproduced in any form or by any electronic or mechanical means, including information storage and retrieval systems, without permission in writing from the publisher, except by a reviewer who may quote brief passages in a review.

FIRST EDITION

This is a work of fiction. Names, characters, places, and incidents are either the work of the author's imagination or are used fictitiously.

Library of Congress Cataloging-in-Publication Data

Axinn, Donald E.
Allan, burning : a novel / Donald Everett Axinn. — 1st ed.
p. cm.
ISBN 978-1-55970-915-6 (alk. paper)
1. Architects—Fiction. 2. Indians of North America—Crimes against—Fiction. 3. Murder—Investigation—Fiction. 4. Florida—Fiction. I. Title.

PS3551.X5A75 2009
813'.54—dc22 2009003697

Published in the United States by Arcade Publishing, Inc., New York
Distributed by Hachette Book Group

Visit our Web site at www.arcadepub.com

10 9 8 7 6 5 4 3 2 1

Designed by API

EB

PRINTED IN THE UNITED STATES OF AMERICA

For Dick Seaver, renowned publisher, splendid editor, and magnificent friend, remembered for his contributions that left the world of quality literature a far better place.

To family and friends. You know who you are. Your support and love are never taken for granted.

For Joan, best and only wife, with my everlasting gratitude for coming into my life.

And for the Miccosukee tribe of American Indians of Florida. With respect and admiration, for your history of courage and perseverence. And for how *Hishuk-ish-ts'awalk* will always be an essential truth.

I suppose that it is not so easy to go home and takes
a bit of time to make a son out of a stranger.

Albert Camus

Happiness is not everything and men have their duties.
Mine is to find my mother, a homeland.

Albert Camus

Fate will bring together those a thousand miles apart; without fate,
they will miss each other though they come face to face.

Chinese proverb

What is life? It is a flash of firefly at night.
It is the breath of a buffalo in wintertime.
It is the little shadow which runs across
the grass and loses itself in the sunset.

Crowfoot

ALLAN, BURNING

1

Allan Daniels gazed down at the scene below, mesmerized by the endless, mystifying expanse of the Everglades. He had thought and wondered about them, but actually being here, seeing their disquieting loveliness, made him feel strange. He pulled down the visor of his Yankees baseball cap to block the blinding sunlight streaming in the front left side of his seaplane. *Mother born down there somewhere . . . Indian structure . . . called it a . . . a chickee.* He lifted the camera from around his neck and took several pictures. *Said her reservation was west of my route.*

The long solo flight from Port Washington on Long Island to Key West had become eerie and at times transcendental. Allan had begun to imagine he was simply watching, observing, floating, soaring, as if he and plane had become one, that this strange, ineffable, and remarkable feeling was happening in a dream.

Without warning, the Cessna 185 shuddered as if it were being strangled, jolting Allan out of his reverie. The engine began to miss, its reassuring monotone compromised.

"Damn it!" he yelled. "Damn it! Why here? Shit! Why now?" He slammed his fist on the leather-padded instrument panel and closed his eyes, trying to shut out the inescapable reality. "OK, stay cool. Figure it out." *Dirt or water in the fuel lines,* he reasoned, seeking an acceptable explanation.

From remembered training, he automatically reached down for the fuel selector switch, located on the floor between the two front seats, and quickly shifted it from "Both" to "Left." The engine continued to cough in spurts, sounding gravely ill. The plane began to lose precious altitude, no longer willing to behave.

Allan peered down at the paralyzing mangrove swamps and groundless marsh savanna. A shiver raced across the back of his shoulders. *Few canals far between. No boat . . . roads. Shit. Should have learned more about them, the Miccosukees, how they managed, how they survived . . .*

He stared intently off both sides in turn. Absolutely nothing except the terrifying brown-green mangrove and algae, swamps that looked like an endless vomit of chaos. No sign that anyone had ever been down there except, he knew, his mother's people. White men? Only someone bent on escape or self-destruction. Someone whose pain had become unbearable, someone whose future appeared futile and hopeless.

Allan quickly turned the fuel selector to "Right." The engine immediately resumed its reassuring pitch and cadence. "Thank God!" He sighed and patted the top of the panel, grinned, bowing his head to an imaginary audience of fellow pilots. He swung the plane back on course, regaining the original 6,500-foot altitude. He banked the right wing and at the same time depressed the right rudder pedal. The compass rotated, the HSI settling on 210 degrees. He repositioned the selector to "Both."

Dirt or water in the line, yeah, that was what I . . . back on track . . . we're go!

In less than an hour's time he'd be setting down on top of the resplendent turquoise water in front of the Key West seaplane base. He fantasized the pontoons cutting two parallel lines into a glistening, unruffled surface, a beautiful finish and well-earned feelings, the result of his mettle and competence.

It was stifling in the plane, even with air pouring in from the two vents on either side, where the front window met the wings. Perspiration soaked through his shirt; his thighs and butt stuck to the seat. The swollen humidity felt like some kind of additional challenge or punishment.

His mind wandered. *She's the one wants to separate, I don't! So I raised some problems about our marriage, but that doesn't mean separation.*

Ferrying this seaplane offered Allan a chance to get away for a few days. Out of the blue, just before he took off, Joyce had announced she wanted a separation. She must have met someone else, must be having an affair. He didn't want to believe that but couldn't shake it from his mind.

Still, marriage does change . . . we used to be close, so romantic. But after Nance and Craig were born, her focus . . . and her career . . . True, she's drifted away, gone in another direction. But I never expected this!

The night before he had departed — flight plan filed, clothes chosen, and gear packed — Allan stood in front of his sink in their bathroom. He began to brush his teeth, gazed into the mirror, and peered at the gray in his hair. His very dark brown eyes looked weary. His long, angular face was drawn. A dark stubble made him look grizzled and tough. His body's movements usually flowed and were the confident ones of an athlete. He straightened up, brought his face close to the mirror, and whispered, "You'll get through this." He rinsed, then looked up again. *Some combination . . . that's what you get having a Miccosukee mother and Russian Jewish father . . . quite a package. Joyce sounded so final . . . this trip . . . chance to think things through . . . choices . . . solutions . . .*

Allan scanned the sky. The moist cumuli hung haphazardly, all plumped up like puffed cotton, like whipped cream. But he knew there might be dark dragons lurking, out of sight behind the cumuli, poised to slam any plane that ventured near. He badly wanted the trip to be finished and knew he had to concentrate even more because he was exhausted. No mistakes in judgment now, especially over these treacherous Everglades.

Nothingness. Pay attention, Allan! Only one more hour to Key West.

He regretted not having borrowed a handheld radio. And the plane's navigational aid, a Loran, had been sent back to the factory for repair. Over New Jersey, Maryland, Virginia, the Carolinas, Georgia, and Florida before he reached the Everglades, it had been relatively easy to compare a sectional map on his lap to what he was flying over: highways, a town or city, lakes, rivers, railways, radio towers, or the coastline. Particularly airports, especially the bigger ones, or a large plant, all located exactly where they were supposed to be. Key points to confirm his position, but here . . .

Allan liked being alone, but there were times when being completely alone for too long felt like being homeless. He recalled as a youngster in the Boy Scouts getting lost in a forest. He had to spend the night there but found it wasn't as scary as he had feared.

And his fear of heights. At age eight, at the family's summer house in Pine Hill, upstate New York, Allan had refused to climb to the top of the eleven-story fire tower on Bellaire Mountain. On a day when his sister and cousins had wandered off exploring, he had forced himself to start up the tower. Jaw clenched, he kept moving. When he reached the third level, he looked down, grabbed the rail tightly, sure he would fall. *I have to get to the top at any cost,* he remembered thinking later on (he found that funny). He continued on hands and knees until he reached the lookout platform. He stood up carefully, held onto the railing, looked straight down onto the tops of the evergreens. Tears welled in his eyes. He began to smile, then laugh. When he saw them return, he yelled down in triumph.

And in college, leading six other students in a winter climb up Mt. Marcy in the Adirondacks on snowshoes, on the second day a heavy snowfall forced them to turn back to the previous night's lean-to. Joan had been bringing up the rear. They waited an hour, but she didn't show. He told the others to stay put while he went back up. A few hours later, Allan appeared carrying her. She had badly sprained an ankle. "Hot tea," he ordered calmly. "We'll rig some kind of sled. I'll pull. You guys break trail."

All of a sudden, the engine sputtered, spit one last time, and quit, pulling him rudely from his dream.

He moved the fuel selection gauge, pumped the primer, pressed the starter button. Nothing. "All right," he screamed, "go shit in your hat!"

Eleven hundred miles from Long Island, almost at the finish line. Damn!

A flash of adrenaline ran down one arm. Only quiescence and the swamps below for company. The altimeter began to unwind like a clock running backward. Forty-five hundred feet. He nosed the plane down to prevent losing too much airspeed and stalling, and set the best angle of glide that would permit maximum time before gravity brought him down for good. Four thousand feet. Thirty-five hundred. Three thousand. He banked the plane into a shallow left turn.

Where to put this thing down? You're an architect . . . design a nice big lake to land on, Lake Champlain . . . you wish!

He pressed the microphone button, something he should have done when the engine first began to act up.

"Miami Center, Mayday, Mayday! Cessna floatplane nine-nine-eight-zero-two, approximately one hundred miles northeast Key West. Heading . . . two-one-zero. Squawking one-twenty-one-point-five! Any aircraft! Coast Guard! Mayday! Mayday! Acknowledge!"

Allan realized he was trapped in a nightmare with no escape. He became riveted on finding any span of water long enough to set down on without tearing the plane apart. Not to mention himself.

2

GOING DOWN. No choice. No decision. "Miami Centrr . . . Cessn fltplnn . . . Cannot . . . fixx on yyy . . . Switch too . . . Do you reee . . ." Like a beacon going dark in a violent northeaster.

That was all, except the distressing sound of the wind moaning through the wing struts. The propeller turned slowly, like a broken windmill. In a dream the previous night, in the Hampton Inn near the seaplane base in South Carolina, he was sailing above the exotic, turquoise water of the Florida Keys. Allan wasn't afraid of anything. He had floated over it, arms spread into wings. But, like Icarus, he fell, crashing into the sea. He survived, swam for hours, and finally crawled up on the beach of a swanky resort. All the guests applauded. The general manager placed a garland around his neck.

Always land into the wind, except when you can't . . . put this son of a bitch down on anything watery. Moccasins, rattlers, alligators . . . you'll handle them later. Wait! That channel! There! Real short . . . touch down at the far end where it straightens a little, maybe enough. Plunk it down on the back end of the pontoons in a full stall.

Allan gripped the pilot's control wheel tightly, foreboding adding its contribution. To make sure he didn't overshoot where he'd decided he must touch down, he put the plane into a slip, left aileron and right rudder. With the nose raised, the plane slowed its forward motion. He held it in an attitude just above a stall, continuing to slip into the crosswind, making sure he maintained the necessary minimum air speed. The plane's pontoons would have to plunk down onto the water's surface at exactly the spot he had selected. He removed his hand from the throttle, aware the motor was dead, and quickly switched the fuel selector to the "off" position to reduce any chance of fire. Concentration was matched by anxiety. The plane slid down neatly, just scraping the mangroves. As it brushed the branches, he eliminated the slip, pulling the yoke fully back. A solid, near-perfect landing, the plane's feet breaking through the flat, stagnant surface like perfectly balanced skis marking grooved lines on a blanket of fresh snow. "All right, all right!" he shouted, then raised his middle finger in a "fuck you" gesture.

The seaplane slowed to a standstill. He turned off all the switches and breakers. Rotating beacon, avionics, alternator, fuel pump, mags, master. Absolute quiet. No sound of motor, no rush of air through the vents. Only the slosh of water against the pontoons. "Now the fun begins," he declared with a wry laugh.

White herons, their legs like thin reeds, stood frozen in their fishing stances at the edges of the channel. Twisted mangrove roots spread into the water under their mantles of leaves. The flow of water remained continuous, although not easily discernible. Once in a while, a flurry of motion underneath, sometimes over a wide area but usually a small flip or watery blurb. As the seaplane drifted closer, the herons scattered, unable to cope with the unfeathered pterodactyl that had come to shove them off their habitat. When it didn't attack, they settled back to their fishing stations, the choice locations commandeered by the larger birds.

The breeze blew the seaplane up against the mangrove roots. Allan reached for the door handle and let the door swing open, breathing in the thick, meaty air of the Everglades. Water lapped against the pontoons like the slow beat of a kettledrum. He sat motionless.

Eleven hundred miles but can't make the last fucking hundred. Son of a bitch. I'll string up those bastards who sold me this lousy fuel.

He unbuckled his seat and shoulder belts and took a deep breath. "What now, Captain Midnight?" he murmured. *Stay with the plane . . . no place to go unless you plan to walk on water. That would solve the problem, wouldn't it? Except you're just a bit out of practice.*

Nothing stirred except an occasional heron flashing its head into the water. Something rustled nearby on the bank of the channel. An alligator? A big moccasin?

Too late for search planes. *Tomorrow. No big deal . . . could have been worse . . . could have busted your body into small pieces.*

3

THE SUN SANK LOWER AND PLANTED SHADOWS from the vines, dark curves that looked like writhing black snakes. Allan pulled the small anchor from its storage compartment, stepped carefully out on the front of the left pontoon, and threw it into the breeze; he did the same off the right rear pontoon. He tugged on the anchors until they held, securing the ropes around the cleats. Allan sat, arms around his knees, scrutinizing the mangroves.

Search and rescue . . . tomorrow, for sure.

Newsday *headlines: "Long Island Architect Lost in the Everglades. Search Continues." Pan to Bogart on the* African Queen *. . . cut, bruised, delirious. Daniels staggers through the Swamps of Hades . . . almost gives up but survives against incredible obstacles.*

A sharp, hot sensation ran down his arm as he thought about the last time he put his kids to bed. "Daddy, are you really going away?" Nancy asked with a little sadness in her voice, pouting, her arms crossed. Then she ran across the room, jumped into his arms, and sank her face in his neck. "Please, Daddy, please. I miss you already."

Nance was long and lean and eight. Her face reminded him of Joyce's: large forehead, ears exactly the right size nestled inside soft, almost rust-colored hair. Her eyes were engaging and dark brown like his. She was born with a pronounced birthmark on her right cheek, which they were going to have removed but decided against it. Her teeth were slightly crooked, to be straightened by an orthodontist as soon as they settled on when to begin.

"Me too, me too," Craig cried out as he threw his arms tightly around one of Allan's legs. "Take me with you, Daddy. I will be your best helper!" He looked up with his delicate face, his almost jet-black hair cut into short bangs across his forehead. His eyes were blue-green like his mother's, his chin longer than his sister's. His ears protruded a little. The five-year-old's frown almost made Allan laugh. Allan enjoyed observing Craig's energy and the determination he applied to almost everything he encountered. *I was just like that,* he mused.

Allan reached down, lifted Craig and his sister into his arms. "Hey, my little lambs, not to worry. They've asked me to ferry a seaplane down south. Only be away three days. Four at the most." They looked a little sullen and didn't respond. "Hey, when I come back, we'll go away for a weekend. You know, up to Middlebury. Homecoming."

"Without me, I'm afraid," Joyce said with emphasis as she entered the children's bedroom. "And I'll tell you which weekend." She pulled the kids together, kissing each on the head, then dropped to her knees and hugged them again.

"Bear Mountain," Nance said emphatically, "Bear Mountain!"

"We'll vote on it," Allan said cheerily. "Maybe we can change Mommy's mind." To which Joyce shook her head and mouthed the word "no."

4

BEAUTIFUL JOYCE. EXQUISITE JOYCE. Magna cum laude from Smith. Usually reserved, unpretentious, no makeup, confident with her intellect but surprisingly less assured than when they first met. That changed later. Tall, willowy, auburn-haired, not always constant with her friends but initially single-tracked about Allan. They met when he was a senior at Middlebury, right after he had played in a baseball game against Williams. Her brother, Jay, introduced them.

Allan was immediately captivated. He had trouble taking his eyes off her, and when he did it was only because he didn't want anyone to notice how smitten he was. Her expressions, the way she moved, the way she listened. Her provocative features, seductive eyes, smooth cheeks, sensual mouth, that delicate nose. When she swung her head, her hair made him want to sink his face in it, find all the inviting places on her neck and kiss each one.

She wore contact lenses. "Not vanity," she told Allan after a few dates. "Easier than glasses." To which he responded that her eyes mesmerized him. It was weird. She seemed to know exactly what he was thinking, what he felt.

Joyce had a way of hugging herself, wrapping her hands around her arms. "Hey, stop," Allan said during their umpteenth date, "all hugs now include me. Like this," he added with a smile, squeezing her to him. "I love feeling your body this way," he said, to which she simply giggled.

"Allan," she said a few moments later, "my parents . . ."

"What about them?"

"They're a little concerned . . . about your being . . .

half-Indian. I mean, not that they have any prejudice, it's just so unusual. You know."

"For me, too." He laughed. "Sometimes I look at myself in the mirror. Like I'm split — the Jewish half with the Indian half. Indian and Jewish . . . gets confusing."

"You should talk about it more," she said slowly, turning toward him. "How it makes you feel."

"Look, I don't hide who I am. It's just that I've never been — how should I put it — curious about my mother's people." He drew a couple of fingers over his eyes. "Oh, she's told us about their history and customs. Very interesting actually. And I sure don't want to hurt her. But my life's here, not there."

"Well, if we get . . ."

"Hey, what do you mean *if*? We are, we will."

"Our children, we'd certainly want them to know about their heritage, all of it, both sides."

"Tell you what," he answered, pulling her down next to him. "I'll get you some books." He grinned. "And when I meet your parents, I'll dress up in tribal clothes. Introduce myself as Chief Running Bigshit. Demand restitution for kicking us off our hunting and fishing grounds so you whites could build your sterile towns and crowded cities on our sacred lands. Idiotic and destructive concrete jungles and subdivisions. Drive around in those stupid jeeps and trucks. Attacking and destroying our natural resources. Raping our lands."

"That'll go over really big, you schmuck. But you can understand that my parents had expected someone *one-hundred percent* Jewish for their darling daughter."

"Makum no difference," Allan continued. "Me big warrior, takum you squaw. Parents no like, me havum brothers torch wigwam. Scare shit out of them. They say, 'OK, yeah. You takum daughter. Too much college. Gottum big head, big ideas.'"

Joyce laughed.

"You, me, we makum nice, fat children, lots of them," Allan continued. "More Jewish-Indians." He turned around to face her. "We hitch up, movum reservation. You learn live Indian-style. I build Indian synogogues. Call first one Temple Bris." Allan was clearly having fun.

"Are you making fun of Indians?"

"Of course not. Sorry. My distorted sense of humor. Making it sound ridiculous that Indians talk that way." He shook his head. "*No* Indian talks that way today. A hundred and fifty years ago maybe, when they were forced to learn English."

She grabbed his hand. "You can kid around, but we're lucky this isn't a few generations ago. One of my mother's cousins married a Gentile. Had to move away. Maine, somewhere. Nobody ever heard from them again." She looked straight in his eyes. "But you and I, my sexy Indian, are going to have us a nice, sweet Jewish wedding. And you, my dear, will have to put on a suit. Not your usual jeans and sweater."

He waited a moment, looked at her earnestly, and responded. "Sure, if that's what you want. I may kid around about being half-Indian, but there's not much I can do about it."

"But there is," she responded soberly. "You know beans about your Miccosukee heritage. Find out more from your mother."

Allan shrugged. "I don't know much about Judaism, either. It's not that important, where somebody comes from."

"Really? You surprise me," she said strongly. "Where have you been? People want to know. Business, politics, clubs. You, especially. You wouldn't have gotten those scholarships if you weren't Indian."

"Yeah, I suppose so."

"Don't forget, our children will be one-quarter. That's still Indian." He nodded, kissed her long and deep. And didn't stop.

♦ ♦ ♦

Sexual attraction, pure and very simple. At the beginning, he got only a sense of her body. Great breasts, nicely rounded rear end, flat stomach. Allan liked all of it. Initially, that might have been enough, but when they were together more and more, he realized how they resonated, how what she said and believed added greatly to his understanding of his own thoughts and feelings. He decided he would do everything, anything, to make her his own on a permanent basis. He only hoped she wanted the same.

Those expressions of hers were like doors opening into the rooms of her emotions. He learned to wait and see if there would be laughter, challenge, anger, affection. A swing of her head, what she might say or do next, all part of it. Blue-green eyes, long eyelashes, hair that floated to her neck. Brown freckles on her nose and cheeks that highlighted her light skin. Something particularly catching about her mouth. Lips full but not thick. Teeth very white, perfectly formed, the way they look in toothpaste ads. In the summer, her tan was just right, arresting. It gave her a captivating golden glow that made people turn around and stare.

Joyce had a way of grabbing her nose with two fingers just before saying something, the same habit Allan noticed in her mother. When she felt strongly about something, she didn't care whether anyone else liked it or not. Allan told her never to run for elected office unless she had enough votes stacked with family and friends.

"Your sister," Allan had remarked to Jay that first time, "really lovely. And different. I enjoyed talking with her at dinner after the game."

"She's the bright one in our family," Jay responded. "Knows exactly what she wants. Apparently," he said with a slight smirk, "she must have found you very interesting. Normally doesn't spend that much time with one person."

Allan began calling her. At first once a week, then more often.

He was pleased when she wrote him. At his fraternity house, Delta Upsilon, the day's mail was placed on a small table.

"Hey, Daniels," Jay called out with a grin several weeks after Allan had met Joyce. "Another one for you. I recognize the handwriting." Allan was playing a few hands of bridge before lunch.

"Uh-huh," one of the other guys chimed in. "She must be writing you about the political situation down in Northampton. Or maybe this year's wildebeest migration across New England."

Allan put the letter in his pocket. "All right, you low-class dumb animals, double your two no trump."

Soon he was hitchhiking down to Northampton, or she would take a bus to Middlebury. They stopped dating anyone else.

One evening in late May, they walked along the ridge of the golf course that looked down on the lights of the town. In the east, the magnificent Green Mountains, their distinct silhouette against a sky that poured out a few white and blue stars. Spring scents mingled and wafted around them. The balmy, full moon that broke out from between the clouds seemed to be smiling at them.

"Terrific tonight, sharing this with you."

"What you like, dear boy, is the way we make each other feel. Talk to me a little before we lie down on your blanket. You get very quiet when we do." She giggled. "It's the . . . ," they said together, "the most fun you can have without laughing."

He turned from surveying the speckled night sky, put his hands on her shoulders, and said, "What I'm feeling right now is," he began earnestly, "that there will never be anyone else for me. Butzi. That's going to be my nickname for you. I like the way it sounds. OK?"

"You'd say anything to get into my pants." She gazed softly at him. "But I like when you talk this way. The same goes for me," she admitted. Then, almost in a whisper, "And doing it with you is . . ."

Like magnets. They couldn't keep their hands off.

Joyce was staying for the weekend with Jay's girlfriend in Forest, one of the girls' dorms. The next afternoon after classes, Allan drove her to Lake Dunmore. They parked in a campsite lot and walked to the Falls of Lana, which pour into the lake from a stream coming down from Silver Lake. They sat dangling their feet in the water, engrossed in conversation. Suddenly Joyce became quiet, her face troubled. She shut her eyes and shook her head.

"What's . . . what's the matter?" Allan asked softly. He reached for her hand.

Joyce looked up as if searching for something tangible, something she could hang onto, that would ground her distress, anything that would put an end to her anguish. She shook her head again.

"Please," Allan requested, "tell me."

"I've mentioned my sister, Nancy, but I need to talk more about her." She struggled for words. "She was three years older." The "was" was uttered slowly, like a death knell. "Cancer. Leukemia. My parents and the doctors tried everything. It was slow. She suffered. We thought for a while the remission might become permanent, but then at the end . . . she . . . just after her nineteenth birthday."

Allan rose and pulled her close. "I'm so sorry that I couldn't have met her."

Joyce stepped back. "My big sister was the one I could really talk to. More than my mother and Jay. We weren't always very close. Nance helped me growing up, when I was confused about so many things. What was happening to my body, my thoughts, boys—everything." Allan nodded.

"We were different. She was sort of attractive in her way but didn't have my looks and figure, I suppose. Did OK in school but only in the middle. I was at the top of my class. Sports too. My parents, especially my father, it was clear he favored me. Ever since I was little. Took me to baseball games and tennis matches. We'd go fishing. Nancy didn't want to."

"How did your mother—?"

"Mom tried to treat us the same. In every way." Joyce took a moment. "You'd think Nancy would have resented and hated me. But she didn't." Joyce turned away and faced the mountains. "She was just kind and caring. She was there all those years, either physically present or in the back of my mind. Wherever I was. Wherever I was I knew she was there. And then . . . gone. Nothing. Silence. How can I explain the shock and impact of silence? Seeing her, talking with her. Longing." Joyce looked down. "After she died, I'd have a thought, even talk to her like we always did. I'd imagine her speaking. It was my wanting her to be here. But I'd keep talking with her. I still do, sometimes." She hesitated. "These clothes. They were hers.

"More than anything else I miss her not having opportunities. Like meeting the right guy. Hopefully they'd have married, raised kids. A full life. She should have had more years. Sure, she'd have bad times and failures. But now she has nothing. She *is* nothing. I . . . I lost my best friend. I never realized how much I loved her."

Joyce collapsed to the ground, covering her head with her arms. She began to sob, which became a wail so searing, so discordant, that it frightened Allan, who was at a loss as to know what to do. He dropped quickly to his knees and put his arms around her.

She became quiet, dried her tears with the back of her hand, and took a few deep breaths. "Death is so absolute, so final. It had always been for someone else, someone maybe I knew or had heard of. I watched my father's parents being buried, but even as a ten-year-old I knew that when people get old they are supposed to die. Not the young. But death, the idea of it, the reality of it, never made its way into my head and heart. The last thing Nancy told me was that it was all right, we're not in control. To go and live my life as fully as I could. I remember telling her I would, that she would always be with me. That's romantic, I know, but that's how I felt. That's how I still feel."

Allan stroked her hair and said, "I would think it's almost impossible for you not to feel some guilt."

After a pause, she turned to him and said, "After she died, it was so bad, my parents sent me to a psychiatrist. I resisted at first, didn't want to face how guilty I felt — even though rationally I knew I shouldn't. When those sessions proved so helpful — about two years' worth — I knew I wanted to have a career in psychology."

She became quiet again, then said softly, "Allen, when I become a mother and if I have a girl, I want to name her Nancy. OK with you?"

He nodded. "Of course," he said.

Allan proposed to Joyce on the top of the Bread Loaf Snow Bowl. None of their friends or family was surprised. They were engaged for six months, then married in early June in an intimate outdoor ceremony by her family rabbi at her home in Brookline, Massachusetts. Both families were there. Jay was best man, and Joyce chose Sharon, Allan's sister, to be her maid of honor. As a wedding present, both fathers offered to help with costs of his graduate school not covered by scholarships. They also bought them a slightly used Volkswagen bug. "Our 'M-M' — our make-out machine when we can't wait," Allan had remarked when they first drove it.

One morning before the wedding, Allan walked into his family's kitchen and sat down opposite his mother. She was wearing a housedress, her black hair tied neatly in back. "What's wrong, Mom?"

She looked away. "Your Miccosukee heritage is something I wish you were proud of. Our language, our culture. But you just don't have any interest." She sipped some coffee, then glanced at him. "Our values are as important as they've ever been. These days maybe even more. Your father certainly hasn't been encouraging." She looked at him. "At least your sister is involved." Allan's face did not register anything.

"After your father and I were married by his rabbi, we went down to my family's *ah-mo-glee* for a Miccosukee ceremony." Allan nodded. His mother hesitated, then added, "I was thinking how nice it would be if . . ."

"Mom, I'm not ashamed of my maternal heritage," Allan interrupted. "I mean that. But we're up here in the north. I always have been. I'm going to be an architect. My career's in front of me."

"What's that supposed to mean?"

"Nothing. OK, being Native American did help me get the scholarships, but people don't care that much. You and Dad had that Indian ceremony because, well, it was important to you. It doesn't make sense for Joyce and me. You and Dad met down in Miami," he went on. "You told me both families objected. Joyce's family accepts that I'm half-Indian. It's fine with them."

She sighed deeply. "His parents would not attend the traditional ceremony near our *ochopee.* It was very special — and just beautiful. That hurt him, but me even more. Not to be accepted. There's still a lot of prejudice. You're wrong, Allan," she remarked, shaking her head. "People care. I hope you and Sharon won't ever have the experiences I've had. Look at me. *Hica ee-tees.*" Then she said evenly, "I know what I'm talking about."

A few days after the wedding and before starting summer jobs, Allan and Joyce loaded up their Volkswagen with a few valises of clothes, tennis rackets, cameras, hiking boots, a small, two-man tent, Coleman stove, pots and pans, and whatever else they could think of.

"The Greens and Whites are OK," Allan said as they turned onto the Massachusetts Turnpike, "but I think we'll enjoy the Adirondacks much more. Very few roads, lakes all over the place, great camping, and challenging mountains to climb. Nothing else like it here in the East. Most of it is virginal — like the two of us."

"Not even my grandmother would believe that," she teased.

Joyce leaned her head against his shoulder. "I'm glad we made love these past few months. But there's a lot we don't know about each other yet."

"Yeah, it'll be fun finding out," he said, laughing. She nodded.

"You're doing seventy-five, you know. Allan, we don't have time for jail."

"I can't get this car to go any faster, except maybe downhill."

Joyce turned to gaze at the landscape out her window. Vibrant green fields, trees in full leaf in clumps and in forests. Then, without turning back, she said in a tone he almost couldn't hear, "My first time. It was pretty bad."

"How so?"

"Well, you know. About to begin my junior year in high school. One of the last ones who hadn't. Typical story. There was so much pressure. I finally decided to do it. I wanted it to have meaning, not just a schtup. My family always takes a cottage on Cape Cod at the end of August."

"You want to talk about it?"

"Not really — but I will." She looked over at him. "Allan, I believe the more we know about each other, what happened before, experiences, important ones, it will bring us closer."

"Sometimes it's difficult to talk about these things," he said, "but I'll try."

"You'd better, because this will not be a one-way discourse." She paused for a few moments, gathered herself, and continued. "So we're out on a pretty night on this beautiful beach. Three couples. Sand dunes, blankets, and beer. This one guy, a couple of years older, Jamie Davison, was about to go back to Boulder, Colorado, for his sophomore year. He was sort of cute. I'd been dating him — if that's what you want to call it. So he puts on this campaign about how screwing is so great.

"The other kids were taking their blankets around the dunes, out of sight. I didn't tell him I'd never had sex. We started kissing, petting. He was really excited. I guess I was, too. But when he got on top of me, I dunno, something, I didn't want to. I told him that. 'I'm not ready, I don't really want to,' I remember saying. 'Look, kid,' he said, 'we're not leaving here until . . . but I promise it'll be all right. You'll really enjoy it. And I'm using a rubber.'

"It wasn't rape or date rape. I let him. But it hurt and wasn't much fun. He came pretty quickly and it was over. Big deal. I wasn't a virgin any more. Big fucking deal."

Which made them both laugh.

Allan pulled over on the shoulder of the expressway, turned to her, and said, "We all know that sex can be good or it can be bad. But when you love someone as I do you — there's nothing better. Of course it's physical, but also . . ."

"The act that completes the relationship," she said, finishing what he had begun.

"Trust," he said as he drove back onto the expressway, "the good feelings, then the good sex. What's very important to me is that you're fulfilled, too."

"How did you get so . . . fucking knowledgeable?" she asked.

"Readum books. Watchum movies. Tribal elders, the big shtarkers, talkum to young boys in sweat lodges. Indians likum sex big time. Good schtupum OK when both understand just doing it like animals. But with squaw, special. Early and often. Makum closeness."

"Listen, Big Running Bigshit, you never heard that stuff on any reservation." She glanced over at him and placed her left hand on his right. "And your first time?"

"Many, many first times," he answered smugly. Then, "All kidding aside, I will tell you about it, but not today. OK?"

She nodded. "OK. But *soon*."

♦ ♦ ♦

Allan matriculated at MIT's School of Architecture for a three-year bachelor's degree, graduating in the top 20 percent of his class. The requirements for a license were very demanding. Long hours, weekends, summers as an intern with an architectural firm, time as a draftsman, then extensive exams. But he and Joyce were happy, settling for quality over quantity time.

Joyce had double-majored, anthropology and psychology, but had nowhere to go without a graduate degree. They lived in a small apartment in Cambridge, walking distance to MIT. Joyce took a position as a secretary in a dean's office at Harvard.

"Sweetheart," she said one day while he was shaving. She walked over, put her arms around him from the rear, her face pressing against his well-formed back. "Do I have to worry one of your female classmates is going to try to jump you? If you didn't have to go to class and I didn't have to be in my office, I'd suggest a nice way to begin the morning. Start the day right."

"You're a minx, did you know that?"

"When it comes to you," she said, puckering her lips and sitting on the closed toilet cover. He came over and sat her on his lap. "Remember that time in the parking lot?" she half whispered. "Outside my dorm. Started kissing, then hands. Got me so hot, we did it in the back seat. Good thing it was snowing hard, all the windows fogged up."

"Don't remember any such thing." He looked over and grinned. "I didn't lay a hand on you until we were engaged. Always been shy about sex."

"Listen, Mister Pervert, we're lucky *we* didn't get *me* pregnant. Condoms don't always work."

"You couldn't have. I never came in you."

"Such a liar. You probably broke all the records for . . . anyway, Mister Architect, you complain about putting on some weight, but you're still very, very attractive."

Allan looked at himself in the mirror and nodded in agreement. "Hey," he said, jumping up, "My eight o'clock."

"Allan."

"What?"

"It's OK for me to be second fiddle while we're here," she said in a strong tone, "but when you're out and established, the old gray mare is going to have a career of her own. Besides wife and mother."

"I know that. You remind me three times a week."

"Just don't want you to forget." She kissed him very slowly on the lips.

"That old movie we saw last week," he said a little somberly. "*Casablanca.* Reminded me how much I hate being controlled."

"As long as you remember, dear boy, I feel the same way," she responded. Then, after a pause, "I'm very proud of how hard you strive, your goals." She went over and kissed him again. "And living together, married . . . I never expected it to be this good."

That was then. But in recent months in Cambridge, their love-making often had not been as fulfilling for Allan. It lacked something. At times, it seemed to him he was just . . . performing. He wasn't sure exactly why, but he was reluctant to discuss it. Were they losing their intimacy? Is this what happens to most couples after a while?

"Wait a minute. Take this coffee mug. And tonight, if you behave, there'll be something else besides dessert," she said with a wink.

5

After Allan graduated from MIT, they moved to Manhasset Isle on Long Island, into a pretty two-bedroom apartment overlooking the bay. He used one bedroom as an office.

He worked first as a draftsman, then took the formidable exams and obtained the esteemed license. He and a classmate opened their own firm but differences soon deteriorated into disharmony. Allan was more ambitious, worked harder and longer hours than his partner. A year later, they split up. Allan immediately established his own practice and succeeded from the outset.

When Joyce no longer had to work to supplement their income, she went to Hofstra, earned a master's and a doctorate in clinical psychology, trained at the C. G. Jung Institute of New York, and obtained a license to practice child counseling and art therapy. She set up an office in Manhattan and quickly developed a reputation as a very competent and effective analyst/therapist.

The years at the beginning of their careers were pressured and strenuous, but they were relatively happy. They had differences and disagreements on occasion, but when a daughter arrived and then a son, they felt more fulfilled than in any other way.

"Always tell me," she said one evening when they were returning home from dinner at his parents', "if ever you notice anything I'm not doing right with Nancy or Craig."

"Sure. Absolutely."

A few moments passed, then he said: "You're great with the kids, you really are. I'd point out anything detrimental. Joyce?"

"What?"

"Recently," he began, "you're . . . you get to a point . . ."

"What point?"

"You hold back."

"Well, you do too, my friend," she shot back. "I'm glad you brought this up," she added with some hostility.

He ignored her comment. "I'm beginning to feel unimportant."

"Bullshit. After all those years of *my* supporting *your* career?"

"I appreciate that, I do. But this last year or so. You're in the city more and more. At home you let patients call anytime. Plus now that they've made you a big mucky-muck in the APA, you're away a lot on trips."

"Hey!" she retorted. "I have my career just like you do. Women are finally getting to do the things men always did and controlled."

He pulled into their driveway, shut off the motor, and said in a measured tone, "That may be, Joyce. I'm for that, except—"

"Except what?"

"The price is pretty damn high. I know how much you love the kids, but even *they* feel you're not spending enough time with them."

"That's absolutely not true," she snapped.

"And between us," Allan continued, "you've changed. Your . . . involvements." He looked down. "I have to add this. I feel lonely."

"Are you trying to analyze me? That's my field."

"Psychologists and psychiatrists usually have problems, I'm told. . . . That's the reason they go into that profession."

"Oh for Christ's sake," she flashed back. "You're trying to put me on the defensive. That's an old trick." She paused. "You sure forget. When you were at MIT, swamped with work, you preached quality over quantity. Remember?"

"Any way you want it. But we've got a problem. I'm certainly not asking you to give up being a psychologist, but if you don't want our marriage to deteriorate, you'll do something. Balance things better."

"It's late and I'm very tired. What I want to do is go inside and get some sleep. But I'll think about what you said."

"Will you? Or will you put it off?"

"There are times, Mister Daniels, that you give me a swift fucking pain you-know-where."

"The truth hurts, Joyce."

"Good night, Allan! That's quite enough."

6

THE NIGHT BEFORE HIS FLIGHT, Joyce walked into their bathroom wearing a large, white terry cloth bathrobe and stood next to him. She leaned her hands on her sink and confronted him in the mirror. "I don't understand you. Tell me exactly why you're making this flight? You're such an enigma. Scared of heights, but you enjoy flying planes. That doesn't 'fly.' Pardon the pun."

"When I was a kid, looking down from a thirty-story building was a problem, but not anymore. And flying is very different. I can't explain it." He turned around to face her. "You've been giving me a hard time, and now you're challenging my going as if you actually care. And why have you been so damned angry?"

"Failure. I guess I'm angry with failure."

"Whose? Yours or mine?"

"We've discussed this," she said with continued annoyance. "You have trouble with what I'm doing, my career." She said resolutely, "I don't want this family broken up, but it is failing. We're failing. Mostly because you won't accept change." She looked away. "I am *not* going to give up my career — what I've worked so hard for."

"You forgot, Joyce, to include 'wife' and 'mother' with 'career'. If it wasn't so important, this would be like some soap opera. Almost comical." He rubbed his chin. "You and I were really happy, not perfect but pretty damn good. Now you're fucking it up, big time." He turned to her and blasted, "Maybe you've met some super hotshot psychiatrist —"

"That's just plain stupid," she snapped. "But *you*, Allan, come up *very* short."

"Like what?"

She leveled at him. "Your inability to grow. Which should

include supporting *me.* And, if you don't mind a psychologist's considered opinion, you are completely unexamined. I've urged you to do some therapy. You're stuck with . . . I don't know. . . some immaturity. Narcissism maybe. You're unrealistic and excessively self-involved. Little if any real insight."

He countered. "That's psychobabble." He came over and put his hand on her shoulder. "Look, Joyce, I believe — "

"You believe what?"

"We can get our relationship back."

"How? I'm afraid we've drifted too far apart."

"Does this have anything to do with . . . your family or friends . . . my being half-Indian?"

"That's absurd! I've never had a problem with that. Never, and you know it. I certainly understand bigotry — even among so-called liberals." She gazed at him. "There's something important you need to understand, Allan." She took a deep breath. "I may love you, Allan, but love is . . . not enough."

"What the hell does that mean?" he said. "This has to do with your inability to prioritize your life."

"And what exactly is *that* supposed to mean?"

"Things like calls from your patients. Evenings, times during the weekend when we're alone. I start discussing problems in my office or when things go well, sharing them with you, hoping they'll bring us closer, and you, you're on the goddamn phone half the time! How do you think that makes me feel?"

"You keep harping on that," she said. "There've been plenty of times we've been completely alone. You're right, it's not the way it used to be. You function on too superficial a level. It leaves *me* feeling *empty.*"

They brushed their teeth. He finished first, looked at her in the mirror, and said angrily, "Maybe you really *did* meet someone. Maybe you're even sleeping with him for all I goddamn know! But in this marriage, putting your ass in two beds is the fastest way to end it!"

She peered at him, searching for something to say.

"I'm sorry I said that," he said a few moments later in a different, gentler tone. "Look, when I get back I'll take some time off, meet you in the city, take in a matinee, enjoy a quiet dinner, a play, ballet, do things we both like. There's an excellent retrospective we can go to. Mies van der Rohe, Phillip Johnson, Frank Lloyd Wright. Or whatever you want."

"I don't know," she began slowly. She turned away, reflected for several moments, then said flatly, "Allan, even before this conversation, I have to confess, I'd been thinking about a separation agreement."

Allan felt as if he had been slugged in the stomach.

"Don't act so surprised. This has been coming for a long time."

He closed his eyes. "No. No, no, no!" he blurted. "All we need is some time to get close again. Besides . . . think of Nance and Craig."

"I've already thought about that," she said quietly. "It's definitely not what I want, but I will not live a fabrication." She gazed at herself in the mirror, her finger tracing a line from her cheek to her mouth. "You'd better get used to it." Then, sincerely, "I'm very sorry."

Allan's thoughts turned to the children and the games he had invented over the years. Especially the ones at bedtime. They liked most the one called Taking a Pow. Giggles and laughter when one of their stuffed animals said he or she had to "make." And did so on top of Daddy's head!

He would look in on them at night, so peaceful, the day's events washed away by exhaustion. When they were babies, he changed their diapers. When they were older, he hugged away their nightmares. He encouraged their fantasies, suggested meanings for stories they created, designs in mud pies, with paints, with their dolls and animals. Prizes for the prettiest stones and clouds. For leaves and sticks they would make collages from. For silly snowmen who always had names.

That's what a father does, he thought, *but not if I'm not here.*

Allan remained in the bathroom, closed the door, and sat on the toilet seat cover. He sank his head into his hands. Tears filled his eyes.

God, she doesn't even want to try . . . family . . . MY family. Feels like it's all going down the sewer.

He got up, and before turning off the light thought, *Maybe she'll change her mind while I'm away. Give it a chance . . .*

7

ALLAN PULLED OUT THE EMERGENCY locator transmitter from its small compartment in the rear, set up the aerial on top of the wing, and waited for the test light to glow. It didn't. Then he remembered he had not only failed to check the battery before he departed, he had forgotten to take along spares.

That was stupid, he thought. *Real stupid. Well, old chap, simply hop around the corner to the nearest Walgreens and pick a few up. You don't even have to swim . . . simply walk on the water . . . you're a real comedian . . .*

Allan had brought a collapsible spinning rod. During the next several hours, he tried fishing, without success, hurling curses across an obviously indifferent channel. As the afternoon aged further, he listened more and more intently for an airplane or helicopter motor. He became increasingly hungry, partially from anxiety. He had eaten the last of three packages of cheese crackers he'd purchased at Pahokee, his last fuel stop. Allan needed to get his mind off being stranded, lost, and hungry. His thoughts turned back to Joyce.

Should have explained better what flying means to me. Up there time seems to stop . . . breathtaking . . . spiritual . . . the outside world absent . . . nothing else like it, except maybe sex. And the weather . . . mysterious . . . always fascinating . . . unpredictable.

When he flew, Allan concentrated on the clouds and their formations. Some were tranquil and cauliflowered, their edges wispy with opalescent contours. Others were murky and ominous, harbingers of doom. Cunning, hiding thunder and lighting. Or ice-filled, poised to rip apart pilots who had become too cavalier.

Allan learned from his studies that changes in temperature are the basic factor in the creation of weather. Systems try to equalize.

Lows and highs and fronts. Differences in barometric pressure create wind. Wind cannot be seen, only what it affects. If weather's messages were read more carefully, its telltales would be better understood.

He had to be very attentive when he flew. Make the correct choices, some small and insignificant, others thick with meaning. Otherwise he could fall out of the sky. Like Icarus.

8

ALLAN NOTICED OYSTERS clinging to the mangrove roots. They reminded him of swarms of monarch butterflies congregating before the long trip to their winter reunions in Mexico. Not big, fat, succulent oysters like the ones he'd had at the Harvard Club a few days earlier with his older Middlebury roommate, Bob Parker. Bob had gone to graduate school in Cambridge after yet another stint in the Navy, at Harvard Business School.

Allan had phoned Bob in his midtown Manhattan office, using Bob's private number. "Need to talk to you."

"You sound upset," Bob answered.

Allan heard the sound of pages flipping. Bob's calendar? "Sure. What about tomorrow? Three in the morning?"

"Very funny, but this is serious. Shit, today, Bob. I'm flying a seaplane to Key West Wednesday."

"Yeah, I know. All right, my club at, ah, make it one. How will I recognize you?" He teased, "Oh yeah. Daniels, the guy who's that ridiculous combination—a Jewish Indian. The one who went off the charts when he took those preference/aptitude tests when he was trying to decide who he was—or should be."

"Good-bye, Parker, you goofball," Allan responded. "As a comedian, you stink! One o'clock."

Allan raced into Manhattan through the Midtown Tunnel. He pulled into a parking garage on Sixth Avenue, handed the attendant a five-dollar bill to keep his car up front, and walked rapidly east on Forty-third Street, past the Princeton, Explorers, and other private clubs before entering the Harvard Club. The receptionist told him his host was in the dining room. *This club, perhaps past its prime but handsomely designed,* Allan noted as he entered. *Elegant, restrained, classy.*

Allan found Bob at a corner table, slumped in a cushy chair, sipping a cocktail, wearing a button-down white shirt, Harvard crimson tie, and a blue blazer that made him look as if he was on his way to some chichi cocktail reception. Allan couldn't see his pants but knew they'd have to be chinos — to complete the uniform he maintained he despised but wore anyway. Robert Monroe Parker, his long, wavy hair beginning to gray, had been raised in Old Greenwich, Connecticut, the son and grandson of Annapolis career naval officers, both admirals. He decided not to go to Annapolis but to Officers' Candidate School at Notre Dame, then, after service, he finished college at Middlebury. He also fought in the Vietnam War on a destroyer. When the captain and his senior officers were killed in an explosion from a shell from an enemy ship, he immediately took command. Due to his swift actions they escaped additional hits. As a result, a number of his men were spared. He received the Navy Cross and ended up as a three-stripe commander in the reserves.

Bob possessed an unmistakable self-confidence, an ability to make quick decisions, some for immediate action, all to be reflected upon later. His leadership qualities propelled him to being elected president of Delta Upsilon fraternity and captain of the tennis team, on which he played number-one singles.

Solidly built but only five feet nine, he could not be considered Hollywood handsome but exuded strong masculine characteristics. He was always clean-shaven, except when he was traipsing around up in the mountains. Most of the time with Allan. A glint in his eye was quite evident in his reaction to some attractive coed or a faculty wife who might have engaged him in conversation. His female conquests were legendary, but not his grades. In their fraternity, the brothers decided he had somehow talked his way into the B-school, which was probably true.

"Daniels, you look like you've been dragged through day-old garbage," Bob greeted Allan. "You don't do drinks at lunch, but I'm having me a sizeable Beefeater martini. Maybe two. Five olives, bless them, soaked in eighty-proof alcohol. Prepares me for an afternoon with idiot clients. Money management gets very dull, except when one has a sexy female client, of course."

He flagged the waiter, who took their order. Their meal began with Alaskan king crab legs for Allan, Blue Point oysters for Bob.

Allan began telling Bob about some innovative concepts for lobby designs, then traded a few crab legs for some oysters.

"C'mon, hotshot, you're not here to give me an academic analysis of your latest creation," Bob said, looking straight at his friend. "You and Joyce, right?"

"I feel so damn shitty. Had this nightmare last night. I was in a completely bare room staring at two little white coffins. Nancy and Craig. Joyce was wailing in the background."

Allan choked up a little. "She's terrific with the kids." He looked away. "Used to be involved with and devoted to me. Her career's taken off. I told her I feel neglected. She said she does, too."

"Shit. So who doesn't at times?" Bob responded. "What's wrong? You sound like some asshole masochist who doesn't know how to work out his most important relationship."

"Two nights ago Joyce — " His voice caught.

"What? Joyce what?"

"She said she was no longer sure about our marriage . . . wants a separation agreement. Maybe a divorce."

"That doesn't make any damn sense. You two always seemed as close as love-of-my-life teenagers. Maybe something else going on?" Bob demanded, eyebrows raised.

He frowned and stared at Allan long and hard, reached for his martini but didn't pick it up. When Allan didn't answer, he continued. "I have to ask you this, kiddo. I mean, shit, you're not involved with anyone else, are you? Some babe in your office, some client's secretary? Maybe at the club? A guy once said, 'When the dick gets stiff, the brains go straight out the window.' I mean, most guys are not averse to a little extracurricular schtupping, but, tiger, you never were dumb enough to confuse an exciting piece of ass with love and marriage."

Allan shook his head and continued wrestling with the crab legs. "No, nothing like that." He hesitated. "I've become — how to put it? — lonely. And Joyce feels the same way."

"A guy we both know," Bob went on, "absolutely convinced himself this other woman — would you believe it, his father's secretary — was everything his wife was not. His perfect opposite number." He looked straight at Allan. "So this stupid schmuck dumps his fifteen-year marriage, which sure seemed as good as any. I mean, his wife is really attractive, bright, head on straight, personable, athletic. And she adored her husband."

"You mean the Nortons. Joyce told me."

"Oh. Anyway, guess what? His new marriage is already down the crapper, if you haven't heard."

Allan gazed across the room, at the other tables. Everyone deeply engaged in conversation.

Each in their own little universe, Allan thought. *Indifferent to everyone else's situation and problems except their own . . . human animals struggling in an animal world.*

"So, Mister Daniels," Bob said, noticing that Allan's mind was straying, "it doesn't add up, you and Joyce." Almost a question. "You're a good guy. I mean decent, caring, involved. Everyone likes you. I've seen you with Nancy and Craig."

"I guess I'm not good for Joyce anymore." He lowered his head, eyes closed. "When she told me she wanted to separate, it hit me like a swift kick in the balls." He looked up squarely at Bob, his eyes urgent. "A legal agreement. Shit!"

"Look, I hate to suggest this, but maybe *she's* found someone else."

"I brought that up. She rejected it out of hand, but who the hell knows." Allan struggled to crack a crab leg, put it back on his plate and grabbed another, which he crunched so strongly a piece of shell flew across the table. A shot across Bob's bow.

"She tells me I'm too remote. Not supportive enough. I *am* very involved with my work, but I also try to make sure there's time for us." Allan sighed. "Jesus, Bob, she hadn't said a thing about this until the other day."

"Very strange," Bob said, shaking his head. "Joyce is anything but the type who keeps quiet when something's wrong. Here, have another oyster," he said, lifting his plate toward Allan.

Allan waved it away. "I asked her why she hadn't told me earlier she was so upset, so dissatisfied. Maybe she didn't for a reason." He sighed feebly. "Shit," he said, almost in a whisper, "she apparently doesn't even want to *try* to get things back on track.

"Bob, I admit I don't always see what's really going on. Very possibly because I don't want to. And I can be defensive when I shouldn't be, I know that. Joyce has been after me to go into therapy. But." He hesitated. "That feels like dropping into a pit filled with cobras. And I doubt it would work."

Bob drained his martini and glanced up. "In what way?" he asked evenly.

The waiter arrived with their entrées, bringing a momentary lull to their conversation. He hovered. "Everything all right?" he asked with the mandatory smile.

"Fine, thanks." Bob waved him away.

"Well, for example, this whole fucking thing being half–American Indian, half-Jewish," Allan said, shrugging. "Who I am. To me. To everyone else. My sister has no trouble with it. People in our part of the world aren't involved with anything Indian. Plus we've pretty much assimilated. But Mother's always reminding me about my heritage. When people learn I'm Indian, you know, they give me that funny look."

Bob reached across the table and laid his hand on Allan's. "If I ever hear someone making any snide remark behind your back, I'll beat the crap out of them. But on the matter of Joyce," Bob asked, "how can I help you?"

"Maybe I just wanted to hear myself talk. God, I sure don't want to see my marriage break up."

Bob pushed back his chair. "The cliché, my dear friend, is that life is too damn short to perpetuate mistakes, especially big ones. The problem is knowing what they are and admitting when we get things wrong." He stopped and shook his head. "Now I sound like some jerk psychiatrist. Take my case. When Polly and I got married, I was completely convinced I was getting hitched to my life partner. Except that after two years she decided I was a bad disease she was starting to catch. I thought it was all over. *At least we don't have kids* went through my mind. Then we both changed enough to be able to reconcile. But honestly? We still have problems."

Outside the club's entrance, Bob grabbed Allan in a bear hug and said, "You've been there for me a hundred times. I'd kill for you, buddy. Let me give some serious thought to all this. In any case, take your time, OK? On your flight, play it all out. Life without Joyce and the kids. What that would be like. What you can do about it."

Allan shook his head. "Doesn't look like it's going to be up to me."

"Then start thinking about how to get the relationship back. There are ways. Find them. I can't feel your feelings, but you sure as hell know I care."

Allan put his hand on Bob's shoulder. "Yeah, I know that, I really do. And believe me, it helps. Thanks, pal. I'll call when I get back."

9

THE FAINT AND UNEXPECTED SOUND of a small motor startled Allan from his reverie. An intrusion into the silence, one of the enchantments offered by nature. But not a sound he didn't want to hear. He strained as it became louder, craning his neck like a young tern waiting to be fed. A small boat approached from around the bend. Allan smiled, raised his arm. The young man guiding the boat was brown and unshaven. He did not smile. Allan stood erect, left hand tightening instinctively into a fist. *Who is this guy?*

He wore old army pants, greasy and torn in several places. One leg appeared slightly shorter than the other, as if mangled. His plaid shirt was buttoned all the way up and looked as if it had never been new. No shoes, no hat. He was medium size, lean and hard, and seemed ready to spring like a coil. Black hair stuck to his forehead, blocking part of his left eye. An ugly scar jagged down from his right temple across the entire length of his cheek. Skin the color of burnt almonds.

As he drew closer, Allan could see that his left hand seemed crippled, turned inward, the fourth and fifth fingers curved back, the other three straight. His left arm hung oddly from his shoulder. The whites of his eyes were clear, irises deep brown, almost black. He glared at Allan. *Miccosukee or Seminole*, Allan speculated. *Surely Indian.*

"Heard your plane. Goddamn lucky I saw you," the boy said and spat. He looked Allan up and down. "If you want to come with me, make it snappy. Got things to do."

He pointed to the seat in front of him. "Place about half-hour. Name's Tommy Handley." He sniffed. "D'ya know it?" he asked, studying Allan's face.

Why should I know it? And good God, what's he doing out here? "No, I don't," Allan responded as he reached forward to shake hands. Tommy did not respond. "Allan, Allan Daniels." He waited for some response, but there was none. "If you can take me to some spot where I can get out of here, I . . . ah . . . I'd be glad to pay you. Come back later for the plane."

The boat bobbed on the small wake that crossed underneath, waves lapping against the plane's pontoons. Tommy nodded, a slight grin turning up the corners of his mouth. A low, flat sound emanated from him, not a grunt but a form of expression Allan could not interpret. He pointed again for Allan to sit in the bow. A bird shrilled from the mangroves. Tommy turned in its direction and spat again into the water. He pointed again to the boat, his eyes narrowing.

Allan swung around to the cabin of the plane, reached in through the passenger door, snatched his duffle and small ditty bag, secured the windows, and removed the key from the ignition. He changed his mind, replaced the key, rechecked the rows of breakers, made sure all the switches were turned off, and placed the control pin through the stem of the wheel yoke as he would after any flight. *Pull out one of the radios, maybe use it as a portable,* he thought. *Don't think I can get the compass out.*

"What's the radio for?" Tommy asked with what struck Allan as a sneer.

"Maybe rouse a search plane or helicopter."

"Leave that fuckin' thing here. Nobody's gonna see or hear us."

"Look, it could prove useful . . ."

Tommy glared at Allan. "Stays here." He started the motor. "If you're comin' with me, mister, get the fuck in the boat."

Jesus, Allen thought, *This guy sounds like trouble. Frying pan into fire?*

He put the radio back on the pilot's seat and managed to scribble a note without Tommy noticing: "Picked up—young Indian — Tommy Handley." He threw the ditty bag in the bow, sat down facing forward. Tommy dragged the plane under the overhanging mangroves, the front of the fuselage and most of the wings out of view. He tied it to a large mangrove branch.

"What are you doing that for?" Allan asked.

"The fuckin' sun," he grumbled, pointing up, which didn't make sense to Allan because the day was closing down.

As they set off, bright sunlight flashed through the swamps, its beams splashing among the dark shadows of the mangrove vines. They alternated in unsymmetrical patterns. Most of the time the light came from their right, which meant they were heading south. Allan had always been fascinated with light, especially twilight, the variations in color and intensity and their relationship with the time of day. Now bands were thrown across the sky, at the bottom sanguine red, then carrot and marigold oranges, yellows and a curious olive green, then higher, magenta topped by peacock and sapphire blues. He studied the sky intently, wanting to capture it before it faded and disappeared.

Tommy did not speak or look at Allan, which made him feel even more uneasy. *Feel like a caged animal. This . . . shit.* When he was very young, Allan felt controlled by his mother. She warned him that if he did not do what she said, there would be trouble. All kinds. It confused him because he did not always know what pleased her. Her behavior, the Miccosukees', was so different and disconcerting. Allan did not understand quickly enough when she changed her mind. Signals he never properly learned and grew to have difficulty trusting.

Try to remember the route he's taking . . . impossible to relocate the plane except from the air. The sonorous ride began to affect him like a narcotic. Tommy sewed the boat through channels, weaving, the motion more and more hypnotic. Allan's mind began slipping. Daydreams, reveries, unconnected words, flashes of pictures, everything ephemeral and impalpable, distracting him from the seemingly unreal situation he was in. He was floating, wrapped in pleasant remembrances. Of women who affected him, ones he'd had fun with, laughed with, had sex with. Most he had not become very close to in high school and college. Until he met Joyce. Before her, he had been too self-involved to commit and unwilling to share feelings, except those that would lead to sex.

Allan knew his perceptions and behavior had been fashioned to a great extent by the first woman in his life, his mother. There were other mysteries, like darkness. Like when he witnessed his father's parents being lowered into the ground. Like what did girls look like naked? What about his sister's blood-stained underpants?

"Don't bother me about these things, Allan," his mother once said when he was exploding with curiosity. "You're much too young to understand *taygees.* I will absolutely not discuss them with you. I'll . . . I'll get you a book. Or your father will talk to you."

Allan glanced up briefly from his mind's journey. Tommy was completely focused on guiding the boat.

"Say, do you think . . . ?" Tommy either didn't hear him or was not going to respond.

Like a dream. A real lousy one, he mused.

10

AS THEY ENTERED A THICK MASS of mangroves, Allan watched the last vestiges of sunlight withdrawing from the world. Not a word from Tommy. He glanced at Allan once or twice, the look of a trapper. Or patient spider.

Stop. You're imagining things . . . only the way he behaves.

The boy who conducted them on the water trail remained fixed, rigid like the boat.

They came to an aperture large enough for only a small craft. Allan began to feel like a spelunker whose headlamp had stopped working. "Keep your goddamn mouth shut," Tommy ordered, as if he could smell Allan's claustrophobia.

In the light of an almost-full moon, the dim outline of an asymmetrical, truncated structure. Stars danced in a show, in and out of puffy cumuli. Tommy eased the boat toward a mass of waterlogged ground. He did not move a muscle. His entire being seemed concentrated on every sound, movement, and smell.

A short dock, well hidden in the mangroves, fed onto a trail split at least three ways. A maze. You could get confused quickly. Allan banged into his guide, who stopped as if frozen. Allan felt embarrassed, like a child caught not paying attention. They had arrived at a moat. Tommy reached up, grabbed a rope with both hands. "Swing across," he hissed. "This fucking way." *The smell of sulfur.*

The clouds separated, curtains parting, moonlight pouring through. Tommy's shelter, built under a giant cypress, was constructed in a rudimentary but classic post-and-lintel configuration. The roof was covered with irregular pieces of corrugated metal. It looked like an adult's playhouse. Tommy's tank-house, his hermitage. Allan remembered a paper he had written at MIT on primitive construction methods. Tommy must have understood what Allan had studied, that a hurricane could quickly convert a structure back into its original materials. He had located his shack between two shorter, red-barked gumbo-limbo trees. To secure his home, two large ropes were laid over the top, the ends fastened around the bottom of the trunks. The three-inch-thick ropes that Tommy had found washed up on the coast had probably been woven in the Philippines or Brazil.

Allan listened to the disparate sounds of the swamp. The breeze seemed strange, uncomfortable and agitated. The ground was moist, but not like a forest floor after heavy rains, more like a bog, a marsh. *Quicksand here? Better be careful.*

He crossed a clearing cluttered with flotsam Tommy had scavenged from shores and beaches, then followed him into the dwelling. The pungent reek of excrement emanated from the right of the entrance, from the direction of a blown-down tree. Allan assumed from camping experiences that Tommy, and now he, would stick his tail over the log and let go into a hole. If Tommy had bothered to dig a hole.

Inside, a fifty-five-gallon drum, one end hacked off, stood upright next to the center post to collect rainwater. A hose with a crude spigot was placed over a number-ten can. *That water must be stagnant,* Allan thought. A worn, whitened pallet supported by two upended logs simulated a table. For light, kerosene lamps.

Tommy handed him an aluminum camper's plate filled with food ladled from a pot. "Sit there. Fish, other shit. What I can lay my hands on. Not fancy shit like where you're from, I'm sure." He skulked into the far right corner. Allan heard the sound of a bottle's cork being released.

Why's he so damn belligerent?

"Want some of this stuff?" Tommy asked, laughing. "Don't

bother, it'll fuckin' blow your head off. Homemade by some of my cozs on the res. On their *ochopee.* Ha, ha, ha . . ."

Allan watched him lift the bottom of the brown bottle above his head. "What are you so angry at?" Allan asked, surprised at the acrimony in his voice. "My mother is Indian."

"What'd you say?"

"I said, my mother is Indian."

"You shittin' me? You ain't no fuckin' Indian."

"Half. Miccosukee."

"Yeah, sure. Like I'm half-Chink."

Allan looked down and shook his head. "She was born on the reservation. Met my father in Miami. Worked in a hotel behind the front desk."

"How come you don't look more Indian? Your skin's too fuckin' white."

"Believe me or not."

"Well, *Yankee,* I don't. Say something in Miccosukee. You're just shittin' me to get me to help you get the fuck out. Hey, I ain't here because I want. I have to. But that's OK."

Tommy put the bottle down, wiped his mouth with the back of his hand, glowered at Allan. There was silence, as if time had been suspended. Neither man said anything, just studied each other. Tommy took another swig.

"Take what you're gonna eat." Another directive, this one firmer. "But no more'n that. I don't waste fuckin' nothin'. Except the time I gotta spend here. Shit, not even that." Then he added slowly, "I make out. Yeah, now I do," he said with a chuckle. "A little side business and no fuckin' taxes."

Allan tore at his food, not caring about the strange tastes. A combination of something like a green vegetable, crustaceans, and pieces of meat taken from swamp animals, all mixed in a stew. He might have thrown up if he wasn't so hungry. But he gorged like a survivor who wasn't sure of his next meal, using his fingers instead of the crude utensils Tommy had pointed to.

Allan remembered youthful experiences in the Adirondacks, how he learned to enjoy the outdoors. Camping on Paradox Lake, an "all-men trip" with his father, pan-frying and eating their day's catch of perch and sunnies. With his family on the Otter Creek near Middlebury. Along the White River in New Hampshire, tearing his leg on the barbed-wire fence while trying to catch a lamb, seeing his blood spurt. His father always encouraged him to grow up strong, conquer the elements, be tough, be a leader. He tried to wear clothes similar to his father's.

"Hey, Indian," Tommy said, pausing to swallow, "how'd you like to fuckin' live alone in this place? Last two fuckin' days. Maybe less." His eyes were fixed on the bottle. He sat straight-legged, back against the pallet. "Nobody can do this here shit as good as Tommy Handley." He tapped his thumb against his chest. "I'm like fuckin' them, the animals," he continued, pointing. "They know me, I fuckin' know them. Ha, ha. *Ee-chos, laa-le, chen-tes, ke-hay-kes.* Yeah, learned from my mother. My old man. Fuckin' white man ran away with my mother. People made them lots of trouble, around Homestead and Immokalee." He got up and turned on the spigot over his cup. He moved to the entrance, stood and sniffed at something wafting across the clearing.

"Sister died. Goddamn fuckin' Indian medicine didn't work. Another ran away. Doin' real good. Somewhere up near Fort Myers. The fuckers sent me to white school. Near Okeefologee. Lousy shitty place," he said with a sneer. "Those white boys an' teachers. All that stupid talkin'. Lots of fights." He was beginning to slur his words.

He wheeled, stared at Allan, his face suddenly devoid of aggression. "Ma, she died. Moccasin, I guess. Maybe coral. Too far gone when I finally found her." He blinked, then said sadly, "Thrashin' around somethin' terrible. Old man was drunk, the fuckin' bastard. Couldn't find his goddamn boat key in time. Son of a bitch drank after that, maybe went loco. Some father. One day he don't come back. I took his fuckin' skins. Came back once, but I kicked him the hell out." He took another swill, spat. "School, real shit. Ran away. Swiped stuff. Got caught. Judge, that motherfucker, said I needed lessons up at the work farm. *Ochopee.* Goddamn whole year."

He checked a trap outside, then drained more of the bottle he held under his arm. "People don't want half-breeds with fuckin' records. Tampa, Fort Myers, Pahokee. Dishes, cleaning cars. Citrus, that's something else. Crummy work, stinkin' pay. Hate those shit jobs. My swamps. My *okees.* Let them bastards try an' find me. When I need stuff, my mother's people'll trade with me."

Tommy pulled his left arm forward, which he dragged more than raised. "See this? Two years ago. From a goddamn 'gator. Lucky it's still on. But I got the fucker." He turned over a second trap and began to mend the netting. "Better no fuckin' people. Decide when to fish 'n' hunt, sleep. *Nobody* gives Tommy Handley no trouble no fuckin' more. Not here in my swamps. My *yahg-nee.* Those jerk-offs can't find me. Keep tryin' but too fuckin' stupid. Not here. Not in my 'glades."

He leaned against a post, processing some thought, then burped. "Trouble is no women, but now, got me a friend over on the res. Nice ass. Real sweet to me. Great blow jobs." He finished with the trap, lifted it up, and said, "Now, this here's a great fuckin' trap. Nothin' gets out. I make great fuckin' traps."

Another grab of the bottle, sucking on a glass teat, even though it looked empty. Allan shook himself. *Like a Grade B movie. Be out doing something... not see a rattler, coral, or a moccasin latching on... become confused. If he didn't get the poison out quickly with his knife, goodbye Tommy. Maybe he'd get an infection . . . wouldn't take much. Who'd give a shit? Good riddance, they'd say . . . one less Indian. Kinder ones might say he's better off.*

"Don't you have anythin' to say, mister, or am I pissin' in the fuckin' *fah-blee-chee?*" Now the booze was talking. "Hey, Miccosukee, my grub ain't good enough for you?"

"I was just thinking. Ah, listen, I have to tell you. I admire the way you get along. I mean, out here, and — "

The muscles in Tommy's jaw pulled tight. He spat. "You don't know fuckin' nothin'! Just like the rest. Got 'coon and snake in there." Tommy laughed. Allan's eyes widened in disbelief.

"Yeah," Tommy yelled, "I buy food! With my fuckin' hands, that's how! Where the hell you from, anyway?" His words ran together, a continuum of disconnected thoughts.

"Long Island, in New York. Wife and two kids." He began to pull photos from his wallet, changed his mind.

"Shit," Tommy said. "A real fuckin' dude." The words drawn out like clothes on a line. "Don't really know fuckin' nothin'. Like how to survive." Tommy sought the brown bottle again, forgetting it was empty, then threw it across the shack. He crawled over to the pot and attacked the food in it, killing again the animals he had killed previously. Allan watched, mesmerized.

Tommy ate slowly, savoring each morsel. Allan tried to guess what was going on in his mind. After he finished eating, Tommy boiled water, threw coffee grinds into it, and drank some.

"Going out an' take a shit," he mumbled.

Allan inspected the shack. A large, broken footlocker reminded him slightly of a coffin. Several machetes and large knives dangled from nails on a wall. Traps were in the process of being assembled in a corner next to several half-broken fishing rods. *Were there guns?*

A torn newspaper article was pinned to a wall in the corner, almost out of view. Police and rangers looking for the person who had shot the owner of a remote general store on the outskirts of Fort Myers. Peter Clancy had come back unexpectedly, surprised the robber. Two shots, in the right chest and leg. The victim was in shock; the assailant escaped with packaged food, bullets, fishing and trapping equipment. Candy dispenser thrown into a mirror. Feces on the floor. The police thought they might know who it was. "Anyone having information . . ." Allan stopped, not wanting to get caught reading. Lucky, because Tommy walked back in just as Allan returned to where he had been sitting. He tried to appear nonchalant, innocently poking into his ditty bag as if looking for something.

"Gets dark later here than up north this time of year," Allan commented, trying to make sure his voice sounded normal.

"So fuckin' what?" Tommy responded.

"Nothing. I gotta go," Allan said as he exited the shack.

To the west, the horizon was lit by occasional flashes of lightning that resembled trees with asymmetrical silver-white limbs. Moments later, following the laws of physics, thunder cracked. The cracks and booms came with varying degrees of loudness.

How do I get away from here?

Allan found the log. It was all he could do not to throw up.

11

ALLAN SLEPT THE SLEEP of several days' exhaustion. Tommy's was the result of inebriation, but he stirred just before dawn, rose, and commanded, "Hey, Yankee, get the fuck up. Gotta take some skins and meet my friend. Me and him trade stuff."

He peered at Allan, who just stared at him. "You're comin' with me," Tommy said sharply. "Don't want you here by yerself."

"Maybe your friend can get me out."

Tommy heated up last night's stew and coffee. When Tommy motioned toward a plate, Allan shook his head, but pointed to a package of muffins he had seen on a shelf. Tommy nodded and raised a single finger.

When he finished eating, Tommy tied a bunch of skins together and waved for Allan to follow him to the boat. He placed the bundle in the bow, indicated for Allan to sit in the middle, then pulled the engine cord and cast off the ropes.

After what seemed like an endless ride, Allan said, "Sorry for asking, but when do we get there?"

Tommy spit, laughed, then almost shouted, "I ain't no fuckin' tour guide. When we fuckin' do, that's when."

Tommy navigated the boat around numerous islands, following a convoluted route to his destination. Eventually they arrived at the sandy shore of a hummock. He nosed the boat up onto it. Allan rose and began to lift the skins out. "Get away from them! I'll do that myself!" Tommy yelled.

Allan was startled by blue-gray smoke snaking upward a short distance away, from a cluster of gumbo-limbo trees. He thought he heard the slow beat of a drum. *I must be going crazy.* They walked to the place, Tommy dragging the bundle. An Indian sat cross-legged, his right hand tapping a small drum between his legs, his left at his side, holding something. He seemed transfixed, his eyes staring into the coals.

"This here *nog-nee* is —" Tommy began.

"Sit down," the man interrupted in a calm but strong voice, without looking up. "I've been expecting you." He paused. "*Both* of you." His words were firm and measured. He wore faded jeans, boots that had seen better times, an army shirt, and a rain jacket. On his head was an old, beat-up khaki hat, its front bent back. He stood and focused on Allan and Tommy. Middle-aged, tall and lean, he seemed in excellent condition. His skin was dark over his high cheekbones, large nose, and ears, which were also oversized. His eyes were slightly slanted, dark irises, very clear. He wore his long, jet-black hair tied back. He looked like he could have been an Indian chief in an old Western.

"I brought skins," Tommy offered. "Got the stuff for me to take back?"

"My name is Osceola," the man said matter-of-factly, paying no attention to Tommy. "James Osceola. Just about the last shaman around here. Our young people aren't much interested in Miccosukee culture. I badly need to find someone to follow me, perpetuate and preserve our languages. There are two. Understand and pass on our heritage."

His speech, manner, and word selection were those of a man with keen intelligence, and perhaps a first-rate education.

When Osceola walked over and stood close, Allan noticed they were roughly the same height. "You are supposed to have come," he said quietly and put his hand out to shake Allan's. He spoke in a strong tone, examining Allan's face as if he knew him from a previous life. "Your eyes are like ours. You are not a stranger. What is your name?"

Allan thought that somehow he must be dreaming. "Daniels.

Allan Daniels." Osceola waited. Allan cleared his throat. "My m-m-mother," he said with a slight stammer, "w-was born down here. Miccosukee. Went north after she met my father. Converted to his religion."

"Your *wáàche.* She is still Miccosukee," Osceola retorted earnestly. "That makes you Miccosukee. Comes down through the maternal side."

"Suppose so," Allan responded with a smile. "I guess I'm sort of an accident."

"*Nothing* is an accident," Osceola continued resolutely. "Sometimes it may seem so, but everything we see, everything we are, all is part of the whole." He brought his hands up to the level of his head, palms facing upward. "All things are equal. All part of a totality we Indians accept but do not fully understand. Everything always was. Everything is. And everything always will be. The Great Spirit creates and is part of everything. Every thing — small, large, alive or not — has a soul. That's our basic belief."

Allan listened, struck by the simplicity of his words and the sense they seemed to make. "What you said, that the mother determines the religion —"

"Sit down," Osceola said, almost ordering. "There is much for you to learn." He took a deep breath.

"Hey, Jimmy," Tommy interrupted, "what the fuck. I got my skins for you. Let's trade up. No need to spend time talkin' to this fuck. He ain't really one of us."

Osceola fixed Tommy with a stare and nodded for Allan to sit next to him.

"Perhaps you know this, perhaps not. We Miccosukees are descended from fewer than two hundred who survived the third and last Seminole War in eighteen fifty-eight. Didn't trust the government, what they promised. When they wanted to ship us out to

Oklahoma. We had learned what happened to Geronimo and his Apaches out there. Our people hid out deep in the Everglades. They finally gave up trying to get us. We were too creative, too resourceful. Do you have any idea how difficult it was for us to survive, especially at the beginning?

"Daniels," he continued at full vent, "do you at least know what your mother's clan is? Her maiden name? *i:ci,* Deer. *Fah-blee-chee,* Wind. *Ko:wî:,* Panther. Or *chen-te.* Snake. One of those? Where did they live, exactly? What is her Indian name?" His focus on Allan's eyes was unequivocal.

"She told us her last name was Tustenuggee. Panther clan. Her village was on the Tamiami Trail. She told my sister and me things about her life before she left to work in Miami. Before she met my father."

Osceola remained stock-still. "I guess," Allan went on, "she's pretty much accepted that we were not all that interested. I mean, Long Island's such a different place. She wanted to fit in. Decided it would be better for her children to follow my father's religion. But she still has great pride being Indian. No other Indians like her up north, where we live, anyway."

"There are American Indians everywhere," Osceola countered. "Sadly, most have assimilated. Through intermarriage, they're down to an eighth, a sixteenth, thirty-second, or even sixty-fourth." He gazed over at Tommy. "One of our leaders, James Billie, and another, Ruby Tiger Osceola, said a while back that in a hundred years, there probably won't be any of us left. All swallowed up by the whites. Gone. They believe — I do too — that we must fight to hold onto what little of our culture and blood are left. Convince Indians they should be proud to have Indian blood in them. What we are, what we know about living properly with nature, should be emulated." He stood, arms extended, and looked ahead. "We must help our young people, push them to get educated, convince them to take their place and succeed in society *but remain Indian.* That is absolutely imperative."

He pointed first to Allan, then to Tommy. "Look at the two of you. Miccosukee. Miccosukee. Both of you. On your mother's side, where it counts. But you couldn't be any more different."

That's for sure, Allan thought.

Tommy said, "Yeah, you're sure right 'bout that. For me, nothin' but trouble bein' half-breed. Shitty old man, a mother who couldn't handle him. Didn't get much of a chance, did I?" His voice rose, then calmed. "You, Jimmy, you kind of made it. Raised up on Pine Island Ridge in Davie. By that white family. Put you through school an' all, didn't they?"

"Damn lucky about that," Osceola agreed, looking away. "But I had to work my ass off through college. Graduated with a degree in accounting, but companies' doors were pretty much closed. I'd come in for an interview, they'd see the color of my skin. Maybe things have gotten better, but I wouldn't count on it. Not yet, anyway."

Allan asked, "Why do you live in the Everglades?"

Osceola ran his fingers over his eyes. "Wife died. Cancer. She was Seminole . . . our kids . . . I don't see much of them. One over in Everglades City. Two others in Chokoloskee or Immokalee, another doing well in Pahohee. Drugs got three of them. Can't help them anymore. With them, I had been hoping." He turned away, his lips tightening. "But that's over." He sat again and stirred the coals. "Tommy here, well, he got in some trouble. All he can do now is live deeper, back in there. For now, anyway." He reached over into his backpack and pulled out bread, ham, and some American cheese. He laid it out on his jacket, then said, "*Impigee.* Help yourselves. There's Pepsi, too."

Allan and Tommy quickly made sandwiches. Osceola smiled and continued. "No doubt, Allan Daniels, you think you're listening to an old codger unwilling to accept new ways. Stuck in the past." He pulled a cigarette from a pack and lit it, cleared his throat. "Today the American dream is bathed in greed and craziness. I know, I know. Look, obviously we mean shit to the white society. A bunch of stupid Indians with strange customs. But we're beginning to fight harder for self-determination. And redemption and reclamation.

"That Mandan up in North Dakota. Arnold (Bear Comes Back) Cade. A helluva guy. His great-grandfather, Cherry Necklace, saved Lewis and Clark that terrible winter in 1804. In 1943, those bastards in Congress abrogated the treaties with just about all the sovereign Indian nations. Remember, we were *sovereign nations.* Took the Mandans' bottomlands to build a dam. Shoved them into destitution. Terrible conditions. Tarpaper shacks. No water, no heat. Just about amounted to genocide. So here's this youngster, Arnold, the youngest in a family of ten, gets a scholarship to Stanford, does so well, gets one to Yale Law School, after that gets another to Harvard for a master's in public policy.

"And listen to this," he said, winding up, "fights for years for his and other tribes. With that dam, the Mandan Hidatsa and Arikara tribes, former enemies, were forced to combine in order to survive."

His face turned angry. "You cannot possibly imagine the terrible conditions we Indians faced all over America. Even now for so many. Tribes pushed onto the worst lands, off their farms, ranches, and rivers they'd been living on successfully, some for a thousand years or more. Just about all their bison decimated. So," he paused for a moment, then said gravely, "guys like Cade have become our leaders. Someone said we should call them Coyote Warriors." Looking sharply at Allan. "God knows, we need them."

Allan looked down at the fire, glanced at Tommy, then gazed across the hummock before coming back to Osceola. "I never knew about this, these things. I mean —"

"You damn well should, Daniels. We Miccosukees and Seminoles have a better sense of time and history than whites. Other tribes do, too. And especially about nature, its significance. The whites have been slowly decimating Florida ever since they came to settle. Our chairman said it best: "The Everglades is our mother, and She is dying." Sure, people move down, nice weather, jobs, easy living. But what's happening to the magnificent Everglades?" he asked, his voice rising. "Our incredible natural resources and wildlife, freshwater that's been flowing southward for tens of thousands of years? Those sugar bastards and developers are siphoning it off, that's what. Sons of bitches. Some day we'll probably need desalinization. Look around. Other parts of our nation are also being trashed. Acid rain spreading northeast, killing those beautiful forests. Overgrazing. Overfishing. And, very significant, pollution and the climate. It's happening slowly, but happening!"

He drew on his cigarette, looked up, and shook his head. "Soon it may be too late."

"What do you expect me to do?" Allan asked.

"I'll tell you what, Daniels," he said. "At least learn where the hell you come from. Learn about the significance of the Green Corn Dance. The Hunting Dance. The Snake Dance. Become involved. You could be an important voice. Make a difference. You could help continue our oral history. Miccosukee is our tongue. There's another, Hitchiti. It's unwritten. The older folk, who live more remotely, some still speak it."

Osceola looked away. His forehead furrowed. "There is something else."

Allan asked, "What? What is it?"

Osceola glared, then said very slowly, "You have a problem."

"I do?"

"Yes." He looked away. "You think too much in the present."

"Doesn't everyone?"

"You've got to understand yesterday but go beyond today. You have to be more into tomorrow. You have to think in the future. If you can do that, learn that, you can be an effective member of our tribe. And," he said, putting his hand on Allan's head, "you will. I know this to be true."

"Well, ah . . . that's not possible. When will—"

"Do not ask that," Osceola answered. "You will know when, Allan Daniels. You will know."

"C'mon, Jimmy, for Christ's sake," Tommy pleaded, "he ain't the fuck interested. I gotta get goin'. Too close to the law here."

Osceola nodded, rose, and walked over to his boat. "There," he said, "take a look, Tommy. Same as last time: dry stuff, the muffins you like, coffee, some cans of gas, engine parts you talked about, a new knife. A few more things I threw in."

Tommy examined the items, counted some of them, smiled, then went down to his boat to load them.

When Tommy was out of earshot, Allan turned to Osceola. "Can I go with you? Get to where I can call the seaplane base in Key West and the FAA? I need to tell them where I think the plane went down. Let my family know I'm all right."

Osceola shook his head. "My boat can take only one person. And now I've got to make room for the skins."

"Can you at least make some calls?"

"There's no telephone where I live, and if I tell them about you, they're liable to find Tommy's camp." He waved his hand side to side. "Couldn't do that to him. He'll take you out."

Allan glanced over at Tommy tying up the goods. *God, I hope so,* he thought. He turned to Osceola. "Thanks for . . . for sharing with me those things about the tribe." Osceola nodded, and the two men shook hands.

"We will talk again, Daniels. There will be another time, I am sure. Maybe several." With that, Allan climbed into Tommy's boat. As they headed down the channel, Osceola waved them on.

Yes, Allan thought, *there will be another time.*

12

BACK AT TOMMY'S CAMP, after some food and banal conversation, Tommy suddenly said with a laugh, "You, Miccosukee, sleep there, same as last night." Allan dragged boughs to a spot opposite Tommy's on the other side of the fire and placed a tarp over the boughs. *Gotta stay awake. Make the fire bigger. Watch him.*

"Hey!" Tommy said. "Don't keep puttin' wood on the fire. Ain't got a shitload, y'know. And hard enough to fuckin' get."

"I'm cold, thought I'd keep the fire going."

"I said no more wood!" Tommy yelled. He threw Allan a slicker, which smelled fetid, musty. He put it down.

Allan had risen at 4:30 the previous day in Charleston. He was worn out from the flight, but more from the bizarre events since he had gone down. To better protect it, he had placed his wallet in the pocket of his jacket, which he wore for warmth and to fend off mosquitoes. He propped himself against a bench to make sure he remained uncomfortable. It worked for a while, but soon his lower jaw dropped and he fell asleep.

Allan stirred at the sensation of groping hands. His heart pounded as he felt his wallet being slipped out of his pocket.

Tommy was crawling away. Without thinking, Allan grabbed the closest object, a piece of firewood. Tommy threw his hand up to deflect the blow. Too late. The blow struck, not on the top of his head, where Allan had aimed, but just behind the right ear.

Allan heard the thud. He imagined the blow may have torn into Tommy's skull, flattening all patterns of reflex. An ooze began to appear at the edge of his mouth.

Allan had taken his one opportunity to strike his aggressor, he reasoned. It was instinct. *Son of a bitch shouldn't have taken me for granted.*

"Ahhhhh . . ." Tommy hit the ground, his body folding, his mind gone blank.

"Oh, God," Allan cried, standing over Tommy with his club, not ready to put it down. *This boy is dying. What the hell did I do? Oh, God.*

Tommy writhed like a snake trying to shake off a wound. Then the groaning stopped, replaced by erratic breathing, spurts of air pulled in and pushed out, a weak bellows slowly losing momentum.

A .38 pistol had jolted from Tommy's belt. *Oh, the little son of a bitch! He would surely have gotten rid of me, no question.* Allan picked up the gun and sank down on a stool. Tommy lay dumbly on the ground, legs skewed, chest and head twisted. Yellowish sputum bubbled from the corner of his mouth.

Tommy was still breathing, but his breath was labored. Allan put logs on the fire, covered Tommy with clothes and tarps, and lit the kerosene lamp on the table. He tried to sit out the long night but kept dozing off, forever waking to the sounds of Tommy's spasms. The light ripened slowly.

OK, getting out of here, back to where I went down . . . the radio in the plane. No, better go south to Florida Bay, the Keys . . . fishing boats . . . Coast Guard . . . spotted from the air. Go, just go.

Allan rose, peered outside then back at Tommy. He knelt down, appalled at how flaccid Tommy's body had become, his face sagging, his mouth hanging open. His ocher-colored skin looked ghastly. Blood matted his hair, a huge swelling where the blow had landed.

Allan dragged Tommy to the dock, carefully placed him into the boat, laid him gently face up, put some clothes under his head, and covered him with a tarp. He brought an extra gas can, rolled some food into a shirt, and filled a thermos and a plastic bag with water from the drum. *What else?* He scrutinized the shack, the clearing, then pushed off. Within moments he turned around, back to camp. He went inside the shack, took the pistol, grabbed two torn straw hats, put one on, then covered Tommy's face with the other.

The morning air felt refreshing, a light breeze flowing from the southwest. Cumulus clouds were tinted with the pink of sunrise. The sky broadened as the water pathway widened. Allan hoped the weather would hold up. Squawks and caws emanated from the mangroves, the same he had heard from his downed seaplane.

He chose the widest channels, around one island, then another, and another. Tommy lay motionless. The day heated up rapidly, the light clarifying the horror of what had happened.

After about an hour, Allan shoved the gear lever into neutral to check on Tommy. He removed the hat and gazed at his head. The spot where the blow had landed had the deep red of rage, an insult Tommy's body didn't seem to be able to handle. The corner of his mouth was thick with spittle and dried blood. He made sure his head was cushioned with clothes against the front seat. He recoiled at the chalky face, the color of life bleached out.

Several hours later, the channel finally opened onto Florida Bay. Further out still, he selected a mangrove island and put in. He knelt down, straddling Tommy's body. The boy's eyes were shut, his breathing more labored than ever. Allan leaned closer and cradled the young man's head gently in his hands. "Hang in there," he said, more to himself than to Tommy. The eyes opened, but were glazed.

"You'll . . . you'll be all right," Allan said. "I'm taking us out so we can get help." Tommy's eyes widened in fright. He tried to raise himself but immediately collapsed. Allan stroked his matted hair, clammy forehead, and cheeks.

"I would have given you money, tried to help you . . ."

Tommy's voice came in whispers, his words slow and hushed. "I shot . . . a man . . ." His eyes seemed to focus on something beyond Allan. "They'd . . . get me in there . . . or . . . die . . . here . . ."

"No, Tommy, no! Don't die on me."

Tommy moaned, his face a mask, his eyes shut.

God, please don't let him die. Allan leaned forward, held the wasted man in his arms, his cheek against Tommy's head. The boy's eyes fluttered open, then shut again. Allan heard what he believed was his final exhalation.

Allan rocked back and forth, back and forth. Tears streamed, blinding his sight. "Oh, no, no, no . . . ," he muttered, then slumped forward, his head shaking in disbelief.

13

ALLAN SKIRTED A SAND BAR but had to cut back about ninety degrees. So many islands, part land, part water, with mud flats and sometimes sandy fringes. It was difficult to delineate land from water. He idled the motor, stood up, and took note of the Number Three marker. The continuous mangled mangrove roots of the shore of an island, if it could be called that, came closer. Allan searched for a place to land and noticed a very small beach.

The craft coasted until its hull met the sand underneath. Allan jumped out, lifted the propeller out of the water, dragged the boat up onto the sand, and tied the bowline to a thick root.

Flaps of white blur jumped up out of the mangroves. Allan recoiled from the sound. Snowy egrets, their bristled plumage tucked in, bounded away into smooth flight, slim and assertive. Cormorants, all black except for orange throat pouches, spilled out. Nearby, three roseate spoonbills, large and pink with flattened bill tips, also rose, their wings gulping large quantities of air.

Something else stirred that was not so pretty. Mosquitoes. They did not fly away. Scouts checked him out, sent back a report. Allan clamped his hat on, pulled out his repellent, traded slaps for bites.

He climbed up into the mangroves, then made his way through the vines to the northernmost point of the island, dragging the tarp with Tommy inside. It was slow and difficult work. He hid the body where it would not be visible.

My God, what have I done?

Instinctively, Allan looked around again, then collapsed into a sitting position on some roots. He felt his heart beating hard in his chest.

There were large animals in the 'glades. Alligators, a few Florida panthers, saltwater crocodiles, bear, deer, some foxes and coyotes. But few if any here in this area, he was pretty sure. The mosquitoes more than made up for it. They set upon him as if they hadn't had a meal in weeks. Allan pulled the repellent out again from his pants pocket and patted it vigorously onto his damp clothes, neck, and face. He scrambled from the vines, raced to the water, submerged, rose, and ran as fast as he could to the boat. He dragged it out, pushed the back of the engine down, jumped in, and pulled the cord hard to start the motor. It broke.

The attackers did not waste time, little affected by the repellent. He dropped the anchor, dashed back into the mangroves to the tarp. He unfolded it and ducked under.

Allan shuddered from the thought of sharing it with Tommy. In short order, he decided to race back to the boat. *My shoelaces tied together. Or better, a piece of line.*

Some thin line, knotted at one end, worked. The engine started.

It had all taken too much time. The afternoon was emptying out. Allan decided he would have to spend the night drifting and fighting the mosquitoes.

Allan was caught in the sun's relentless scorch. It became even stronger reflecting off the still water. Tommy's hat blocked some of its fire. All the fresh water had been consumed. His jacket and shorts did not cover enough skin. He could feel the burn. Every so often, he sloshed water on his legs, even though he knew that salt water makes sunburn worse.

Allan began to hallucinate. He was floating on a mysterious body of water. A little like flying a few days before.

I will survive. I will survive. I will . . . His mind shifted to what had happened with Tommy. *Oh, my God . . . Paddle to that island . . . overhanging mangroves . . . out of the sun. Lie down on the bottom of the boat. Cover up, rest . . . rest . . . Oh, my God. What have I done?*

14

AT FIRST HE COULDN'T BE SURE if he was imagining it. But when the sound became louder, he lifted himself up to see a fishing boat speeding toward him, three men on board. He dropped the pistol quickly over the side of the boat, then started to clap.

"You're lucky, buddy, damn lucky. We were headin' back," said the captain with a smile. "I'm Norm Seltzer. Almost didn't see y'all. One of the guys was lookin' around through my binocs." The man was tall, about thirty-five, his body bronzed and leaned by a life on the water. His face was prematurely lined, grooves fashioned by the unremitting sun mirroring off the salt water. He wore a cap with ISLAMORADA FISHING printed on it. The expression in his eyes was that of a man whose curiosity and purpose were tempered by patience.

Allan looked up at him with fuzzy eyes. Seltzer reached down over the gunwale, his arms strong and welcoming.

"Here, grab my hand. Y'all look like you've been out here for days." Allan handed up his duffle and backpack.

"What'cha doin' out here? Where the devil were you headin'? Wouldn't want to be in that thing if a storm came up. We get some bad ones. Hey," he continued, "some blood on your ear, an' some more on the back of your jaw. You get hurt?"

Allan instinctively put his fingers against his jaw and rubbed, trying to remove the blood, but stopped himself.

"Ah, it's from . . . from an Indian boy who found my plane." The three men stared at Allan as if he were having some kind of apparition. "Went down way back in there a couple of days ago. Ferrying a seaplane. I bought the boat from him." Allan was shaking.

"Said he'd been fishing and caught his finger on a hook. Pretty deep. Bled a lot. I had a kit.

"Can't tell you how thankful I am you found me," he blurted. "Name's Daniels, Allan Daniels. Man, that sun was turning me into dried fruit. I'm bushed. I'd appreciate some water and a place to lie down for a little while." After he'd drunk some bottled water, one of the fishermen offered him a flask of Jack Daniels and a sandwich. He refused the flask.

Below, in the small sink in the boat's head, Allan washed away whatever was left of the blood, then dropped onto a bunk. When he closed his eyes, the patterns of light and shade on his eyelids came in through the porthole. He quickly fell into a deep sleep, aided by the engine's steady rhythm.

When he woke up he was a little lightheaded, so he carefully walked up the steps. He held onto the rail and took a couple of deep breaths. He glanced at his watch: it was about an hour since he had collapsed on the bunk.

"Hey, Daniels," the captain said from the helm, "you better sit down. In the shade. An' drink some more water so you don't get more dehydrated. Where'd you come from in there?"

Allan sat down opposite Seltzer. "Engine went dead. Had to make a forced landing," he said between sips.

The two other men stood near him. One of them said, "Must have been scary. Wow, you look shot."

"Yeah, a little. Came out of the swamps somewhere northeast of here. I guess I chose the right channel. The Indian boy who found me didn't want to take me out, so I bought his boat. Told me to keep heading south, I'd hit the bay, then you saw me. God, what a place. I mean it's awesome in there . . . the boat conked out once or twice. Probably lousy gas like I had in my plane."

"Yeah, you're the guy," Seltzer exclaimed. "They've been searchin' all over. I called in an' told them we'd found you. Glad you made it, buddy. There've been guys who've gone down and were never found. Alive, that is. I'm a guide. Fishin' parties is what I do. Pretty good today, hooked two nice tarpon. Catch an' release, but we got some trout. Eatin' fish." He kept talking. "Tomorrow we'll be out for bonefish. Spooky on the flats. Have to stalk 'em. Gets excitin'." He seemed pleased with himself, smiling a little boy's smile.

"You really saved my ass," Allan said. "Under that sun, I was beginning to lose it." Allan gazed ahead at the seemingly numberless mangrove islands, then back across the stern. The huge expanse of water seemed to spill over the horizon. "Hey, why are you towing the boat? Nothing worth saving except the engine. We could take it on board."

"Haskins — he's the sheriff — will want to see everythin'. Doesn't mean anythin', just the way he is." Seltzer lit a Salem, crushed the pack, and turned from one channel into another. Allan watched the compass swing south-southeast. "Headin' to Islamorada," Norm said with a smile, "where I'm out of."

As they approached the marina, he announced, "After we pull in, I'll drive you over to the sheriff's office. Billy said I should. Right off. For a motel, Trade Winds is the place. An' the Tiki Bar. The guys hang out there after work. Good place, good prices. Plenty of beer an' laughs.

"You'd be one of those pilots I see flyin' tourists around the Keys? I watch you guys. One day I'd like to go over to the Dry Tortugas and Fort Jefferson. Quite a place, you know. Kept those poor bastards there durin' the Civil War. Bein' in jail is one thing, but those guys just rotted." He shivered at the thought.

"No, not me. Just ferrying a plane down from Long Island. Have to get back." His eyes shifted toward the distant islands, which looked like dark green bubbles sliding on top of the turquoise water.

"Want some more to eat?" one of the fishermen asked. "How about a shot of bourbon or an Amstel? That'll fix you up."

"Another sandwich if you have one," Allan answered. "No booze, thanks."

They reached the marina. Seltzer backed the boat perfectly into its slip at the Islamorada Yacht Club and tied the lines. His clients stood next to him with cash in their hands while he filleted their catch. Then he began to hose down the decks.

"After y'all finish over at Haskins', you'll see the Trade Winds a little ways back down the road. Come to the Tiki. We'll down a couple."

"I sure will," Allan replied with a tired grin. "And, by the way, drinks are on me. See you in a minute," Allan added. He walked through the yacht club's darkly lit bar and slipped into the door marked "Sailor's Head." He glanced around warily. He was alone. *Make sure it's all off,* he thought as he checked the mirror to make sure no blood had escaped his earlier effort.

15

As they got into his pickup, Norm told Allan, "Ain't very far. Good sheriff, Billy Haskins. An alright guy. An' real dedicated. We all grew up together."

"Islamorada sure isn't like Brookville," Allan observed as they pulled away. "On Long Island, where I live."

"Been to New York one time," Norm said. "Ain't my kind of place." He threw his half-finished cigarette out the window. "You, ah, seem a little nervous. Should be just, you know, routinelike."

Allan studied everything he saw. He noticed the Greyhound bus-stop sign at a gas station, by Moose Lodge Number 141, "God Bless America" painted on the stucco. A group of five small stores.

"Bus makes four trips a day, two west an' two east," Norm said.

They came upon the one-story, tan-and-white Monroe County municipal building. Town clerk, tax collector, and sheriff's department. Two red-tile steps connected the walk to the concrete structure. On one side, a barbed-wire fence surrounded a hundred-foot radio tower. A sign on the other side read "Prisoner Intake Parking Only." The jail was a small rectangular appendage to the main building. Allan noticed several small windows with black bars.

"Get many prisoners?" he asked nonchalantly as they pulled in.

"Naw, nothin' heavy. Those guys are sent up to Miami."

Allan slid out of Norm's pickup and shook hands. He stepped behind the sheriff's Plymouth Gran Fury, Florida official plate 6888. The short walk to the front door was bordered by green ilex.

Allan hesitated, took a few deep breaths and straightened his shoulders, then opened the glass door and walked through the small lobby. He stood there for a few minutes, completely unaware he was mouthing words: *Keep cool. Calm . . . decisive. . .*

A middle-aged black woman in an old, shabby dress sat on the bench next to a man slumped forward, his hands between his legs.

Allan knocked on the second door inside and opened it. "Sheriff?" Allan asked.

"Ah, Mister Daniels," Haskins said, coming out from the rear office. "C'mon in. We'll talk a bit. You want some coffee?" he added in a sonorous, friendly voice. He smiled, his crisp, blue eyes carefully inspecting Allan's for any reaction. "Nobody gets a job around here unless he knows how to do good coffee." He laughed. "'Course, he's gotta know a few other things, too."

Allan judged Haskins to be in his middle to late thirties. Thinning brown hair, his broad face starting to hang from weight, folds in his neck, rivulets like baby fat. His belly bowed out, which Allan assumed was the result of too much beer. But his stance was erect, his movements effortless.

A black leather jacket hung on the aluminum clothing tree next to the doorway. A conspicuous, sewn-on patch read "Florida Sheriffs' Association." On the wall behind his desk, pictures of a bowling team, a man standing next to a large fish hung by its tail, and an older photo of a man with a boy, presumably Haskins with his father.

"Cream and sugar? No? Well now, Mister Daniels, let's just look at a few things." The sheriff sat in a frayed swivel chair and put his feet up on an old desk. Under his carefully pressed uniform, Allan could see the white ends of his long woolen underwear protruding from the bottom of his trousers. "You said you were picked up by an Indian. Recall his name? Maybe show me on this map here where your plane went down? Ah, and that camp of his?" The sheriff leaned back in his chair, its leather seat splitting, the white stuffing ready to ooze out. "Norm mentioned some blood on your face when he picked you up." Haskins took his pencil and slowly placed it between his two index fingers. "You get cut or somethin'?" he demanded more than asked.

Allan stood next to the window. The contrail of a jet extended east across the sky. *Slow and easy,* he thought. He put his coffee mug down as he sat and said carefully, "Look, Sheriff, it was a little hectic out there. He kinda mumbled, but I, ah, think he said his name was Tim . . . or Tom or something. Yeah, Tom. I went down somewhere about . . . here." Allan drew a fast, wide, circle with his index finger on the large Coast and Geodetic Survey map on the wall behind him. "And as far as his camp, too hard to tell. In those swamps, everything looks the same, at least to me." He stared at the sheriff, whose face remained impassive.

"As far as the blood, as I told Norm," Allan said, as convincingly as he could, "the kid said he'd caught a hook in his finger just before he came over to my plane. I had a first-aid kit and fixed him up. Bleeding was pretty heavy. Must have gotten some on me."

"Uh-huh." Haskins leaned forward, the chair's front legs striking the floor with a noisy thud. "Tell you what. We're gonna scrape off whatever may still be in the boat. Do a little lab test. Just might be the Indian's. Now, that there boat you were in and that camp of his . . . well, hold that for a bit." He leaned forward, then rose and walked across the room to face Allen. "You know, Mister Daniels, you look pretty damn bushed. Imagine you'll be stayin' at the Trade Winds." He brought his face closer to Allan's. "If you don't mind, I want you to write out exactly what happened. How and when. With a full description of what that boy looked like. Could be one of those bad ones. Got a couple in there. Miccosukees or Seminoles. Goddamn hard to find; they sure know the swamps. Learn from the animals. Become animals themselves."

Haskins raised his coffee mug and drained it, without taking his eyes off Allan. Then he led Allan to the door. "Talked to the Coast Guard. Haven't located your plane yet. Told them where you'd be in case they need to get ahold of you. Want me to drive you over to the motel?"

"No thanks. I need the walk." Allan shook the sheriff's hand firmly. His father once told him that showed other men you weren't weak. They should understand that about you right away.

Allan stepped into the sun, its light, like his energy, draining, its rays beginning to create soft colors for the sunset. His walk to the motel felt unnatural. He stopped a few times, looked cautiously around to see if he was being followed. *Stop being paranoid,* he thought. A hearse drove by, a Cadillac that had seen better days. He supposed it had once been in a city somewhere and ended up here, the end of the line.

The clerk was expecting him. "You don't have to sign the card, Mister Daniels. Gave you a real nice room. Second floor. Looks out over the ocean. Nice and quiet. Here's your bag; Norm dropped it off. Oh, ah, if you have a credit card, I'll just stamp it blank, fill in the amount when you leave. That all right?"

Room 213 was clean, pleasant, and comfortable, but not elaborate in any way. A small balcony with two aluminum chairs overlooking the pool, the wide, flat beach, and the Atlantic curving over the horizon.

Joyce wouldn't like Islamorada, he thought. *Bored. A day or two on the beach . . . She'd prefer the ambiance of Key West . . . Tennessee Williams . . . Key Largo . . . old Cuban section, shrimpers, Navy, gays, shops, food. For me, Islamorada . . . except . . . damnit, what happened back there . . .*

Allan placed his things on the bed, stuck his head under the faucet in the bathroom. He let the water run as cold as it would. He plopped down on the bed, picked up the phone. "Hi, Joyce. Couldn't call earlier. Had a rough couple of days. How are you and the kids?"

"Allan. We were concerned when you didn't arrive in Key West," she answered with an audible sigh. "The seaplane base in Florida just contacted John O'Neill at our base with the news you were found. I talked to your parents but didn't say anything to the kids about your—"

"Good," Allan cut in. "I'll call them later." He paused. "Joyce, I'd really rather be home."

"Craig had . . . he fell and cut his arm. Needed eight stitches. Could have used your help."

"Damn, oh, I'm sorry. Let me talk to him, all right?" He continued, "I . . . after I went down in the Everglades. Crash landing. Lucky I'm alive . . . and then it was rough getting out. I'm in a place called Islamorada. First chance I had to call."

"I was up all night with Craig," she responded, apparently annoyed by his dramatic tale. "He wants his father."

"I'd come back today if I could, only, well, the sheriff down here says I have to stick around. The boat I got out in . . . an Indian boy's . . . it's complicated."

"I do *not* understand a word you're saying," she said. "Tell him your little boy needs you."

"Sheriff's pretty hard-assed." Allan took a deep breath. "Joyce, believe me, I don't *want* to be here. Can I talk to Craig, then Nance?"

"Call your parents," she said. "They're very worried. I spoke to Bob and Polly."

"OK, I will. And listen, the way things are with us . . . this couldn't have happened at a worse time."

"I think you—" Joyce began, but instead put down the phone and called, "Craig, honey, it's your father."

16

He found Norm sitting alone at a table in the Tiki Bar. The room's shellacked pine walls were dotted with photos of smiling fishing captains beside their boats, a few with trophy fish displayed next to them. Several overhead fans circulated the air, which was heavy with the odor of beer and cigarette smoke. Allan wondered why there was no air conditioning.

"Hey, Daniels. Sit down and have a beer. How'd it go with Billy?"

Allan slipped into a chair. "Surprised me a little," Allan said. "I'm not used to sheriffs. Seems determined to dig into every detail. I need to be on my way. Family matters. But it looks like this may take a while."

Norm signaled a waitress, who brought frosted mugs of Red Stripe, a lager-style beer from Jamaica. "I guess you oughtta know somethin' about Billy," Norm offered. "No secret around here why he's considered the best sheriff between Key West and Miami. Good guy most of the time, but watch out when he thinks he's gettin' crossed. Hell, state of Florida gave him some big award a few years back."

"That right?" Allan asked.

"Damn bright," Norm went on. "I should know. Friends since we was kids. Could've gone to college an' maybe law school up to Gainesville. Billy used to work at Pinder's Department Store. George Pinder offered to pay the costs but Billy turned him down. If there's a man cut out to do what he does, sure is Billy Haskins. What he is has a lot to do with his dad. They was real close. Used to go fishin' in the 'glades." Seltzer lifted his mug to his mouth and took a big swig. "I remember Billy tellin' me about a time when he was, oh, I guess about ten, eleven. Got caught out there. Had to wait out a big storm. Didn't make no difference, because they liked being together so much. Spent the night holed up against a big old cypress in a lean-to his father rigged.

"Anyways, sometime before light, his father woke him. He'd gone out to check their boat an' didn't see the moccasin before it bit him. Was real calm as he talked. The bite hurt an' had to be taken care of, but the important thing was not to get excited. You need to slow way down, so you could think straight an' make the best decisions."

He took another swig of beer and checked the bar to see if anyone was listening. "Billy watched his father remove the snake kit from his sack, take the knife, an' cut Xs in the area of the bite, squeezin' out the blood, getting the venom out. Keepin' the pain to himself. Do what he had to.

"Couple of months later, a terrible thing happened. His father owned a gas station at the edge of town. Billy was helpin'. Just after dark, four black men drove in, shoved them into the back room, pistol-whipped Billy's dad, an' went for the cash register. When his daddy resisted, they knifed him an' sped off. Billy called on the phone for help an' they took his dad to Fisherman's Hospital in Marathon, but it was too late."

"Damn," Allan said, shaking his head, "how horrible."

"Anyway," Norm resumed, "Billy was never the same. All he talked about was how one day he would find a way to do somethin' about the kind of men who killed his daddy. So when he was sixteen, a sophomore, Billy became a real good boxer an' wrestler. Filled out, trained with barbells, ran. Played first-string offensive end on the football team but was an even better defensive linebacker. Loved tacklin', knockin' down passes, sackin' the quarterback.

"Worked two jobs, one after school at Irene and George Pinder's Department Store, the other on Saturdays at his father's old gas station. Sometimes, Friday after work, he'd hitchhike up to Florida City, just south of Miami, where he'd stay with his cousin, Bobby Joe. Got into fights, him an' Bobby Joe. Bobby Joe got ten stitches in his head one time, one of the black boys he was fightin' got a broken arm an' another suffered eye damage. The black kids claimed Billy an' Bobby Joe started it, which they probably did. Our sheriff, Johnson, told him he couldn't get back at the men who killed his father by beatin' up Negros. The sheriff told Billy he had somethin' special goin' for himself. Everybody in Islamorada knew Billy was bright."

Norm picked up his beer and drained it. "Billy told Mister Pinder he wanted to be a sheriff. That was it. Anyway," he said, "one time some guys robbed a store at the end of a day. I saw them leavin', racin' over toward Plantation Key. Negros. I called Billy. He told me to cut 'em off before they got away, said, 'Get those motherfuckers! Nail 'em!' Told me to keep watchin' them. He'd be listenin' from his car. He moves faster than you might think for a big man. Billy can sweep up his pistol and holster with his left hand, his hat with his right, an' in a flash he'd be racin' down U.S. 1.

"It'd been cloudy that day, rain heavier by evenin'. The half-moon visible the previous night was shinin' somewhere else, I guess. I could see Billy's flashin' red lights reflectin' on the wet concrete of the bridge. Anyway, we cornered them, all right, but they turned off U.S. 1 into a field an' started runnin'. Billy yelled for them to stop. Kept runnin'. Two shots. The first caused one of them to straighten up, the second shot dropped him. Slumped an' dropped, folded in half like he was doin' exercises. The men all stood still, like you see in a church or a cemetery, us hopin' he had just been wounded. 'Holy Christ!' someone yelled. We started walkin', then ran. The other man tore free, ran to the one lyin' face down. Haskins caught up with him, big hand on his shirt collar. They made a circle as Haskins, still grippin' his prisoner, turned over what appeared to be a teenager. The man fell to his knees an' put his arm under the boy's head.

"I'll never forget what he said. 'Robby, Robby, my Robby,' his face pressed against the boy's head, against his neck. Blood spillin' out from the kid's mouth. 'Lord, Lord, no, no!' The others stood, hardly believin' what had happened. The man rocked up and back, moans an' cries right through the worst of the heavy rain.

"'He's only fifteen, oh Lord, Lordie, no! He's just made fifteen!' Haskins motioned everyone away. They walked slowly to their cars. The deputy ran to the phone in his car.

"Ten minutes later, an ambulance comes, siren wailin'. Covered the boy's body an' lifted it inside. The second bullet had torn into the kid's heart. Haskins led the father to his car, into the back seat, separated from the front by heavy steel mesh. I could see the father weepin'. Billy just stood there, shakin' his head, but his face said it all: white as a sheet. I always wondered if he was thinking about his daddy. Thinkin': did I overreach? Don't know till this day, though. Billy never talks about it. And I'm sure never will."

17

A couple of Norm's friends joined him in the bar. One was short, bearded, and wiry, the other taller and on the heavy side. Both wore ISLAMORADA FISHING caps.

"Hey, Seltzer, who's this guy, another dumb Conch like you up from Marathon?"

"No, you jerk, he's not a Conch. Name's Allan. Allan Daniels. Fished him out of the bay. On some Indian's boat, for God's sake. Came right out of the fuckin' 'glades. Pilot. Lost his seaplane in there."

Allan stood and shook hands with the two men. They introduced themselves. Harry Slade, the shorter, Cal Howard, the bigger man. They asked Allan what had happened with his seaplane.

The waitress brought a round of beers. The men began to share their day's experiences, exaggerated tales about bonefish and tarpon they had caught, and the ones that got away. And the construction jobs they were working on.

The waitress swung her hips and smiled at Allan. On a trip from the bar, she brushed against the back of his head. When she came by again to ask if they wanted another round, she leaned over, smiling, her breasts visible in her low-cut blouse. "I'm Peggy, honey, and if I can do anything for you, just let me know."

Allan looked up at her, smiled, and said, "Thanks, I'll let you know."

The banter among the locals at his table began to wear on Allan, like a song played repeatedly, losing its appeal. He missed Joyce, missed the kids, the perfect family he thought they had been. He thought about the many things they enjoyed together: symphonic music, avant-garde shows, classic theater: Shakespeare, Ibsen, Shaw, Chekhov. Talking. Weekends with the kids, skiing at the Middlebury Snow Bowl. Vacations at the Basin Harbor Club on Lake Champlain. That special weekend in Washington. When the kids were babies, feeding them at all hours, changing Nance's diapers, bathing Craig. Showing them off to family and friends as if no one else had ever before had similar feelings.

Suddenly someone threw a swizzle stick across the table, bringing him back to reality. "Big Norm, did ya let some whoppers get away today?"

"Listen, Cal, you clown," Norm fired back, "if I were you, I'd stick to tryin' to be an electrician an' not for one second pretend you know the difference between a tarpon an' a bonefish."

"You know, Seltzer," Cal countered, "listenin' to you is like listenin' to my mother-in-law. Can't turn her off, but you I can." He thumbed his nose. "Hey, have another beer, 'cause today ain't your turn to pay."

Howard seemed like a man who'd be content to spend his entire life in Islamorada. "I don't know who was luckier today," he said, turning to Allan. "Big Norm findin' you, or," he proffered a big grin, "you findin' him. More than likely he was lost himself." He took another swig, playing it for all he could. "An' didn't even know it. Findin' you made him have to look at his compass, which he never could figure out. We never let him go out to the Atlantic. He'd end up in Cuba for sure. Or some island in the Caribbean eatin' grouper an' coconuts with some native broad."

"You're such a damn bore," Norm shot back. "Everyone knows you can't tell an outlet from a switch."

"We all went through school together," Cal explained. "He's as much a dumbass today as he was back in kindergarten. We're small townish down here an', well, Conchs. Like it that way."

"Hey, Allan, what's that? Yeah, that thing around your neck?"

"A Star of David." Allan removed it and handed the medallion to Norm.

"You're Jewish?"

"Yeah. Also half Indian. Miccosukee."

After a moment Norm looked at him wide-eyed and said, "For real? You don't look or act like one."

Allan stiffened. "Indian or Jew? We get so mixed up, you can't tell one from the other." He thought that pretty funny, but apparently his new friends didn't.

"No, well, I mean, just that I thought Jewish folk were a little different. An' a guy like you, flyin' a plane an' all, the way you seem, you know . . ."

How's he going to get out of this?

"Anyway, don't make no difference to me, OK?" Norm grabbed the waitress's arm as she passed. "Another round, Peg, for me an' my friends."

Allan left and walked outside. The sun had set, and the first stars were starting to appear in the darkening sky, flickering pin lights pointing the way to the universe. There was Jupiter, or perhaps a small failed star. Nearby, Venus, the evening star, and Mars, exhibiting its iron-reddish tint.

Back in his room, he opened the sliding door to the balcony. A moist, mellow breeze swam in. He inhaled its salty, musty flavor, leaned against the doorjamb. He tore the paper that said SANITIZED FOR YOUR HEALTH from one of the glasses on a tray on a dresser, poured Cutty Sark from his flask, ran in some tap water, and stepped out onto the balcony. The lights from a ship slid along the horizon. He took a sip. A tanker or freighter. Another sip. Men heading to Central or South America, maybe Asia. *What would it be like going there on that boat?*

A few more sips. He took off his clothes, turned on the water in the shower, and stepped in. Water splattered his head, startling him. He stood with his back to the stream, letting its warmth hit him on his shoulders, back, buttocks, and legs. He urinated, unwrapped the thin bar of soap, threw the wet wrapping over the top of the curtain, and soaped under his arms, chest, genitals. He remembered his last night at home, wanting to but not having sex with Joyce. That great feeling. He rinsed, stepped out, dried himself, drained the contents of his drink. He reentered the room, dropped down on the bed, and stared at himself in the long mirror on the closet door.

"Shit," he muttered with a grin. He leaned forward toward his reflection and made a face at himself. "I'm getting good and fucking high." He lay down on the bed and closed his eyes. His mind returned to the Everglades. *At least you're out of there alive . . . but Tommy's not.*

He was floating on top of the Scotch, being drawn into the mirror, slipping through and drifting slowly to gruesome places. *Carrion cages in fog-filled rooms, supernatural walls preventing orientation or even balance. A judge and jury lurking somewhere that could be heard but not seen. The murdered staring with their horrific, piercing eyes. Close up. The murderer would have to look back at them. Forever.*

Excuses or explanations were not permitted. Language was devoid of recognizable words. Allan's punishment was to carry an impossibly heavy barbed icon. Like Sisyphus pushing his boulder up a steep incline.

And God. No explanation would be acceptable. Somehow, life and death were interchangeable. Coinciding. Existence — if that's what it could be called — was different than he had ever imagined.

Someone or something had a seared scar that ran from both eyes across his nose, its end torn off and oozing greenish-yellow. Tommy? No, it was Allan, his face so ugly others turned away in disgust.

Heavy, deep, whispering, not human, emanating from separate places. "Any moment, any moment, your death. Can happen at any time. You will never know when . . . You, Allan Daniels . . . you!"

He struggled to pull himself back, back through the mirror. He lay face up on the pillow, panting and sweating. Minutes passed before he felt relieved. Then stillness. Then sleep.

18

ALLAN AWOKE AND SHOWERED AGAIN, scrubbing again the places where the blood had been.

Man, I am hungry, he thought. Norm had recommended the Green Turtle. *Good dinner might pick up my spirits.*

He dressed in khaki pants, a plaid sport shirt, tasseled loafers, no socks. He walked the half mile to the restaurant. Roxy, the owner, showed him to a table. She looked about fifty, with gray frowzy hair cut roughly in line with her chin. Most likely she had been pretty before she became chubby. She spoke with the same accent as the other locals.

"Got fresh dolphin an' yellowtail. Snapper's always good, but tonight I'd go with the dolphin. And, of course, our own special turtle soup."

Menus tucked under her arm, she stood between Allan's table and one occupied by an attractive young couple. "Fresh this mornin', you know. Sid—he's my husband—an' I never serve anythin' but fresh fish. Sid's inside doin' the cookin'. We've had this place over twenty years. Not fancy, but the food's the best in the Middle Keys."

She turned away and said, " 'Bye now, Jane, say hello to your mom for me. Tell her I hope she feels better." She turned back to Allan. "Folks tell us that. Everybody comes here, tradespeople, locals, professionals. Ain't that right, Doc?"

"No question. You and Sid have made the Green Turtle into a remarkable institution." The man laughed and added, "Absolutely no other restaurant anywhere near like the Green Turtle."

Allan had noticed the man she called Doc as soon as he'd walked in. He looked English or Scandinavian, middle to late thirties, tall, trim, with nice features. He had thick walnut-colored hair, well-groomed. He wore khaki slacks, a light blue shirt, a plaid jacket, and no tie. His black-rimmed glasses looked too large for his face. Premature darkness hung just beneath his eyes. He seemed communicative, uncomplicated, self-assured.

Allan's gaze then fixed on his companion. He couldn't help being taken with her. Her manner appeared reserved but not unfriendly; she wore the hint of a smile. She was stunning, exuded femininity. Her sandy, shoulder-length hair curled slightly at the bottom. A narrow nose that was just a little long on her otherwise perfectly proportioned face, a small beauty mark on her right cheek. He focused on her eyes, the color a mixture of Persian and powder blue, if that were possible. She sat erect in her white blouse, her shoulders back. He imagined her breasts. Her motions seemed fluid, like those of an athlete. "Ken and Sue Watts," Roxy said. "Our local doctor. Sue's a writer. What did you say your name was?"

Allan stood up and walked over to their table. Ken Watts rose and shook his hand.

"Daniels. Allan Daniels. A defrocked ventriloquist. Before that I was a cardsharp. That's the problem when you're an escaped psychotic." They looked puzzled, then broke into congenial laughter. "Not really. Nice to meet both of you." He paused. "Back up on Long Island, I'm an architect. On the side, a struggling poet," he said slowly, looking at Sue. She registered a small smile.

"Business or pleasure?" Ken asked. "People come down for the weather. Some for fishing, although *I* never seem to have much luck with fish."

"I was ferrying a seaplane to Key West," Allan said. "An hour or so from my destination, the plane developed engine trouble, and I had to make a forced landing in the Everglades. Only a couple of days ago, but it seems like years." He stopped, shifted his weight, trying to appear taller than he was. "Somehow I got out of there to the bay, where Norm Seltzer picked me up. Know him?"

"Sure do," Ken said. "One of our best guides. Lucky he saw you. You look OK for what happened. Maybe a little played out. Be happy to check you over if you like."

"Thanks," Allan said. "If I develop any aftereffects I'll give you a call." He retreated to his own table.

Roxy brought Allan soup. "I don't think I ordered this," he said, looking up at her.

"No, you didn't, but it's our own special turtle soup, an' with what I hear you've been through, you'd better have it. No charge."

"And I thought my mother was in New York," he said with a grin. "I'm sure it's full of good things. I'm fine, really, just a little worn out. A good night's sleep and I'll be fit as a fiddle. Thanks, though."

His eyes caught Sue's, and she gave him another smile. Ken ordered coffee, his wife herbal tea.

Allan spooned some soup, coughed from the sharp spices. He glanced around the room, trying to seem nonchalant. "Wow."

Roxy laughed. "That's the Tabasco."

"How long will you be here in rainy . . . Seattle?" Sue asked, adding to the light moment. "What kind of writing did you say you did?"

"Poetry," he responded. "My first book was published last year by a small press in Minneapolis. *The Hawk's Dream.* Poems in some magazines out West. Started a novel, but that'll be a while."

Ken pointed to one of the seats at their table. "Why don't you join us?"

Allan nodded and moved over. "What kind of medicine?" he asked Ken.

"I'm a GP."

"Writer?" he asked, turning to Sue.

"Yes. Fiction, short stories, some essays. A few published. My first novel hasn't been." She shook her head. "I just signed on with a great new agent, Nadine Halpern. She's strong on my short stories."

"Everyone knows that a lot of mediocre stuff gets published that doesn't deserve to," Allan broke in, "while too often really good material is turned down."

"It takes oh, so long." She sighed. "All the writing. And the rewriting. And rewriting."

"How long will you be here?" Ken asked.

"Not really sure. Depends on what shape the plane's in, when the Coast Guard finds it. Then flying it out. Some routine stuff with Sheriff Haskins."

He watched, waiting for a response from her. Ken looked over at his wife. "Well, Allan, if you're around tomorrow night, we're having a cocktail party. You're most welcome. You'll be refreshing for us locals."

Roxy broke in. "Allan Daniels, phone. Coast Guard. Trade Winds had them call here."

"Be right back." He hurried over to the telephone.

"Allan Daniels."

"Mister Daniels, Lieutenant Kim Sparks here, sir. One of our helicopters located your plane. Not easy finding it. Only the tail was visible. The first search and rescue craft missed it."

"Thanks, Lieutenant. I'll arrange to be dropped off in another seaplane from the Bone Fish Seaplane Base farther down the Keys. Or maybe a helicopter. I'll bring a mechanic." Allan wondered, *Will I be able to get it out of there?* "Otherwise, they'll have to take it apart. Oh, by the way, did they, ah, observe anything else?"

"No, sir. Nothing. Only one or two Indians in that area. They've had run-ins with the law, so they keep out of sight. That's not our jurisdiction, unless there's been an accident or something. We need you to file a report. Similar to the FAA's."

"I understand. Thanks for the call, Lieutenant." Allan imagined Tommy's body where he left it on that island, maggots picking at it, bloated, slowly rotting in the mangroves.

He walked back to the table and forced himself to shake off his dark thoughts. "They found the plane," he said to Ken and Sue. "Have to go to the seaplane base on Sugar Loaf Key tomorrow morning, arrange to get another seaplane in there, and try to fly mine out. But I might have to go in by helicopter."

"I have office hours," Ken said with a smile, "but Sue has to drive to Key West." He laughed. "They say Kay-o Wesso around here. We need a few things for the party. What do you think, Susan? Why don't you give Mister Daniels a ride? It'll give you a chance to talk about writing."

"It will be a change for the children," she said pleasantly. "We have two. Josh will love to hear about flying. We're always tripping over his toy planes."

"I couldn't ask you to do that," Allan said. "There are taxis, and—"

"Not at all," Ken interrupted, "taxis here are outrageous." He glanced at his watch. "Well, time to head home." They rose, and Ken shook hands with Allan. Sue told him she'd pick him up at his motel around nine. Ken added, "Tomorrow at our place, around six-thirty?"

Later, in the motel, Allan sat on his balcony, feet up on the rail, soaking in the moist warmth of the Islamorada night. He stared out on a sea unmarred by whitecaps. He inhaled deeply, thinking. *All this . . . so strange . . . like a dream . . . a bad dream . . . Tommy . . .*

He noticed the almost-full moon slowly making its way up over the horizon from the east. *Should have told the sheriff right off exactly what happened. I'm not good at lying. But what would that do to everything I've worked so hard to become? More important, the kids . . . and Joyce . . .*

"You shithead," he shouted into the night.

Allan went inside and flopped down on the bed fully clothed, his right hand over his eyes. He fell into a deep sleep, as if drugged.

Allan and Joyce were together in a black rowboat dressed in black bunting, drifting through an endless swamp. Gray-green Spanish moss clung to him like cobwebs. She was talking, but Allan could not hear her, except for a word or two, phrases he could not understand. A noxious smell seared the air. He strained to breathe, but the oxygen was waning. He reached out to Joyce, but now she seemed to be Sue. She looked at him but did not take his hand.

Suddenly Allan turned full face up against a giant spider web. A monstrous tarantula, its hairs quivering, began to envelop him, spewing orange sulfur vapors, the poisonous gas inhaled by convicted murderers. He gasped and emitted death sounds.

Haskins was the huge spider, twice as large as a man. It motioned with one of its arms for Allan to come toward its horrendous mouth. Behind it somewhere was Tommy. "That's him, Sheriff Haskins. Daniels is the one that did it to me . . . to me . . . to meeeeee."

"No," Allan screamed, "you have to hear my side. You must listen to —"

"I," pronounced the spider, "hear nothing."

19

THE NEXT MORNING in the coffee shop, a call came in for Allan. "Well, how you this mornin', Mister Daniels? Hope you had a good night's rest."

None of your fucking business, Allan thought. "Fine, Sheriff. Just fine."

"Well, real glad to hear that. Now, I'd like to see that report I spoke to you about. Important it be fresh in your mind. To get it right, know what I'm sayin'?"

"I'll work on it. A lot to cover. And I do know what you mean," Allan answered, a little sarcastically, though he was sure the sheriff wouldn't pick up on it.

"I'd want it this afternoon, except I have a meetin' up in Key Largo," Haskins said. "But Mister Daniels, very first thing tomorrow mornin', OK?"

"Sure," Allan said, then paused before he added, "Look, for me the sooner the better. I have a lot of commitments back home."

"Right now, Mister Daniels, the only commitment you have is *right here,*" Haskins said, emphasizing the last two words.

Sue picked him up promptly at nine. She drove a new green Ford wagon. Her son, Josh, was eight, tow-headed, lithe, long-limbed, with features like his mother's. He asked endless questions about planes and flying. Samantha — or Sam — his six-year-old sister, had blond hair the color of butter. She was adorable, precocious, sassy, and moved with almost endless energy. Allan couldn't decide which parent she looked more like.

She edged onto Allan's lap, looked straight into his eyes, squeezed his nose, and asked, "Are you going to kiss me?"

"Samantha! Whatever possessed you to say that? Leave Mister

Daniels alone. Go play in the back with Josh. We are not leaving until you do," Sue said firmly.

"Oh, Mommy, Josh is so mean! Do I have to?" Reluctantly, she climbed over the seat to join her brother.

They headed southwest on U.S. 1, the only road through the Keys. The day was gentle, as if resting between moods. The deafening roar of a few diesel tractor-trailers broke the stillness. Allan looked left several times and caught glimpses of Sue. They passed Bud & Mary's Fishing Marina, the Holiday Inn, and Poppa Joe's Lounge and Restaurant before crossing the long bridge to Lower Matecumbe Key. An osprey carrying a small fish in its claws landed on a twig nest on top of the telephone pole next to the eighty-mile-marker sign.

"If you have the chance, try Poppa Joe's," Sue suggested. "Doesn't look very appetizing, but the food's great. The Lorelei's good, too." A smile, small, polite. "You're very quiet. Not like last night. You do have a nice sense of humor."

"I am? Oh, sorry. My mind's full of questions. And not enough answers. Anyway." He paused. "I appreciate your taking me."

"You said that when you first got in."

"I did?"

"Yes. Are you OK? You must be exhausted."

"Got a lot on my mind. Didn't sleep very well. Confusing dream. Actually, a nightmare. It seemed so real."

Her lips creased into a smile. "They always do, don't they? Want to talk about it? You might learn something."

Allan glanced over at her but didn't answer. *Can't do that.* He turned his head to take in the scene.

He caught the sight of a small skiff, a Boston Whaler, skipping over the copper-brown flats, its wake lit sharply in the sun. The turquoise blue and green water was pinned with dark shadows created by small cumulus clouds, which he knew were moving, but from the car he couldn't see exactly in what direction or how fast. Road and bridge construction was beginning to slow their pace. They drove in the one open lane across another bridge onto Long Key. A sign announced the Shark Institute.

Samantha leaned forward between them and uttered a long "Wooo" from inside a Halloween mask. "Mommy, I have to make. I always have to when *he* pushes me."

Sue pulled into the parking lot of the Fishermen's Hospital on Knight's Key in Marathon. Josh declined his mother's invitation to go to the bathroom, content to walk around with his new friend, who held the boy's hand. Josh wanted to know about the antique DC-3 transport plane parked at the airport across the highway. Allan explained that DC-3s were the country's first major airliner.

"What does DC-three stand for?" Josh asked.

"Well," Allan answered, "it was the designation — the name — that the Douglas aircraft company used."

Minutes later, they continued driving southwest, past the Disabled American Veterans' building. A sign on a tan stucco building read, "Son Shine's House," and underneath, "God in Action." They reminded Allan where he was. Additional construction work backed up the cars and trucks. A flagman waved them down to ask for a cigarette. They shrugged. In the rear of the car, the children were deeply engaged in some sort of game.

"Your children are adorable," Allan said.

"Sam, well, she's quite a bundle. And Josh has really warmed up to you. He doesn't with everyone. What about *your* family? You said something last night."

"Yes, two children. I miss them."

"And your wife?"

"What?"

"You *are* married, aren't you? Not a single parent?"

He laughed. "No. Yes, but . . . there are . . . a few problems." *Why did I have to mention that?* he asked himself.

"Oh, I see," she said with a hardly noticeable smile. Then, in a quiet voice, "I'm sure everyone has some."

He expected something more, but she left it at that. A few moments later, she said, "I'm curious. Why did you decide to become an architect? Please excuse me, but writers are always asking all kinds of questions."

"It fits me, even though I wasn't sure through most of college. It might have been professional baseball. I was a little confused, so during my junior year one of my professors suggested NYU's testing and advisement center. They offer it to the public."

"And?"

"Seems I excel in mathematics and science, with an aptitude in art and literature." He cleared his throat. "It presented some tough choices. After a scholarship at Middlebury, I received another one for architecture at MIT. My mother is one-hundred-percent Indian. Miccosukee."

"She is?" Sue asked slowly, wide-eyed. "You mean, in a sense, you're from here. A native."

"My mother was born on their reservation."

Deciding to tell her, he said, "In the dream . . . it started with my wife, Joyce. In this grotesque swamp, in a rowboat. I was miserable. Then *you* were there. I couldn't hear what you were saying. I reached out but you didn't seem to see me." He stopped, then added, "I'm sorry, I don't mean to get personal."

They exchanged glances, then both looked straight ahead. Allan shifted in the seat.

"It's different for you here," she remarked slowly. "Islamorada is not the real world. For you, that is." She paused. "In some ways, not for me, either."

He glanced over at her. "You, uh, seem so . . . empathetic. Maybe we were kindergarten bed mates. Or adjoining cribs."

"Now there's a thought." She laughed. "Where's that humor come from? From the Miccosukee side?"

"No, mostly Jewish. On my father's side. Been keeping us going for five thousand years." Allan sighed. "The Deep South doesn't get any deeper than here, does it?"

She shot him a sharp glare. "Hold on, partner, people here don't have a particular corner on bigotry." She looked straight ahead and asserted, "For the record, I am, too. Half. Like you."

"Hard to believe. I'd conjured you as some southern debutante from Charleston, an exclusive private school, then Clemson, Vanderbilt, or SMU."

"What an imagination," she replied, shaking her head. "No, Radcliffe. Raised in Scarsdale and Connecticut. Your mother is really Indian?"

"Southern Florida. Tamiami Trail. I may be the only Jewish-Indian in the U.S. No, my sister is, too."

"Now that *is* some combination," she said, laughing. "Great excuse to be schizophrenic!"

After Bahia Honda State Park, another long bridge onto Sailor's Key. Tacky stores and homes only slightly better than shacks. He stared at a sign that read "Sailor's Key Road Prison." Men were working on the road. He shut his eyes and shivered, envisioning himself with a shovel, baking for years under a deadly sun.

Another sign read "National Wildlife & Key Deer Refuge."

"Interesting place," Sue commented. "You take a canoe and a guide leads you all around through the islands. Wonderful birdlife. Huge white herons the size of small ostriches. Roseate spoonbills and several kinds of pelicans."

"Whoa, roseate what?"

"They're pinkish." She laughed, then said with a twinkle, "Don't worry. We'll ask them not to bite you." She added, "Wonderful wildlife in the Keys, particularly *under* the water. We do a lot of snorkeling and scuba diving."

Allan looked to his right, to the southwest. In the distance, islands sprouting pines seemed to float and drift. Above them, clouds had fully massed, gray and thick. A line extended across the length of sky in a typical formation, northeast to southwest. On the far side, unrestricted, incorruptible blue. A cold front.

They arrived at the Bone Fish Seaplane Base, about twenty miles northeast of Key West. Allan asked for Guy Mitchell.

"Ain't here. Went to pick up a plane," the attendant said.

"What? Damn it! *My* plane. He was supposed to wait for me. And I was supposed to fly it out." He hit the countertop with his fist.

"You must be Daniels. Now hold on. Mitchell said to tell you he had to go over at daybreak because . . . in case the engine took a lot of time. Went in a 'copter. Wanted plenty of light. Suppose I ask him to give you a call when he gets back?"

"Yeah, all right. Trade Winds in Islamorada. I damn well want to know why the engine quit." He started to leave, turned, and extended his hand to the attendant. "Sorry I yelled."

Allan and Sue continued into Key West, down North Roosevelt Boulevard. Sue offered, "It's close to lunchtime, and my animals are at that point. Been here before?"

Allan shook his head.

"I know a place. Not fancy but super shrimp and fish. Game to try?"

"Sure. Whatever you suggest."

Sue turned north off Palm Avenue to the shrimp docks and parked in front of Jack's Seafood Barn. Painted on the building was "Come and Get 'Em!"

Inside, they selected a corner table covered with red-and-white checkered oilcloth. The waitress remarked that they were a lovely family, prompting Samantha's declaration, "He's not my daddy." The waitress stared, then retreated rapidly to the kitchen. Allan and Susan looked at each other and burst out laughing.

After lunch, they drove west toward Old Town, the main shopping area.

"We'll park here," Sue announced. "Front Street and Duval are always jammed. C'mon, kids."

"Mommy, Mommy," Samantha gasped, "you promised the toy store. Mommy!"

When her shopping was finished, they drove south on Whitehead, past the renowned Casa Marina, tycoon Henry Morrison Flagler's 1920s watering hole, past the long beaches on the Atlantic Ocean and the salt ponds inside South Roosevelt. Runners jogged alongside the International Airport, where Air Florida's early afternoon Boeing 737 swooshed off the concrete runway, burning a path through the salt-laden air. They turned onto U.S. 1, driving past the navy's jet base. The children lay on a quilt in the rear, Samantha conducting a conversation with imaginary friends, Josh examining plastic airplane parts.

The children sat up once in a while to see where they were. The adults had not spoken since they left downtown.

"Your writing," Allan said. "Your novel. I'm curious."

"Didn't work."

"Why?"

"A woman falls deeply in love with someone — he happens to be an Orthodox Jew. His parents prevent the marriage. She rebounds with someone she's . . . she's . . ."

"Sounds appealing. What was wrong?"

"Got bogged down. Couldn't decide whether to give it a happy ending or not. Putting the story onto paper was too difficult, too . . ."

"Couldn't project yourself in that situation?"

She didn't respond immediately. "It was my situation."

"Oh," he said.

"We're supposed to write about things we know best, right?" she said. "I do better with short stories — my book is titled *You'll Never Know.* I dig into the personas of my characters, as an observer, at a distance. Completely dispassionate. Circle around, nail them with provocative situations that require them to make choices, behave differently. Change."

"John Cheever?"

"A little, I guess. Updike, too."

"Your title says a lot."

"Where do *your* poetry themes come from?" she asked.

"From all over the place. Things I witness and feel. Flying, the weather, people. What they are and do. A lot about nature. The mystery of time, existence. The poems come out first in a 'vomit draft.'" She laughed.

Allan shook his head. "I'd like to believe that a few, maybe, are as good as what I read in, oh, *The New Yorker.* In my lifetime, maybe, if I write three or five really exceptional poems, I'd be content with that."

"In college one summer," she said, "I went to the Bread Loaf Writers' Conference, up in the Green Mountains. Very heady. Demanding teachers. Like John Gardner, John Irving, Jay Parini, Galway Kinnell. That's how I landed the job with *The Paris Review* after I graduated."

"You went to Bread Loaf?" He glanced over at her. "They talk about that place as one wild adult summer camp."

"You know what, everyone?" Sue said, changing the subject. "We're on Bread Loaf. No, no, Sugar Loaf. There's a nice beach. But only for a few minutes, because we have to stop at the dentist for Josh." With that, she drove into a parking area that fronted a small, quiet bay. They all got out. "You can take your shoes off," she said. "See if you can find interesting shells. I'll watch you." The children ran ahead, playing follow-the-leader. Samantha complained until she got to lead.

Sue glanced at them, satisfied they were OK. The two adults sauntered toward the water's edge. "You said you were half-Jewish," she said. "How were you raised?"

"Reform." He ran a hand across his cheek. "My mother converted. A little rough for her when she came north to Long Island. Most people assumed she was a light-skinned black. From time to time, she talks about her Indian heritage, but my father — I'll make it short — his parents were Orthodox, born in White Russia. Huge families. Typical story. Very poor, eked out a living. But they had rich spiritual lives in their shtetl and were steeped in their traditions. You know what a shtetl is?"

"Yes, of course I do."

"My dad told me stories his father had told him. During the pogroms, Jews were really catching it from the Cossacks. Stealing stuff, raping the girls. So, with just enough for third-class steerage, off to America by way of England.

"Dad never had huge ambitions, ended up owning a drafting business. He's done pretty well. Easygoing. But not my mother. She can be a tough piece of work."

"What do you mean by that?" Sue asked.

"Maybe 'tough' isn't the right word. Strong, disciplined, very sure of herself." He thought for a moment. "Always expected a lot from us, not willing to accept excuses. Demanding. But when I succeeded at something, she rarely said she was proud of me."

"Maybe that motivated you more."

"Possibly, but I could never feel she was . . . there for me."

"Why do you think she was that way?"

"From the way she had to grow up. Her people had to learn to survive. In the 'glades, cut off from developed areas. She told us that her parents made sure she and her sisters knew they had to depend on themselves. Nobody else really cared except her tribe. Few, if any, in white society."

"We had it a lot easier, didn't we," Sue replied, more of a statement than a question.

"My mother wanted something better than having to live her life on the reservation. An hour each way to high school, but she finished, then went to work behind the front desk in one of the big hotels in Miami, where she met my father. He was attending a convention. I respect my mom a lot, I really do. But I can't get her to understand that I'm not the same as her. No, let me add something: her values are appealing, but I'm not into the spiritual part.

"Dad and I are close. He's proud I'm an architect. I have a sister, five years older. Used to be a political-science professor at Hofstra University. Now she's teaching in Connecticut. We don't see each other much."

"Back up a little," she said. "What about high school?"

"Well," Allan answered, "see these long arms, hands, and fingers? I was a pitcher. Top batting average, too. At Middlebury the coach switched me to center field. Decided I'd do more for the team hitting than pitching. Two major-league teams made offers. I'd have to start out on a farm team, of course."

"My father was a rabid Yankee fan," Sue said. "How did you choose between baseball and architecture?"

"Dad laid it out for me. 'Good money for signing,' he said, 'but give up any idea of a career in architecture. You gotta make up your own mind.'" Allan shook his head. "Probably never would have studied architecture if I had known what I'd have to go through. Years and years before you actually become one. Wall Street would have been a helluva lot easier."

"A bit stultifying. Somehow I don't think it would be for you," she conjectured.

They looked at each other; Allan wondered what she was thinking. For several seconds they stood close, motionless, then Sue moved over to where the children romped in the shallow water. She bent down, about to splash them, then let them escape, screaming.

She stood, turned to Allan, and gazed at him for a few moments, forming a half smile. He walked toward her, slowly. Both hands were in his pockets, his pants rolled up, shoes back at the car. "What a lovely place. So wonderfully tranquil. Almost unreal."

They remained side by side. The wind was becalmed, the only sounds from the children splashing. He pointed to two white herons gracefully in flight. His hand grazed Sue's. Allan glanced at her eyes. They were closed. She looked like she was struggling to say something.

She opened her eyes, then called, "Come, Josh, time to go. Let's go, Sammy."

Josh and Samantha ran back to the station wagon and presented their shells. Sue complimented them on such interesting finds, then wiped the sand off their feet.

As they drove past Little Torch Key, Josh and Samantha began to shout at each other. "Children, if you don't stop that I'm going to pull over."

Allan smiled. "They remind me a little of mine," he said.

Josh and Sam lay down on the blanket in the back.

"If we keep our voices down, they might fall asleep," Sue advised. She pointed behind her. "You haven't said anything about your wife."

He hesitated. "Joyce. An up-and-coming psychotherapist. And a very fine mother."

When Allan didn't add anything, Sue changed the subject. "So, when you went down in the Everglades, was it frightening?"

"Something happened," he said slowly. "It was . . . very bizarre."

"Oh?"

Allan looked across the bridge. Afternoon light bounced off the water's surface. His eyes scanned the sun-flattened coral bays as he recalled the horror in Tommy's camp. He shook his head.

The adults saw the soft-ice-cream stand in Marathon before the kids did. Allan wanted to change his mood, so when they stepped into the parking lot he swung both children onto his back. "I'm a giant horse. You can make me go by saying 'Giddy up, horsey.' I do this with my kids," he yelled to Sue. He circled twice then galloped away from the kiosk until the kids' screams directed him back to the window.

Back in the station wagon, Josh said, "Mommy, I like him. What should we call him?"

Allan broke in. "Well, my nephew and nieces call me Uncle Bear because I growl like this: *Grrrrr.*"

"Uncle Bear? That's funny. But you're not *really* a bear," Samantha said, giggling behind her dripping ice cream cone. "Or are you? So I'll call you Uncle Bear."

The dentist's office was located on the second floor of a small building next to an all-you-can-eat seafood shack. Sue went upstairs with Josh and Samantha, who insisted on watching what the dentist was going to do to her brother. Allan waited in the car.

An old van pulled into the lot. An obese woman exited from the driver's side and straightened her tattered dress. She looked worn out. Skin like Tommy's. *Seminole or Miccosukee,* Allan thought.

She gazed around, ill at ease, then saw Allan and came over. "There's supposed to be a clinic here. For folks who has . . . problems. Alcohol." She pointed to the van, where two teenagers sat quietly, "I need to get my boys help. Real bad." She took a step closer. "Sir, might you know where it is? Real important. Please, sir."

"Sorry, no, ma'am. I don't live here, but somebody'll know. Here, ma'am, please take this. It might help you a little." He thrust three twenties into her hand. At first she shook her head, but Allan closed her hand over the bills. "If you need help," he said, "why don't you ask in the dentist's office." He pointed to the building into which Sue had disappeared. "Second floor. They'll know where to direct you."

20

IT WAS LATE AFTERNOON by the time Sue dropped him back at the Trade Winds. The phone rang. "What!" Allan cried out before realizing he had drifted off, into the middle of another nightmare. "Hello. Yes?"

"It's Sheriff Haskins, Mister Daniels. Catch you at a bad time?"

"No, I was—"

"About your situation with that Indian boy. Now, I'd like you to tell me where you *actually* left him. I mean, how did he . . . what did he travel in when *he* left *you*? Or did *you* leave *him*? Exactly where was that again?"

Allan needed to clear his head. "Just a moment." He stood, swung around to gaze through the sliding glass doors. It was an in-between hour, when time pulls together the day's rich, deep pastels. Lights came on around the pool, and in a large house on the distant isthmus.

"Had to have a way of travelin', now, didn't he?" Haskins continued.

"In his camp." Allan measured his words, delivering them in a matter-of-fact monotone. "He brought me there after picking me up. I left with the boat I bought from him. He had a second boat . . ."

"Uh-huh, so you say. Will you be droppin' off your report soon, Mister Daniels? Kinda like to read it over fully, what happened an' all."

Go to hell. And don't let me stop you.

"It's just about done, Sheriff. First thing in the morning, as we said. I had to check on the plane."

"I know. Mitchell had a devil of a time gettin' the compression up in two cylinders, but the plane is flyable." Allan heard Haskins taking a deep breath. "Now, about that boy, Mister Daniels . . . I was just wonderin'. Why didn't he bring you over to Flamingo, or maybe to a park road? Why'd you need to buy his boat?"

"Apparently he didn't want to have anything to do with park rangers." Allan's jaw tightened. "He was hiding out. Didn't you say so?"

"Don't think so, Mister Daniels."

"Oh, right. It was that Coast Guard lieutenant who said that."

"I'm lookin' forward to your report," Haskins pressed. "When you bring it around, I'll have a couple of other things to go over with you. Call me before you come by. Or I can pick you up."

Allan sensed a smile on the sheriff's' face, his eyes inside the puffy lids, his heavy cheeks rising. "I'll call you in the morning, Sheriff."

"Right, Mister Daniels. Very first thing."

Allan hung up and pressed his forehead against the sliding glass door. His eyes filled with tears. *I didn't mean to kill him . . .*

He turned and pressed his back against the glass, then slid to the floor. After a few minutes, he rolled over and stared at the ceiling. *This is only going to get worse . . . Haskins . . . that bastard . . . I'm lousy at lying . . .*

He rose, poured himself a Scotch, showered, pulled on his chinos and a Hawaiian-flowered polo shirt he had bought earlier in town, where he also had purchased gifts for both his kids and Sue's.

Allan took a taxi to the Watts's home, about a mile away on Upper Matecumbe Key. It was set back from the road, at the edge of the huge expanse of Florida Bay, partially hidden behind Australian pines that howled in the wind, a shrill lament. The rambling ranch house was constructed of blocks covered with white stucco. The corners, of alternating raised panels, were painted canary yellow. Apricot shutters set off the windows. Two tall and trim bottlebrush pines stood on either side of the driveway entrance. Palmettos lined the walk.

Not bad, he thought. *Acceptable when you come down the driveway. Too many houses look like this. Should be more innovative. Architects give in to clients, 'Here, this one from the book.' So what do we get? Boring designs.*

Samantha opened the front door. She wore a white pinafore. "Are you really a bear? Bears don't look like you." She giggled. "You don't have any fur."

"How would you like a certain something I brought for you?" He put her down and picked up a package he had hidden behind the front door before he rang the bell.

Samantha dropped to her knees and attacked the wrapping paper. The large stuffed animal was only slightly smaller than she.

"Well, Sammy, what shall we call him?"

"His name is, ah, his name is — what's his name?" She examined his face. Allan shook his head. "Well, ah, his name is, ah, Mister Bear! Yes, that's his name. Mister Uncle Bear!"

Allan picked up the little girl, who was still clutching the bear, and spun her around in broad circles. Her brother watched from the hallway.

"Well, Josh, you don't think I forgot you, do you?" Allan said as he set her down. A huge smile replaced Josh's worried look when he opened his gift. A miniature airplane on floats. Flights could be made to distant places; on rescue missions; in dogfights with some hateful enemy.

Both children ran off with their new presents.

"Looks like you've come and conquered," Sue observed as the youngsters raced past her. A long black dress clung to her body. She didn't seem to notice his eyes clinging, too. She saluted him with her glass. "Come along, I'll introduce you to our guests. What would you like to drink?"

"Whatever's cold with a head on it."

She pointed to a table, and he grabbed a beer. He followed her through the living room and out the French doors onto a large patio filled with people. A small Flying Junior sailboat and an outboard motorboat were tied to a dock that extended thirty to forty feet into the water.

"This is Allan Daniels," she said to the assembled crowd, "architect and grounded seaplane pilot from New York. Allan, you've already met Ken. These are the Careys, Mautners, Scotts, Botholemews, Cauldwells, and over there, the Wileys. More will be here later. Some are old-line Conchs, the others have only been here for five hundred years. We're not quite locals. They call us freshwater Conchs because we're immigrants who have lived here only eight years." The guests laughed. "I'll let you get acquainted. Be back in a minute."

"We heard about your ordeal," June Scott offered pleasantly. Her smile reminded Allan of a TV saleswoman's grin. "Will you be here long?"

"Not sure exactly. Routine things to take care of. Plane to check out. Everyone has been very nice."

"You'll find people down here very accommodating," June said. "From all I've heard, you're a very lucky man. Or a very fine pilot."

"A little of both," Allan smiled. He took a sip from his can of Heineken. "Excuse me, I see Ken over there."

Allan drifted over to the bar and shook hands with his host, who offered him a tall drink with fresh Key limes. "Maybe later, thanks. You seem to be getting low on limes, Doc. Can I get some for you?"

"Sure, in the kitchen. Sue can show you where. I urge you to try my house special."

"Why not?" Allan answered, deciding to put his worries aside, at least for the evening.

"By the way, are you feeling OK?" Ken asked. "The offer to look you over still holds," he said.

Allan, suddenly conscious of his fantasies about Sue, answered awkwardly, "Ah, no, fit as a fiddle. Just need to unwind."

"I know exactly what you mean." Ken laughed. "Oh, excuse me, I see the Pinders have just arrived. Be right back. Here, try this," he said, thrusting the lime drink in Allan's direction.

Allan took a sip of Ken's house special. *Better clear my head.* He ambled to the end of the dock and sat down, arms around his knees. He looked across the flat, silvery expanse. The last traces of daylight painted the sky, using colors taken from the spectrum: pastels higher, darker shades below, the inexorable darkness pushing the twilight out. Some pale white pins were just beginning to show: stars and planets. He remembered from his night at Tommy's camp that the moon would not rise for another hour.

He lay down with his head on the wooden slats, which were slightly grooved and silkened by rain, salt water, and air. Water lapping against the pilings made a song, but he could not pick out any melody.

He turned his head sideways, observed the retreating vestiges of light around where the sun had slid over the horizon. *Tommy's body . . . on that mangrove island . . .*

Footsteps broke his reverie. He could tell it was Sue from her tantalizing scent. "House special," he said, rising. She looked remarkably attractive. He made sure he didn't get too close to her. "I love your husband's drink," he said.

"I delight in this hour," she noted, reflectively. "So peaceful. Everything's in order." She stood for a moment, then added, "No, that's not quite accurate, is it?"

"What I'm astounded by," Allan offered, "is the way chance and circumstance create events we never anticipate. People come along. Constants become changes. Changes constants. Sounds like a contradiction, constant and change."

"It's important to know what's best for us," Sue responded. She turned and faced the house. "And what is not."

"I suppose so," Allan added. "Oh, by the way, many thanks again for the ride today. And the conversation. I got you a book and something for Ken. Left them on the table in the entry. I gave the kids gifts."

The breeze blew against her hair, the ends touching his neck for a brief moment. "Better go in," she said, almost in a whisper. "I should be with my guests."

21

WHEN ALLAN RETURNED TO HIS MOTEL, he stepped onto the balcony and sat looking out on the horizon. *Peace out there, but not here,* he thought. After several minutes he got up, went inside, took a pad, and sat at the desk. He carefully wrote the events of his experience, recalling the details he had told Norm, Haskins, and the others. *Consistent,* he reminded himself, *must be consistent. And short.* Allan read and reread his report, as Haskins had called it, folded it, and placed it inside the envelope the sheriff had given him. That night he slept soundly, for once untroubled by dreams about Tommy. He was grateful for that.

He awoke early, shaved, dressed, walked over to the sheriff's office, and left his report without seeing Haskins. He returned to his room and called Guy Mitchell, who reported what Allan had assumed: contaminated fuel. Allan suggested that Mitchell get authorization from John O'Neill, who ran the seaplane base back home in Port Washington. Mitchell said he already had. A very experienced local seaplane instructor thought he could fly the plane out of the channel to Key West the following day. To keep the weight as low as possible, he would strip it of everything he could.

Next he called Joyce. "Thought I'd check in," he began. "The kids OK?"

"We're managing, thank you," she responded, coolly, he thought. "Just a minute, Allan." She called out to Nance. "Coming, honey. Be right there. Allan, I have to finish getting the kids ready for school. The bus'll be here in five minutes. You can talk to them tonight. I'll hug them for both of us." Before he could respond, she hung up.

I have to figure some way to convince Haskins to let me get out of here.

He went downstairs and stepped into the coffee shop for some breakfast. "Call for you, Mister Daniels," the middle-aged desk clerk told him. "You can take it over there." Allan's mind flashed. *Haskins. They've found the body.*

"Good morning." It was a woman's voice. "What room are you in? Thought I'd bring you some homemade coffee cake after I drop the kids off at school. In about half an hour? Unless you have something else planned." There was a lilt in her voice that set his mind roving.

"Sue? I, ah, two-thirteen, upstairs to the left, end of the hall. The door will be unlocked," Allan said.

He checked himself out in the mirror several times as he waited. *Schoolboy,* he thought, *acting like a goddamn schoolboy!*

Sue entered his room carrying a small tray with coffee cake in plastic wrap and a carafe of coffee. Her hair was tied back. She wore a blue-and-white striped polo shirt and white, lustrous sharkskin shorts that hugged her every curve. She moved close. "You've gotten to me," she said, almost in a whisper. "I couldn't stop thinking about you last night."

He drew her to him. She opened her arms, pressing her body to his. "I've never done this before," she said softly. "I mean . . . it's—"

Their first kiss was slow, their mouths fully joined. Then they kissed again gently, then more passionately.

He brought his arms from around her back, under her arms, over the rising softness, following the contours, slowly. Their kissing became deeper, longer. He pulled her tight against him.

"No," she said, panting a little, "not here. My house. No one's home."

"Are you sure?" Allan asked. "I mean, maybe we . . ."

"Not here," she repeated. "Everyone pretty much knows everyone else's whereabouts. If I stay for more than a few minutes . . . Besides, there's something very impersonal about motel rooms."

As they drove through town, Allan moved next to her and touched her lightly under her right ear. "Your skin feels like velvet." She dipped her head uncontrollably in the direction of his fingers. "What about — " he began to ask.

"Rounds in Layton and Tavernier. Doesn't return until the middle of the afternoon. Always calls."

She pulled into the carport, removed her hand from his, switched off the motor, and sat quietly for a moment. She leaned over, kissed him on the cheek. "Excuse me, I have to take care of something first." She opened the door and glanced at him. He could tell she was nervous. He was, too.

"Say," he said, "can I, ah, use your . . ."

"Next to the front door."

Allan was excited, but being in her home was making him uncomfortable. After using the bathroom, he strolled slowly down to the dock.

Three pelicans circled the bay. They wheeled. One dove, became streamlined, transformed from the ungainly large-billed bird with clumsy feet and wide, bent wings. It entered the water cleanly at a steep angle, rose quickly, then raised its lopsided bill. Allan could see the bulbous outline of a fish pass down its throat.

God, she's exciting, he thought. *But we're both married . . . this isn't right . . . but Joyce has called ours to a halt . . . or am I simply trying to justify . . . what, something else to feel guilty about?*

The sky had become overcast, stratus-nimbus clouds promising to fulfill the prediction of rain. He caught the strong aroma of salt air. The sun shone through a break several miles offshore, a giant spotlight beamed down through a hole in the ceiling. To the northwest, Allan observed flashes of lightning. As he headed for the house, the sun broke through the clouds again.

Allan entered the living room through the French doors, gently pushed open the door to the master bedroom, then closed it behind him. The curtains were drawn, everything edgeless in soft, tempered light.

Sue stood between the king-size bed and the dresser, her hair unbound, flowing down to her shoulders, onto the straps of a filmy negligee. "Sue, maybe we . . ."

She placed her arms around his neck, raised her head, and kissed him, first lightly, then passionately. She unbuttoned his shirt, peeling it from him little by little. They remained in that position, standing, his chest bare, hers separated from his only by the thinness of her garment.

She brought her hands to his belt, unbuckled it, slowly pulled his zipper down until his pants fell to the floor. She opened her negligee and drew it around both of them. He moved his hands around her back, fingers tracing over her skin until his arms embraced her ribs and waist, then her firm buttocks.

"Stand this way as long as you can." She breathed haltingly. She opened her legs. Her breathing deepened; the center of her quickened where their hips and stomachs pressed. Her body swayed in a circular motion, even her shoulders. Her eyes closed, and she tilted her head back, gulping air. He kissed her neck, moved his tongue up and down lightly against her skin.

He drew the negligee down over each shoulder, first the left, then the right, gently, slowly, until it slid down her body. He pulled back and gazed at her.

"My God. You're magnificent," he said. He put his arms around her waist and lifted her off the floor. She slid down his body. Then he lifted her again, carried her to the bed, laid her carefully down, and moved over her. Her eyes remained closed.

Sue rolled over on him, placed her hands on his upturned wrists. "I like it when I'm in control," she murmured.

She drew up her knees, sat on him, separated her legs and straddled his hips. She brought her right hand down and moved his penis against her wetness, slipped it inside.

They raised her hips up, then down, he with her, in unison. She controlled their motion, at first slow, then faster. Then, without willing it, he arched his hips in a curve extending to the back of his head, his neck stretched, his chin pointed upward, more and more pronounced until the release of his orgasm. His cry was as uncontrolled as his actions. His hands rose to pull her body tighter to his. His surges continued, and as they lessened in intensity, he began to laugh involuntarily. She clasped the whole length of her body to his, both moist from perspiration, her legs around him. They remained locked in that position.

"Have you been somewhere, my sweet?" she asked in a whisper. "Tell me." She stroked his face, and kissed him twice lightly.

"The whole world could be going to hell or heaven, it wouldn't make any difference," Allan responded happily. "Even if we were doing it on rocks or in the snow, which, by the way, I'd like to try sometime with you. But now, you."

They kissed, tongues searching like fingertips. He rolled to the side and faced her. He kissed her again, very slowly, her ears, then lower. He ran his fingers along her neck, lightly between her breasts, then slowly over the left, then the right. He moved his fingers down to her navel and then tickled lightly around the slim contour of her lower stomach.

Sue sighed as his fingers found her wetness, and she began to shake. She moaned, her movements unrestrained. He timed his motions to her explosions, which continued until she collapsed, exhausted.

"Allan, come in me." He raised himself over her as she spread her legs.

He had another orgasm, not as strong as the first. She did too. "Looks like you've been saving it up," Sue whispered.

"You bring out the animal in me," he said with a laugh.

They lay back and held hands. She was quiet for a long time.

"Anything the matter?" Allan asked.

"I don't know. I'm not sure how I feel about this. I mean, it was . . . ineffable."

"What?"

She laughed. "Fantastic. You have me in another world; that's the first word that came to my mind." She paused, then: "It's all so complicated. And confusing." She thought for a moment. "I know there will be costs." She sighed. "There always are."

"How? What do you mean?"

"I believe in being faithful. I really do. And here I am with you." She turned on her side and said, "A few years ago . . ." She stopped.

"What?"

"I walked into Ken's office unexpectedly one night after dinner. He said he had to finish up some reports and paperwork. He . . . he was with his nurse in one of the examining rooms. They were . . ."

"Screwing?"

"He was distraught. He swore it didn't mean anything, claimed that she'd come on to him, and finally that night she'd seduced him. I decided that I didn't want a divorce, mostly for the sake of the children. It took several months for me to trust him . . . get back together. Ken's not a bad person. A little weak, maybe. So am I, it seems."

They were quiet. Then she said, "Can anyone properly *write* about sex?" She leaned on one arm and asked, "I mean, can they describe the actual passion of it?"

Allan smiled. "Very little of anything I've ever read. Maybe the action, and even that often that leaves something to be desired. No contradiction intended."

"One of my short stories is about a young woman married for ten years or so. Believed she had a fulfilling marriage, a good sex life. She unexpectedly observes her husband fooling around with one of her best friends at a party, in a darkened cabana behind the swimming pool. She's dumbfounded but doesn't break it up. Pretends nothing is different. Fakes her orgasms.

"She starts to wonder how good she actually is in bed if her husband is looking for it elsewhere. At another party, weeks later, she gets the opportunity to drop a few hints to her friend's husband, whom she has always found lively and attractive. Guess what? She has terrific sex with this guy. The husband uncovers a note from the lover and is ready to kill.

"'I just can't understand you,' the wife says to him. 'I saw you a few weeks ago making out with my friend. I assumed you'd want me to find out how good great sex could be.' That took him aback, but you know what? In the story I made them get closer because of it.

"After I have my characters set comfortably in their ways, *bang, bang,* some surprise — self-made or otherwise — uproots their lives. Of course, plots are easy. All depends on how good the writing is."

He chuckled. "Kind of funny, you writing that."

"What do you mean?"

"Could that story have something to do with the author, by chance?"

"I can tell you," she went on, "that, for me, once in a while there's a fantasy. Some are very elaborate. Today with you. I was on top of an Inca pyramid. With Atualpa. He was screwing me. Part of a ritual. Hundreds were watching us from below. Sounds silly." She stopped and smiled at him. "I never told anyone."

"I guess I'm honored," he responded.

"Shhhh. Just sleep a little." She kissed him softly and stroked his face. They fell asleep peacefully like two exhausted puppies.

When they woke, she snuggled against him. "I have to confess," he said. "At your party, even with you in another part of the room, I would strain to listen to what you were saying."

"You're such a romantic. I think if we were with each other all the time, you'd quickly get tired of me. Or," she said, giving him a nudge, "maybe I would of you."

He leaned over and kissed her again. She tasted sweet. They dozed off in each other's arms.

"My God. One-thirty!" She woke with a start, jumping out of bed. "Time for a quick shower. I was going to give you something to eat, but another time. I'll run you back and be here before the kids arrive."

Two messages awaited when he arrived at the motel. One from his parents, the other from Haskins. He dialed his parents first. "Hi, Mom. It's your delinquent son asking you not to tell him he's a bad boy." He didn't wait for an answer. "Where's Dad?"

"We were so worried," his mother said. "Your flying, Allan. I want you to give it up. Please, for me. The papers are always showing pictures of little planes in crashes. Joyce called when she heard you were alright. Your father and I have been over to help out. Nance and Craig are staying with us Saturday."

"Dad around?"

"You should have called us sooner," she scolded. "And you might talk to your sister."

"Sharon? She stopped giving a shit about me when she couldn't control me anymore."

"I will not have you using that language. Your sister loves you, even though you've convinced yourself she doesn't. You don't even try with her."

"That's your point of view, Mother," Allan said. "I wish it were better between us, but it's not."

"You can do something about that," she advised. "Your father's on his walk. I'll tell him you called. Promise to take care of yourself."

"I met a Miccosukee shaman."

"Really? You did? I hope you told him . . ." She didn't finish.

"His name is James Osceola."

"Common name for our people."

"He told me many interesting things. Mother?"

"What?"

"I'm sorry I'm so different from what you want."

"Let's not go into this again. Now that fate has brought you in contact with my people, maybe we can talk about it when you're back here. Good-bye, son," she said, then hung up.

Allan put the phone down, stepped out onto the balcony, and leaned against the railing. A family was having great fun in the pool. A child jumped into the water at the shallow end, ran up the steps, jumped in again, over and over. The father held another youngster, who wore water-wings and flailed her arms and legs. Suddenly he wished Nance and Craig were there.

Allan shivered as he thought about Haskins and his seemingly relentless determination. He felt the adrenaline coursing through him. He grabbed his notebook and wrote:

But inside the wood cages
the gruel is seasoned with
the cut-off ears of men

who have heard too much.
Their feathers are soaking
in blood, in excrement.
Not one will fly away.

Allan put on his warm-up suit and went for a hard run, first along Route 1, then into a maze of local roads.

22

ALLAN WALKED OVER TO THE TIKI BAR to wash away the negativity, escape from Tommy's whispers and Haskins's stalking. Chatter pervaded the room, an occasional solo song of laughter, often answered by another, both sinking into the swim of sound.

Here everything faded, the day's episodes washed slowly into the haze, merging into the smoke. It was good to get away from the horror of Tommy, his own guilt, his inability to find a solution.

He was lost in contemplation when Norm asked, "Hey, how about some darts? Cal is always braggin' about how he can beat me with his eyes shut. Such a bullshitter. Come on, we'll get in a few throws before he gets here. He must've gotten tied up."

"Guess I'm not in the mood right now," Allan said.

"Yeah, all right. Say, how'd it go with Billy Haskins? Get it all worked out?" He turned to the bar and lifted an index finger to the bartender. "Another Red Stripe?"

Allan shook his head. "I don't know what's taking him so damn long. My son needs me. I'd like to bring him down here someday. My daughter, too."

"That'd be terrific," Norm responded warmly. "Get them out for some back country fishin'. I love when kids take to fishin'. Helps keep 'em out of trouble. Got two teenagers myself. Started 'em early. Matt, my son, is into fishin' big time."

Norm's beer came.

"Changed my mind," Allan said. "A Red Stripe for me, miss. OK, let's give your wild game of spears a try."

They played six games. Allan won the last. "You're catchin' on fast, Yank," Norm remarked with a grin.

"That's because I throw with my eyes closed. Must come from my Indian heritage."

The din broke, weather inside the room changed. Men left, in twos or threes or alone, returning to their homes where, later on, they might reflect on things said, half sentences and expressions, their reactions and feelings. Allan returned to his room, chose not to go to the Green Turtle, deciding he'd be better off alone. After a Scotch, he walked down the road, bought a bag of Kentucky Fried Chicken. He ate every bit of meat, then broke the bones with his teeth, sucked out the marrow, and chewed off the knobbed ends. He ate while staring at the news on TV, most of which just floated over him.

He took his notebook and sat on the balcony, examining the twilight flooding the Atlantic. He fantasized about islands beyond the horizon. A single-engine tail-dragger, a tandem two-place Piper Super Cub, flew by, making its way southeast, perhaps heading to Marathon or one of the small, private airstrips along the length of the Keys.

Allan learned to fly when he was eighteen, at the beginning of his freshman year at Middlebury. His father was an amateur pilot. "I have an offer for you," his father had said after he and Allan's mother had driven him up to Vermont from Long Island. "If you agree not to smoke, I'll stake you to flying lessons. It's a bribe, I know, but this way everyone wins."

"I'm not happy with the thought of you becoming a pilot," his mother added, "but your father convinced me it's safer than tobacco. Promise me you'll be careful."

In high school, he had a buddy whose older brother owned a World War II Stearman biplane. It was exhilarating being in an open cockpit, wearing a helmet and goggles, flying along Fire Island and over the Hampton beaches at two hundred feet, wiggling the wings at young women in bikinis who waved back at the intrepid airmen, observing geese and swans on ponds, flying low over potato farms and pine forests, that special feeling of venturing freely through the sky; landing at airports for coffee or a sandwich. A few times, old veterans from the war would walk over to touch the Stearman's fabric, smile broadly, and share stories.

He accepted his father's offer, joined the Middlebury Flying Panthers. Twenty students purchased an old Aeronca Champ, two seats in tandem. One of the club's members happened to be an instructor, another mechanically inclined. Both were paid for their time.

The airport in Middlebury on Route 7 was a combination cow pasture and airstrip. The club plane did not have an engine starter. It required hand-spinning the propeller. If you were alone, you had to jump in before the plane went off on a flight of its own, or else tie the rudder down before propping. Cross-country flights were made to practice navigation, most of it dead reckoning. He didn't actually get his private pilot's license for several years. His first passenger was his stunning, willing girlfriend, Joyce.

Sometime in April, an in-between month in Vermont—on the verge of spring but not yet finished with winter—Allan got caught in bad weather, the visibility little or nonexistent, the view of the ground sporadic. Allan had pushed the plane out of the barn, Joyce helping him. He didn't bother to check the weather forecast, assuming he knew the wide Champlain Valley well enough and could always return to the airport. Or, if he really had to, put down in a field or on a county road.

Fifteen minutes in to the flight, all Allan could see was snow swirling in front of the plane. Hearing was difficult without headsets. "Allan?" Joyce shouted.

"Yeah," he yelled back. "Should break out ahead."

"Aren't we near mountains?" she asked, worry clear in her question.

He didn't answer, not admitting he had made a serious mistake. He was well aware that pilots can get disoriented in clouds or in snow, unless trained and licensed for instrument flying, which he wasn't. Besides, the Aeronca had only minimal instruments.

A minute later, the sky cleared in front of them, and, to his great relief, Allan could see the college to the east. He picked out another familiar landmark, then Route 7. They landed and put the plane away. Very few words were spoken.

The next day, the club's flight instructor sought Allan out. The plane had been seen flying low over the campus. He told Allan he was tempted to ground him but decided he had learned an important lesson. He added that if Allan wanted to show off, he should do it anywhere else, not in a plane and not in marginal weather. It was a lesson Allan would not soon forget.

23

ALLAN PEERED OUT ON A SEA that had worked itself up into an angry lather. The wind, water's ineluctable companion, was complaining bitterly, thrashing the waves into heightened, foam-tipped crests. His mind turned to Sue. *Wonder if she'll create a short story about us, or about me, about cheating, ambivalent thoughts, guilt . . .*

Allan suddenly wanted to write a poem, to touch his feelings, transform them into words, images. *Fantasies . . . they're free. You'd like that, wouldn't you? Washing reality away with poems. Write one, dreamer, about "now," where the hell you are . . .* He sipped some Scotch to release images and associations.

reality and fantasy are twins
more like adversaries

you're making love
fantasy is winning but reality waits nearby

like it was with her when you were
unconscious oblivious drugged

the drug of passion has no memory
no responsibility until later

when reality creeps in and pounds the door
you didn't hear before but do now

He titled it "Twins."

24

HASKINS CALLED AT 7:15, the first voice of the day, a voice that stirred Allan to sudden attention. "How you doin' today, Mister Daniels? Pretty nice weather all day. Uh, say, Mister Daniels, I was wonderin' if you'd stop by this mornin'. Like to go over your, uh, report." His words were spoken calmly but with authority.

Haskins's call was no surprise, but that he had called so early was. Allan wondered, *Has he learned anything from the blood sample? . . . An inquest? Then what?* "Yeah, sure, Sheriff," he replied in a strong tone. "After some coffee and breakfast. An hour or so?"

He took a breakfast tray up to his room, opened the drapes, and stepped out onto the balcony. The sun shone on another new day. He remembered how sleek and provocative Sue had looked in the drench of light two days ago. He wondered what time Haskins had gotten up, what he had eaten for breakfast. Irrelevant thoughts impinging.

Allan used the walk to Haskins's office to prepare himself. *Concentrate . . . calm, convincing.*

The sheriff wore the same uniform: drab, mud-colored, three stripes on his sleeves. He gave Allan a long handshake and longer scrutiny. "Been readin' over your report, Mister Daniels." Haskins flicked through the papers on his desk, stroked his chin, continued to scrutinize Allan, who waited anxiously for him to continue. The sheriff eased into a slouch. Finally he said, "You don't go into a helluva lot of detail here, now do you, Mister Daniels." Not a question.

"All you asked me to do was describe the young man and roughly what happened. I thought I did that."

Round one, a draw.

"Uh-huh. I see you remembered his first name. Kinda strange he didn't give you his last name, isn't it?"

"He did. Hampton. Something like that."

Haskins rose from his chair, walked around Allan, and sat on the edge of the desk, a judge peering down from on high. A small smile graced his face. "Kid's name's Tommy Handley, Mister Daniels. Tommy Handley. Thought you'd like to know that. That's what you wrote in the note you left in the plane! How come you don't remember?"

"OK, so his last name was Handley, not Hampton. I don't see what difference that makes. Look, Sheriff Haskins, what are you getting at? I told you what there is to tell."

Round two, Allan.

The lawman eyed Allan intently, almost aggressively. "Well, now, Mister Daniels, just doin' my job. I kinda thought that's who it was from the description you gave me. Real bad one, that boy. Mixed up, evil gotten into his bones. Been lookin' for him for quite a spell."

"What does that have to do with me?" Allan declared.

The big man was not deterred. "Sometimes," Haskins asserted, "when you're checkin' on one thing, you get two, know what I'm sayin'? Yes sir, rough one, Tommy Handley. Been trouble all his life. Course, we haven't seen him. But up the mainland, around Fort Myers, he's involved in some really bad stuff. Drugs are a part of it." Haskins lifted his huge body up from the edge of the desk, walked over to the window, looked out, and returned to his chair. "Shot a storekeeper durin' a robbery. The kid hightailed it back to the swamps. Been there ever since. Doesn't know the old man pulled through." He drained his mug and slowly lit a cigarette.

"Gotta say it, Mister Daniels, the kid's bad all right, but I sure admire the way he knows those swamps. Half alligator, half bird. Stays in there, at that camp of his, wherever the hell it is — likely more than one camp and several escape routes, case anyone gets too close — does his trappin' and fishin', trades skins with his people.

The law's been tryin' to catch him for several years. Yes sir, pretty amazin', the way he makes out in there."

"That's all very interesting, Sheriff Haskins, but, again, what does this have to do with me?"

The sheriff leaned forward, stood up, and walked behind Allan's chair. "I'll tell you what, Mister Daniels! Your damn story is not ringin' the right bells for me! Now, you said his name *was* Tommy. Why didn't you say *is*?"

Round three, Haskins.

"Way of speaking, Sheriff." Allan said, trying to remain calm. "You know, when you meet someone, unless you keep seeing that person, it's . . . it's natural to refer to them in the past tense." He sighed. "And I'm certainly not going to see him again. What the blazes are you driving at?"

Round four, whose?

"Nothin', really." Haskins grinned like a big, fat Cheshire cat. "The Coast Guard was over, as you know from Lieutenant Sparks. They're involved because of the plane goin' down and all." He leaned back, poured coffee into his mug. He sat in his chair again and swung it around, his back to Allan when he stated, "Those boys called the park service when they finally came across Handley's main camp. When they were also searchin' for your plane. Got in there with one of their marsh boats. Found some blood. Sendin' it to me. I'll pass it on to the lab." Haskins wheeled, looked straight at Allan. "See whether it matches the blood in the boat."

Son of a bitch, Allan thought. *Stay calm, look calm. Say nothing.*

Haskins was closing in. It seemed like the fight was almost over.

"So, you see, Mister Daniels, we sorta have to keep this thing open until there are no questions. About exactly what happened. By the way, you didn't cut yourself out there, did you? Oh, you told me about that." All of it said rapid-fire.

Allan shrugged.

"Well, we'll see, won't we? Just make damn sure you tell me everythin' there is to tell. As far as where that boy is, well . . ." He smiled, took a long drag on his cigarette, and crushed it out on the underside of his desk. "They're not goin' to have much luck findin' him. Least, don't think so. But never can tell. Somethin' may turn up. Sometimes does, you know. Sometimes does."

Haskins grinned and leaned back against the wall, coffee mug against his bottom lip. He just waited, then offered, "Luck is somethin' you have to make sometimes. Knowin' people. What they can take. Know what I mean?"

"Look, Sheriff, I really have to get back to New York. My son got hurt the other day. And my work. My clients and projects need attending to. I'm here too long already."

"I know, Mister Daniels, but you're gonna have to stick around for another day or two. Heard you made some friends, the Wattses and some of the others. The weather's pretty good. You could go fishin' with Seltzer."

Allan felt himself spinning. And burning. Burning. He glanced down, dropped his head, and shook it. He took a deep breath and stood up. "Sheriff, I . . . I can't live with this anymore," he said, shaking his head. He hesitated, then went on: "I made a terrible mistake. I don't mean defending myself. I mean not taking his body with me."

Haskins' eyes narrowed, then he walked over and stood by Allan, his brow furrowed.

"What actually happened," Allan continued as he sank back down into the chair, "was that late during the second night, Handley, Tommy Handley, crept over to where I had fallen asleep and pulled my wallet from my jacket." He took a deep breath. "It woke me up. Instinctively I reached for the nearest thing I could grab, a piece of wood, and hit him. It landed behind his right ear. It was . . . it was just instinctive. Everything was like a bad dream. Unreal. Tommy was unconscious. I dragged him down to his boat, put him in, and shoved off. I wanted to take him to . . . anywhere I could get medical help."

"Then?" Haskins asked.

"Somehow I managed to get us through a bunch of channels and finally out into Florida Bay." Allan closed his eyes. "I begged him to hang on, that I'd do everything I could to help him. But . . . but he died in my arms. I guess I panicked. Took him to an island, wrapped him in a tarp, and left him in some thick mangroves. Norm Seltzer found me a couple of hours later."

Haskins sat on the edge of his desk and brought a hand flat against a cheek, then down around his chin. Then he slammed it on the desk. "You should have damn well told me all this straight off, Mister Daniels," he snapped angrily. "Lyin' to a police officer is serious grounds. You damn well should have."

"He would have killed me after he had stolen my wallet," Allan offered matter-of-factly. "I'm sure of it. He had a gun. Dump my body somewhere near that camp of his. No one would ever find me." Allan buried his face into his hands. "If I had to do it all over again, I would have told you immediately. I would have. I'm not like this. I was confused, in a sort of daze. But I'm not now."

"That may be, but that's not what actually happened here with me, is it?" He stood, glaring at Allan. "You'll need to sign a confession."

Allan nodded. "I should get an attorney," he said, his lips tightening. "Isn't that the way it goes?"

"You can," Haskins commented evenly. "That's your right, of course. But I'm not chargin' you. Yet. I need to go out there an' get the body."

"I understand, Sheriff," Allan said submissively.

"Think you can find the island?"

"Pretty sure. Near Man of War Key and Cluett. Number Three marker. I studied Seltzer's map on the boat."

"All right, Mister Daniels. We'll stop by your motel so you can pick up a hat and jacket." Allan nodded and got to his feet.

"Just a minute." Haskins went over to a cabinet and fished something out. "From now on, while you're here, you wear this monitor around your ankle, so I know where you are." He stared at Allan. "Be pretty stupid to try to leave the area. Real stupid. Know what I'm sayin'? I'll be right back," he added. He left the room and returned a few minutes later, shaking his head. "Checked on the boat. Bein' worked on. Can't go out until tomorrow. Remember, Mister Daniels, stay well within a ten-mile radius or else you're gonna create yourself more trouble."

Allan walked blindly through the control room, waiting room, hall, then bolted out the front door, gasping for fresh air. He noticed a young woman at the edge of the highway, wearing tight pants and a revealing top. She smiled broadly at the cars, her thumb extended in the direction of Key West. Allan noticed her male companion partially hidden behind a telephone pole.

Allan turned in the direction of his motel. He walked back streets, shuffling nowhere, finally sitting down on a crate several feet back from the pavement. Pelicans crossed from the ocean to the lee side of the Key. A dog ran past carrying a large bone in his mouth, followed by another, two mongrels sorting out the day's opportunities. The first stopped, the other nipped at the bone, and they began to tug furiously, growling, snarling. A death struggle over a lousy bone. Then suddenly one gave up and let go. It trotted over and sat down next to him. "Scroungy animal, that's what you are," he said, patting him, "and you stink. But at least you're decent. You don't go around killing people."

He stood up and surveyed the surroundings. Nothing moved. Even the dogs had gone. Allan moped to the motel, hands plunged deep in his pockets. Up in his room, he dropped onto the bed. Eleven o'clock. *Maybe go for a swim,* he thought. *Clear my head. Why the fuck did I have to confess? Probably never would have found the body.* He walked downstairs into the lobby.

The desk clerk called out, "Oh, Mister Daniels, you didn't see this? Here." The return address on the envelope read "Dr. Kenneth Watts." "Allan Daniels" was typed on the face. He took it over to the far corner of the coffee shop and opened it. The note was short and sweet: "The kids want to have a picnic. I know a wonderful place." It was unsigned.

He called Sue. Josh and Samantha were at school until midafternoon. He was instructed to walk down a side street several blocks from the motel at exactly 11:30.

He showered, the water beating warm on his head, shoulders, back, covering his body. *Maybe I'd better tell her we shouldn't continue.*

As he dressed, he fantasized a giant crouching cat. Haskins. *Funny, reminds me a little of Tommy,* Allan reflected. *Both stalk, ready to shoot or pull the cord on a trap . . . relentless. Hunting runs in their blood. Tommy out there in that Florida jungle, Haskins where it's civilized . . . same rules: go after your quarry, then nail his skin on your wall. Me, a city boy who wears a tie and jacket . . . I'm also Indian . . . maybe if I had grown up on the reservation . . .*

25

You don't seem very pleased to see me," Sue began. "You're so . . . so subdued. Anything wrong?" She paused. "I must confess I wasn't so sure about being with you again."

"Sorry," he said, "It's just that I've been preoccupied since seeing the sheriff this morning. He's obsessed about that Indian boy I was with. Wants to know every damn detail, how I got out, about the boat. They've been looking for him ever since he shot a man." His voice transitioned to a more mellow tone. "Haskins ordered me to stick around for another day or two." He looked at her and smiled. "I can sure handle that. Then I really have to get back."

"When did you last speak to your wife and kids?"

"Yesterday. Why? The children are fine. I spoke to both of them. My office, too. The gang will cover for me. I may have to call a few nervous clients, though."

They held hands as they drove through Upper Matecumbe Key past her house, over the bridge to Lower Matecumbe Key, then turned off on an almost-hidden, coral-graveled path that stretched peacefully to a bay. They parked the car in a stand of Australian pines. The wind whistled a single plaintive note in the branches, which swayed to their own rhythms. Sue told him only a few people knew of the place where they were going. It was pristine: no papers, cans, rubbish of any kind. The day was tame, creamy sweet, the smells fresh. The beach formed a small cul-de-sac that sheltered the water. The sandy shore looked as if no one had ever walked there.

They stepped out of the station wagon. Sue grabbed the lunch basket, handed him the blanket, and ran ahead. They pushed and pulled at each other like teenagers, stumbling, tripping until she dropped the basket, spilling the red-and-white checkered tablecloth, food, cans of beer. As she was falling, he threw the blanket over her like a tent. "Aha, Scarlett. I've got you at last and you can't get away," he pronounced in a deep, Rhett Butler/Clark Gable voice. He knelt, arms around the moving mass inside the blanket, hugging it and rolling over with his victim tightly bound.

Allan pulled the blanket off her and stood up, his expression taken from a very different thought. She sat up, surprised. He looked across the flat water to the small, uninhabited keys. "To put it mildly," he began, "this week has been pretty traumatic for me." He sat down beside her. "Nothing will ever be the same. I've had to examine who and what I am, where I'm going."

"The crash and being lost in the 'glades — anyone would be affected," she suggested, kissing him lightly. "Allan," she said in a near whisper, "I've decided that this, with you, yesterday . . . we're not involved, I mean, yet. Otherwise, what happens to my marriage? And my children?" She swung around, knelt, and faced him directly. "And yours? You'd be miserable without your family. Who knows, you might even become closer with your wife."

She held her hands prayerlike. Two terns squawked at each other, adjusted their flight, and dove into the water. One rose with a wiggling fish, small and shiny in its beak. The other came up empty.

Sue lifted her chin, eyes closed. "It's wrong. This. Us. After today, I've decided we shouldn't see each other again. It will only make us miserable. No matter what I've promised myself, I will not become involved. I can't. This is the life I've chosen. Ken, our kids, here in Islamorada. But I have to admit, I missed the storms . . ." She stood, arms at her sides, her lips pressed together. "I'm not good at cheating."

Allan nodded. "Me neither."

They walked slowly to the water's edge. A little farther out the surface rippled, then settled back.

"Fish chasing fry. Mullet or snapper," she said.

"Well," Allan said, "the one thing I'm sure of is I don't want to hurt you in any way."

She sat down and motioned him to sit down next to her. "I believe when one has been in a marriage a fair amount of time, that initial passion, that early love, often does wane. Or is no longer enough. Something has to be added. Things change. I don't have to spell it out," she said, turning away.

"Yesterday, with you, was — how can I put it in words to a fellow writer? — just phenomenal." He smiled. "Anyway, you're right. I don't handle guilt very well either."

"At least let's enjoy today," she said, touching his arm. She shrugged, then shook off her sandals. He took off his pants and sneakers. His boxer shorts looked like a bathing suit.

"What's that above your ankle?" she asked.

"Oh, that," he answered. "Sheriff Haskins wants to know where I am at all times. I think he watches too many movies." They stepped into the water, splashing each other like kids.

After the swim, they dried each other off, sat on the blanket, and munched on crackers with pâté, cheese, artichoke hearts. After they shared a Red Stripe, he lay down, his head on her lap. He felt her hands caressing his tousled hair. Allan got up, moved a few paces away, and stared out toward the islands.

"What's the matter?" she asked.

He seemed unnerved, kicked some sand, and took a deep breath. "Something else. I guess I want you to know what really happened to me out there in the 'glades."

"What are you talking about?"

"Could have happened to anyone." He turned and walked back over to her, then sat down. "That Indian kid, Tommy Handley."

"You told us that the other night. That's how you finally got out."

"Yes, but, there's more . . . something . . . something else." He took her hand. "In the middle of the night, he tried to steal my wallet out of my jacket pocket. It woke me up even though I was in a deep sleep. Happened so fast. I knew he was dangerous because I accidentally saw a newspaper article earlier nailed to a wall. He had robbed and shot a storekeeper. Anyway—"

"Anyway what?"

"I . . . I grabbed the first thing I could, a small log. As he was crawling away, I hit him behind his ear. Just wanted to knock him out. He had a gun and would have found a way of getting rid of me. Of that I'm sure.

"He fell, unconscious. As soon as it was light, I put him into his boat and got us out, hoping that a fishing boat would find us. I was trying desperately to get help. But he . . . he died out there. It was like a nightmare. Someone else's, not mine. All I could think of was hiding his body in the mangroves on one of those islands."

Sue stared at Allan, incredulous.

"I know, I know. Sue, look, I'm not a murderer. It was self-defense. He would have killed me. I couldn't do anything for him. I tried. I swear I would give anything for it not to have happened. What it would do to my family and career."

She stood up, faced him, her hands over her face. "I can't believe this," she said. "I just can't."

"I'm not making excuses. But in that place everything was so crazy, like in another world."

"That doesn't matter." Sue said, "You should have brought his body out." She turned, gathered up the picnic items. "I want to go."

They drove silently along the gravel road. She stopped just before reaching the highway. "I'm sure you weren't trying to get away with it," she said. "I also know you're basically a decent and honest man. But—"

"I didn't murder him. It was self-defense," he pleaded. "Can't you imagine yourself in such a situation?"

"You made a choice. Did you tell me simply to assuage your guilt? You want me to say it was all right?"

She pulled out onto U.S. 1, made a left turn heading back to Islamorada. "Look, I'm truly sorry what you've gone through." She pursed her lips, looked over at him, and said, "But you didn't take the responsibility."

"Please stop for a minute, Sue. The kid died. Nobody could do anything for him. I wasn't thinking clearly. If I had brought his body out . . . my life, my family, my career: all down the drain. At that moment, I didn't think I had a choice." He cleared his throat. "I was wrong. *Very* wrong."

"He didn't physically attack you. You have to come clean with the sheriff."

"I told him earlier today," he said. "What I did isn't going to change anything. If I had it to do over again, I would have brought his body out. Please believe me."

She drove to the street where she had picked him up. Allan got out and stood next to the car, his hand on the open door.

"I'm glad you confessed." She closed her eyes for a few seconds. "I only wish I could help you, but I can't."

He watched her drive away, turned, and walked to a secluded spot on the beach behind his motel. He sat for a long time watching small waves breaking on the shore.

Down a very deep hole . . . no way to get out, he thought as he lay back and fell asleep. *Falling backward through barbed blackness. Ravens have pulled out my eyes . . . they fly soundlessly, dragging them . . . a storm rages . . . lightning . . . run wildly to escape each clap of thunder, not knowing where anything is in the jagged darkness . . . bang into rocks that tear my flesh.*

She has taken away her hand and will not show me what to avoid. She does not care anymore . . . the edge near . . . must know where it is . . . close, can feel it, the cliff . . . fall, bottomless pit . . . Will there be an afterward . . . will it be better . . . will there be wind . . . will the wind be green?

26

HASKINS CALLED LATE THAT AFTERNOON. His tone was commanding. "I'll pick you up at seven tomorrow mornin'. Be ready."

"I will be, Sheriff."

Allan ambled out onto the terrace. The sun was flashing off the water into anything it struck. Pelicans and terns circled, scanning for fish. *Nature balancing life, survival, and death. Since time began. . . Jefferson Prison on the Dry Tortugas . . . burn in that heat . . . how many died during the Civil War? Somehow, I'd try to escape.*

He placed his hands on the rail and leaned forward. The same family playing at the pool. Giggles, screams, slapped water.

Get some exercise . . . go jogging. As he was leaving his room, the phone rang, and for a second he imagined it was Sue.

"Hello? Oh, Joyce. I was going to call." He took a breath. "Look, there's been some trouble. It's taking time. I, uh, didn't want to get anyone upset."

"What kind of trouble?" she inquired.

"With the police. The sheriff here is —"

"The police? What are you talking about?"

"Will you let me tell you? They're investigating what happened after I went down, the boat I came out in."

"Why, did you steal it?"

"Oh, for Pete's sake. Just assume you can't understand what happened to me, OK? I'll fill you in later."

"You're being too mysterious. Hold on," she snapped. "Nance and Craig are anxious to talk to you. Here, Nancy, it's your father."

"Daddy? When are you coming home? We miss you. Lots and lots."

"Well, how's my best big girl? I *am* coming back, but first I have to finish up some business here. I'd really rather be with you, sweetheart, I promise."

"Come home today, Daddy," Nance said.

"Can't, honey. But real soon. Promise. We'll spend lots of time together. I'll dress up as a clown, and you and your friends can punch me in the tummy."

"Oh, Daddy, that's only at my birthday party!"

"I have to go now, but I'll call later. And, Nance, remember that I love you very, very much. Honey, let me speak to Craig."

Joyce came on instead. "He's angry because he couldn't talk to you first. Just when *are* you returning to this part of the world?"

"I'm not in control of that. What I mean is that a sheriff down here, a guy named Haskins — a cross between Frankenstein and Godzilla — is keeping me a couple more days."

"What do you mean, keeping you? Have you done anything wrong?"

"No, not really. I'll explain in more detail later. . . anyway, I hope things are going OK for you at home. I mean that.

"Joyce."

"What?"

He ran two fingers across his closed eyes. "Maybe I should tell you now. I want you to know."

"You met someone. She's twenty and you got her pregnant. You're going off together to Bali."

"Not quite. And not funny."

"What then?"

"In the Everglades, after I went down, a young Indian picked me up, took me to his camp. He tried to steal my wallet, and —"

"What?"

"I woke and grabbed a log. Hit him on the head. He . . . he died in my arms the next morning. When I was getting us out." There was silence on the line.

"You did *what*?"

"He had a gun. He would have killed me first time he had the chance."

"That's terrible! Oh, Allan. What can I do? Do you need an attorney? What will *you* do?"

"I'm not sure." He paused. "I told the sheriff everything. He wants me to take him to where I put . . . the boy's body."

"I had no idea. I'm truly sorry. . ."

"Thanks, Joyce. I'll let you know how things go. I like a little excitement, but this is unreal."

"Look," she said, "it hasn't been good with us, but it doesn't mean I don't care."

"Thanks. I know, Joyce. I'll call as soon as I know more. Don't worry, I'll find some way out of this."

"Bye, Allan. Please take care of yourself. And call me again later. Please!"

27

HASKINS ALMOST FILLED THE FRONT SEAT, but Allan managed to edge in beside him, feeling very small. "Real nice day. This time of year, fall, in between tourist seasons." Haskins noticed someone he knew, waved to him and stopped the car. Through the open window he said, "Won't be able to make bowlin' today, Bobby."

As they continued on through Islamorada, Haskins said, "Real nice town we have here, Mister Daniels. Everybody sort of takes care of each other. Know what I'm sayin'?"

"Yes, sir," Allan responded. "I hope to bring my family down here at some point. I have a girl and a little boy."

Haskins sat up straighter. He sniffed the air. "Need to stop in at my office."

They parked in the sheriff's spot, walked through the back door into his office. "Have a seat." Haskins dropped into his chair, leaned back, pencil between his two index fingers, eyes examining Allan's. "Well, sir, the tests came back, all right, got them here in my drawer."

In spite of himself, Allan's hands clenched tightly.

"You know," Haskins said, "my daddy used to tell me when there's a possum hangin' around, the best thing you do is sit back and wait for him to make a move." He waited, then said, "Because sooner or later he will. Mister Daniels, there may be more to know about this here story."

"I'm no damn possum, Sheriff. If you're driving at something, why don't you say so? I'm beginning to feel harassed. May be time for me to get an attorney."

"Don't get your ulcers in an uproar." Haskins said. "I'm not tryin' to hassle you. Just probin' into somethin' I need to understand better." He gazed hard at Allan. "You don't have to worry if what you've finally told me is the truth. *All* of it." His smile contradicted his words and tone. When Allan didn't react, he continued, "All right, the tests. It's an old boat, seen plenty of action. They said there was human as well as animal blood. But not so clear so as they could know whose, or if somebody got stuck with a hook, or what. I may want to have your blood examined."

Haskins looked out the window at a garbage truck noisily collecting the town's refuse. "We put out an all-points for that boy. No one's seen him in a year or more, so when you reported his whereabouts . . . well, he'd fallen off our radar screen." He lit a cigarette. "*You* were the last to see him, right? Anyway, you put him right back on. No longer a cold case."

Allan stared at the sheriff, his face blank. "I told you all there was to tell," he said.

"I'm real sure you did, Mister Daniels. No doubt we'll find out more when we get to that island." His gaze focused on Allan's eyes. "Want me to run you back to the Trade Winds?"

Allan decided it would be smart to accept, although he wasn't sure why.

"Oh, Mister Daniels," the desk clerk called out as Allan walked into the motel. "This came for you from Dr. Watts's office a day or two ago. Real sorry I forgot to give it to you."

Allan sank into a Naugahyde chair and opened the letter slowly. He realized it had been written *before* the last time he and Sue had been together.

> Let us go then, you and I
> When the evening is spread out against the sky
> Like a patient etherized upon a table.

"T. S. Eliot. My favorite poem."

Allan folded the note carefully, stared out at the sea. The memories of their one afternoon came rushing back: pure pleasure, but tinged with deep regret.

28

THE SKIFF SKIPPED OVER THE WATER, the sheriff guiding it around one island, then past another, staying in the channels marked by red and green buoys. The crisp fall air whistling through the mango trees and the roar of the boat's engine prevented any conversation between the two men. The clouds overhead had turned leaden and spread across the entire sky.

Allan tried to think of something light to say but couldn't forget the reason they were speeding to the scene. He noticed that Haskins was wearing a pistol, a small one, above his ankle. *Why two guns? What does he expect? An attack by a band of egrets?*

When they neared the island, Allan pointed to the small stretch of sand he had landed on. Haskins nosed the boat toward the shore

"Pull the front up higher while I secure the motor," Haskins directed. "Take the anchor and sink it high up into the sand. Deep."

Allan followed his instructions. "Now, which way, Mister Daniels?"

"Toward that end," Allan responded, pointing in a northerly direction. The two men, led by Allan, made their way with some difficulty through the mangroves. He found the tarp where he had left it.

"I want you to see this," the sheriff ordered as he stood over the dark olive canvas. Allan shuddered as Haskins slowly unwrapped the tarp.

Empty.

"What! Where in the hell is he?" Allan almost shouted.

Haskins pulled the sides back over each other and stepped back. "Well, I'm not completely surprised." He sat down on a thick mangrove branch and pulled a cigarette from the pack in his breast pocket. "Those Miccosukees have an uncanny way of knowin' about things. Could've somehow sensed Tommy here. Came an' took the body back to where they'd bury him Indian-style." He drew in on the cigarette and let the smoke slip slowly from his lips, then glanced over at Allan. "Or maybe Tommy didn't die an' got himself back somehow. Tough people, that tribe. *Or maybe, Mister Daniels, he never left that camp of his!*" He stared hard at Allan.

Allan shook his head and muttered, "No, no. I swear I brought him here."

"You're mumblin'. What'd you say?"

"I said I put him *here*. That's the truth."

Back in Islamorada, in police headquarters, Haskins faced Allan. Smoke from his cigarette curled upward before being scattered in the overhead light. The door stood open to the central control room, where the deputy sat elevated on a platform.

The sheriff placed his hands behind his neck, stretched his huge shoulders, grimaced, and yawned. He rose, opened the window, leaned on the sill. "I like this time of day. Moistness seems to pick up the scent of whatever's floatin' around in the air." He turned, peered hard at Allan for what seemed an eternity. "Tell you what, Mister Daniels. I am *not* goin' to charge you. I have to say that since there's no body, there's no crime that can be proven. Manslaughter, maybe, but right now I'm more inclined to believe your story than not. Of course, legally it wouldn't be self-defense because you weren't actually attacked. But unless we find the body, I can't hold you. You can go. For now, understand?" He motioned to Allan to take off the monitor. "My responsibility, well, you know what it is. There are times when it's not clear. Maybe some things I've done weren't right. Suppose I'm tellin' you this because in a way what you did out there that night could have happened to anyone. Maybe even to me." His sigh was heavy and audible.

Allan was surprised by Haskins's openness and sensitivity.

"But, Mister Daniels, I am *not* closin' the case. Not until Handley is found. Alive or dead." He walked to his chair, sat down, and watched Allan intently.

Allan shook his head, his eyes in a blank stare, and said carefully, "I know what I did was wrong. But I never meant to hurt him. Just protect myself. And I should have brought him out, I know that, too." Allan walked over to the window and sat on the ledge. He looked straight at Haskins. "Sometime, later on, I've got to go back in there. Unless I do, it'll always be hanging over my head. Find him. If he's alive, if he'll listen, tell him he doesn't have to stay in those lousy swamps for the rest of his life. If I find him, that is, or if he finds me. If he isn't . . . dead."

"Tell you what, Mr. Daniels." Haskins got to his feet. "I'd be willin' to go with you. Better chance of maybe findin' him. I sure ain't no Miccosukee or Seminole, but for a white man I'm pretty damn good in those swamps. Family's from Everglades City. Lived there when I was a boy. An' if you go in by yourself, you're sure to make a mess of it."

Allan gazed at Haskins for a few moments, a slight smile playing on his lips. "If you came along you'd probably get us lost. Then I'd have to turn from fifty percent Miccosukee to one hundred percent and save your ass."

"Now that sure as hell won't ever happen, Mister Daniels, no siree," Haskins said, grinning. "All right, I'll run you back."

When they reached the middle of town, Allan said, "I need to walk a little." Haskins pulled over. Allan opened the car door. He glanced over at Haskins. "Thanks. I really—"

"Yeah." Haskins cut him off. "I know."

29

ALLAN ADVISED THE DESK CLERK that he would be down on the beach and asked him to keep his bag behind the counter until his taxi arrived. He removed his shoes and socks, rolled up his cuffs, and stood at the water's edge. He checked out a cabin cruiser returning from deep-sea fishing. He heard laughter from the people on board.

The clerk called out that his taxi had arrived. Allan kicked the water with his feet, dried them, put on his socks and shoes, and left the Trade Winds.

The taxi traveled northeast along the Keys for the two-hour drive to Miami International airport. The weather was changing, the sky toughening, the light fading. Thin cirrus and stratus clouds were being rapidly replaced with heavier, darker, troublesome cumulonimbus. The driver commented that the radio reported the weather was getting nasty along the entire eastern seaboard. *Not a problem,* he thought. *Weather's always interesting.*

When they crossed the bridges that connected the dozens of keys, Allan could see Florida Bay to the northwest and the Straits of Florida in the Atlantic. The darkening sky was no longer separated from the water. It looked like a damaged roof threatening to fall.

His flight to LaGuardia would most likely be turbulent. Allan almost welcomed bad weather on commercial flights. He understood the dynamics of a plane in flight as a moving object subjected to unevenness created by varying waves and thermals of air.

When he was nine, he had flown with his father in marginal weather in an old rented WACO biplane. They were flying over the farming district of the North Fork in Suffolk County. Heavy rain began to pummel the plane, and the sky closed in around them. Poor visibility made continuing in any direction impossible. They circled lower and lower.

Finally, his father pulled the power back and positioned the plane for a landing on a farmer's dirt road. This was not at all like their airfield. Allan was frightened. They seemed to be executing a normal landing, but as they slowed, a wheel found a ditch. The tip of one of the lower wings dug in, the plane lurched and spun around. Maybe they'd turn upside down and be pinned inside. Maybe the plane would catch fire.

His father had shut down the engine before landing. The plane spun hard, a severe turn but not disastrous. The propeller stopped turning. It was suddenly quiet, the rush of air gone. Rain poured in, soaking them. Allan had slammed his arm against the side of the cockpit. It hurt, but he was going to keep it to himself. His father helped him climb out. Cars emerged and raced down the road. "It's OK, son. It's called a ground-loop. It happens. We'll call the guys at the airport. They'll take off the wings and tow it back." He looked at his son's face. "Sorry about that. I should have checked the weather more carefully. We got caught. My fault."

At the Miami terminal, Allan dropped into a phone booth and dialed home. "Hi there, Nance. My plane gets in late, but I will definitely, undoubtedly, and surely wake you up and tell you all about Islamorada. And," he hesitated, "I may just have something for you and your brother."

"Tell me, Daddy, tell me," Nance urged.

"Can't. Wouldn't be a surprise. Honey, did you do something fun today?"

"I had a friend over for a tea party. It was real good until Craig came in. He knocked everything over. He's a real brat."

Allan went to the cocktail lounge for a drink. As he sat in the corner next to the window drinking a Scotch, he observed planes at their ramps, one or two with umbilical fuel hoses attached. The arm-like passenger boarding ramps reminded him of praying mantises. The sky became heavier, unloading more rain, obscuring most of the background. Daylight was shut out rapidly.

Allan took his seat on the plane and buckled himself in. Rain pelted the window. He put his face to the Plexiglas and felt the cold on his forehead, eyebrows, and nose. The overhead lights flickered; the engines being energized. The plane was an old Boeing 727. Large engine pods hung down from the wings. *Amazing being able to lift the weight of fuel, plane, and passengers off the ground,* he mused.

As they started to taxi, Allan noticed a man on the ground giving hand signals to the pilot. His hair was jet black, wet, and matted. Allan leaned forward and stared through his window. *Tommy! But it couldn't be him!*

The plane taxied out from the terminal, moved to the end of the line behind other airliners, and waited its turn for takeoff. He laughed to himself. *Don't have any more control over this flight than I had when I went down and Handley found me.*

A not-unattractive young woman, her hands clenched, was sitting next to him. Allan turned to her and said pleasantly, "Hi. You know, we're much safer in the air than on the ground. Much safer than driving to the airport."

"Really?"

"Absolutely. People are just not used to planes. They don't realize cars are much more dangerous."

"Oh. You think so?"

"I know so. Enjoy the flight," he reassured her. "You'll be fine. It's very safe. And breathtaking in a way."

30

WHAT HAD OCCURRED IN FLORIDA touched everything in Allan's life. He struggled not to let torment and despair control his behavior. He became unusually short-tempered and quarrelsome with everyone, even Bob. His sense of humor almost disappeared. Peace of any kind had become an abstraction.

Although Joyce had been pleasant, even solicitous, to him when he returned, she still had not changed her mind: he was to move out. He was not used to living without his family and missed the day-to-day warmth and closeness. It wasn't that he couldn't make the adjustment, but he worried about how his not being there affected Nancy and Craig. *I want what I've been.*

Allan moved into a motel in East Norwich for several days while he checked the market for furnished apartments. One night the kids stayed over with him. He took them out for Chinese food. Before going to sleep, he told them the fascinating things that Osceola had told him.

"And you know, kids, you're one-quarter American Indian. None of your friends can say that. It makes you special. Something you can be proud of."

"They really do all those things, Daddy?" Nancy asked.

"Mm-hmm. They're incredible outdoors, and very smart."

He and Craig shared one bed, Nance slept in the other. The following morning, he dropped them off at their schools.

He selected a pleasant second-floor unit facing east on tree-lined Grace Avenue, near the station in Great Neck, ten minutes from his office and twenty from the house in Brookville. He signed the minimum six-month lease.

"Your problem is," he said to himself while shaving one morning. He stopped and said into the mirror, "Make that problems: one, find out what happened to Tommy. Two: try to get my marriage back. Maybe not in that order."

The following Saturday, the fall balanced the colored splendor of the leaves with a three-toned-gray sky. "What the hell is the matter with you?" Bob asked at the 19th Hole, the grill room of the Meadow Ridge Country Club. "You're as sour as a year-old rotten apple. You couldn't have shot a worse round today." Bob swizzled the three onions in his gimlet glass. "Did you really burn down the local high school?" He noticed a few golfers entering the room and waved. "Hey, one of those guys is a new member. He can't possibly know you're a pyromaniac."

"Not funny, Parker." Allan lifted his glass and sipped his Dewar's. He gazed out the window and watched leaves from a large oak just outside tumble and flit through the air, falling at different rates. "I've been trying to . . . get back into things. It's tough going. I just don't seem to have the same drive."

Bob grabbed some peanuts from the dish on the bar, then offered them to Allan. He turned them down. "Look, buddy," Bob explained, "if you don't like what's going on, change it. Work it out with Joyce. Make compromises. Hell, we all have to."

"Don't think she wants to. It's not only that." Allan slammed his hand down hard on the bar. "I keep reliving what happened to me down there."

Bob poked Allan. "What are you talking about? Nobody's dead."

Allan looked strangely at Bob, pushed back his bar stool, and stood up. "I told you on the phone about my plane going down, right? Well, there's more, a lot more. Got some time? Meet me at Morgan Park."

"OK, if it's that important. I'll call Polly, tell her I'll be late."

♦ ♦ ♦

They parked next to each other and began to walk toward the jetty. Allan noticed several couples looking out on Hempstead Harbor. He pointed to the small, open-sided building at the north end of the park. No one in it. They strolled over and sat down on the bench.

Allan told Bob everything. "I'm still under investigation. Joyce knows about it, too."

"Sure you're not making this up?" Bob asked. "Sounds really weird. Kafkaesque."

Allan stood up. "It's driving me crazy. This sheriff's not quitting, but it's not even that." He paused, looked down at his hands, and said, "The kid's body was gone when I went back with Haskins."

"I gotta say this," Bob said. "You should have brought him out." He put his hand on Allan's arm.

"OK! For Pete's sake, I know that! I did the wrong thing! I panicked. I shouldn't have. I still feel guilty about it every goddamn day."

"Take it easy," Bob said, patting Allan's shoulder. "It's OK. You have to keep perspective."

"Easy for you to say. It's hard to concentrate on anything else." Allan groaned. "A real mess. A fucking mess. *I'm* a fucking mess." He looked out across Long Island Sound. "That's not all."

"Oh?"

Allan didn't face Bob when he finally said, "I met this extraordinary woman down in Islamorada. We . . . we got involved. Didn't plan to. She's not fulfilled in her marriage, and anyway Joyce was kicking me out." He searched for words. "She — this woman — took my breath away. It was fantastic. Stupidly, I told her what happened." Allan watched some gulls fighting over a crushed mussel one had dropped on the rocks. "She was shocked. Terribly upset. I know I've fallen way down in her esteem. We decided to end it almost before it began. Anyway, I'm trying to get her out of my mind. I can handle that part."

"It's one thing, with that affair. . . and *don't* tell me her name. But that kid . . . Hell, not Allan Daniels. Mister Circumspect. Mister Perfect. My best friend. All right, the kid's gone. That's never going to change. As far as the rest, I'll help you any way I can."

"At the time it didn't seem like I had any choice. In hindsight I obviously did."

They headed back to their cars. "Look," Bob said, "you clearly need to unwind. How about dinner with us tomorrow? Nothing big. A couple of drinks. I'll grill steaks. You bring corn."

"Sounds good. I'm taking Nancy to Jones Beach in the morning. We'll come over after that. Thanks, my friend."

Bob closed Allan's car door and said through the window, "Maybe there's some way out of this thing," he said. "And obviously what you told me will remain between us."

Allan nodded. He sat in his car and watched as Bob pulled away, then turned his attention to the sound. A lone sloop beat into the northeast wind, then came about on a starboard tack. Allan watched, mulling over in his mind the physics of sailing, reminding himself of the simplicity of cause and effect.

Nothing happens until it does . . . then you can look for the "why". . .

31

When Allan got home the phone was ringing. It was Joyce.

"Just a minute, Allan. I want to move to the bedroom." He listened over the line for the sounds of his old life. He heard the bedroom door close. "Listen, I've tried to support you through this whole Florida situation. But I hope you know how very difficult it was for me and the kids, you being away just then." When he didn't respond, she added, "Before we were married, you made me feel I was the most important thing in the world. Unfortunately, that seems to be completely gone."

"Joyce, I still love you, you're the woman of my life. I don't want our marriage to end. I've made that very clear. And I'll do everything in my power to make it work again. But I have to make sense out of that business down in the Everglades. It is affecting everything I do."

"You told that sheriff what happened. If he continues to hound you, get a lawyer."

"That's a possibility."

"We all have to move on," she said. "I have to, anyway."

"Before we say sayonara forever, what about a movie later? There's an interesting art film playing in Huntington that got great reviews. Dinner after. That new Brazilian place. Some good wine. How about it?"

She thought for a moment, then said, "The kids will like our being out together. Oh, what the hell, why not?"

"Great. I have some work at the office, but right after that. Oh, another thing. Bob and Polly asked us over for dinner tomorrow."

"Obviously without me," she replied. "Anyway, for tonight,

come by around six. No movie. Just dinner. And don't get any ideas."

When Allan pulled into his — Joyce's — driveway around 5:30, it was dark. He stepped out of the car and stood for some moments contemplating the design. Several magazines had wanted to feature it, but Allan had always refused. "Privacy," he would say. "Maybe when I sell." The house was set back from the heavily wooded street on two acres. Nicely secluded. He had designed earthen mounds of different sizes arranged subtly. Interestingly shaped boulders were integrated with evergreens and flowering bushes. It created the seclusion he had planned. Tall oaks, pines, maples, and a beautiful copper beech filled the property, creating a pleasant and interesting relationship with the house. A magnificent specimen, a blue-green weeping spruce, highlighted the entry. Allan let himself in.

Just inside the door was a planter with water flowing from cascading teak blocks in a series of natural spillways. A two-foot-tall Dubuffet sculpture was positioned in the middle of the flow, partially enclosed by courses of glass block. Behind the house was a pool and a Har-Tru clay tennis court. Multileveled grass terraces were set off with boulders, sculptures, and dark bluestone steps and walks. A Calder-type stabile was positioned nicely in a small area of lawn.

Allan poured himself a Dewar's and turned on the TV. He flipped to a semifinal match of a tennis tournament. The U.S. Open was over in September. The season was coming to an end.

He picked up the phone and called his parents. "Hi, Dad. I just wanted to say hello. Did I catch you during dinner?"

"Well, my boy, as a matter of fact, you're in luck. Your mother is making one of her famous Indian meals. Pompano in a stew with oysters and vegetables. And that wonderful flatbread she makes. Want to join us with your brood? Your sister and her gang are arriving shortly from New Haven."

"Can't, Dad. Having dinner with Joyce. Another time."

"Oh, that's nice. When you have a moment I want to talk with you about . . . I'm a little confused about your situation down there in Florida. Why do you have to go back? Let's have lunch this week."

Allan promised to call him.

Joyce pulled into the garage and came in through the kitchen with the kids. "I'll be ready in a few minutes."

"Sure. I'll put the kids to bed."

"Daddy . . ." Nance said, a sad expression on her face. She sat on her bed, Craig next to her.

"Honey, what's the matter?" he asked, giving her his full attention.

"Daddies are supposed to live with their chidren, and . . . you're not. My friends . . . I try not to tell them anything but they know. It makes me feel bad. Sad. Craig, too." Her brother nodded.

"I know, honey. I'm sorry about it. I think it's just for now." He went over and stroked her face. "I may not be living here right now, but I will never, ever leave you. Never. I care about you and love you both to the bottom of my heart. I'll aways see you. Promise."

Allan and Joyce had dinner at Piccola, their favorite restaurant, one of Long Island's best. He ordered a Barolo suggested by the owner. For their main course, she had rack of lamb, Allan a tasty rabbit.

After a few glasses of wine, Joyce gave Allan a look he hadn't seen for a long time. "It wouldn't take too much . . . ," she began wistfully.

"To what?"

"To remember Bermuda. It was special."

Allan took a long sip of his wine. "What was special was that we never saw that much of Bermuda."

Joyce shook her head. "That grin! You've always got sex on your mind, haven't you?"

"We saw the sights, all right," he continued. "They were in our room. I could never get enough of you, Butzi."

"Well, that was then," she responded, "and this is now. As I said earlier, people move on."

Allan woke up several times that night. He got out of bed at 5:30 and opened the sliding glass door in the den of his apartment. The humidity had broken, the air was crisp, the maples and oaks had begun to color their leaves in the magnificent shades of fall. He turned on the automatic coffee maker, poured himself some juice, then put on his running clothes.

He decided to run at the high-school track near his office. No one was up this early; he'd have it all to himself. Good time to think about what he should do. Had to do.

After twelve laps, he showered in his office, cleaned up some paperwork, and began to sketch the site and floor plan for a new office and warehouse facility in Melville. The various components of the building had to interact efficiently. It should take the minimum time for workers to access different areas. Administration, engineering, and marketing would be located in the two-story office section. The warehouse would be sized in relation to specific equipment and for storage. Allan created half a dozen sketches for his draftsmen.

Once the company accepted the floor plan, Allan planned to design an innovative exterior. He envisioned a series of concave paneled elements textured with blue glass chips alternating with blue-gray windows. The two-story offices would constitute a bold and exciting symmetrical pattern of elements.

Allan called Joyce. "Good morning. I, uh, wanted to catch you before you left for work." He took a deep breath. "I've been thinking."

"So?"

"Well . . . maybe it would be better if I came home. Moved back in."

There was a long silence. "Better for whom?" she said finally. He could hear her erratic breathing. "It's always you and what you need. You still don't seem to get it."

"I'm trying to do what's right for all of us," he said. "I really am."

"Damn you, Allan! In your own unique way, you treat me as if I were a yo-yo!" She paused. "Anyway, forget moving back in, and make sure I'm not here when you come by to pick up Nance. And by the way, has it ever occurred to you that you're creating long-term problems for her and Craig? And now I have to tell them you're going back to Florida? What are they supposed to think? About your obsession down there. Nance will think she can't depend on you. How do you think that will affect her later with men? And your role model for Craig? You're sending both of them the wrong damn signals, Allan!"

"For Pete's sake, Joyce, I have no control over what happened," he replied. "Once the mess in Florida gets straightened out, I'll be able to function better. And for what it's worth, regarding us, you seem to lay the blame for everything on me! Some of it's you, Joyce, and you know it."

"No, Allan, I don't know it!" she exploded. "Now I really want that separation agreement executed! Specific visitation and financial responsibilities. And the sooner the better."

"Oh, c'mon Joyce, you're rushing to judgment."

"I need someone who makes me feel . . . it's called commitment. Devotion. On both counts, dear boy, you come up short. Very short. Do you hear me?"

"I'm trying to. You're pretty tough on me. You might examine your own role in all this."

"Damn you, Daniels!" she shouted and slammed down the phone.

♦ ♦ ♦

When he picked up Nance, Max von Dog, their German shorthaired pointer, was waiting outside. When he saw Allan's Volvo wagon he barked and almost jumped through the open window.

"Maxy! My good old Maxy. I miss you too. *You* find me acceptable, don't you?" He hugged the dog, who licked his face. "Hey, how about a weekend? You'll be my copilot. We'll fly to . . . how about Tahiti? We'll become real beach bums."

Nancy opened the front door. "Daddy, I did my hair myself. Mommy only helped me with the ribbon."

"My, my, just look at you!" Allan exclaimed, stepping back. "You look gorgeous, honey." He swept her up into his arms. "I just love your new dress. But since we're going to Jones Beach, you might be better off in jeans, no?"

"Why isn't Mommy coming?"

"Well, Nance—"

"I know why," she said. "Daddy, it's terrible when you're not with us. Like something else is more important."

Allan looked down and shook his head, his jaw muscles tightening. "It's terrible for me, too, honey. Nothing is more important than you. But you know what happened with my plane. There are problems only I can solve down there. The sheriff has been trying to find the young Indian man. I'm the last one who saw him."

"But *we're* your family, Daddy. You should be with *us*!"

"Of course. I want that, too," he went on. "You and Craig can really be sure of one thing, that Mommy and I love you more than anything else. Always remember that. Always."

Nance fumed. "I'll try, Daddy. But it's hard."

He picked her up and hugged her.

She screwed up her face. "I'll put my dress back on when we come home from the beach," she announced firmly. *Very much like her mother*, Allan thought.

They drove on the Wantagh Parkway south to Jones Beach State Park. Nance wiggled through his arms getting out of the car. "Mommy is . . . ," she began, but reconsidered.

"Mommy is what?" he asked, catching her hand with both of his.

"She was crying when I came into her room." Nance pursed her lips, examining his face. Tears filled her eyes.

He pulled her back inside the car and onto his lap. "Shh, shh, honey, that's all right. I always want you to tell me how you feel."

They walked from the car, hand in hand, the salt-loaded wind raw on their faces. He zipped up her jacket.

"Daddy, you don't tuck us in anymore, and, and . . ."

He stopped and crouched down in front of her. "Now listen to me very carefully. I want to live with you, Craig, and Mommy. Very much. But sometimes parents have problems even though they're married because—"

"Because why?"

"Because, well, things sometimes get mixed up. So they have to work them out just like kids do. But that doesn't mean they don't love each other. Or that they stop loving their children. I keep telling you that you and Craig are the most important things in the world to both of us."

"It makes me feel terrible," Nance said. "My friend, Mary, her parents got divorced. Now she has a new daddy." She looked to him for reassurance.

Allan was not prepared. He wanted to be helpful but didn't want to distort or disguise reality. "Nance, I honestly believe Mommy and I will get back together. Right now she's a little angry with me." He knew not to go into details. "I never want you to ever have a new daddy. I'm your father."

"Maybe you won't be if you don't live with us anymore! Oh, I

hate you, Daddy, I hate you!" She ran to the car and climbed into the rear seat. She lay face down, fingers in her ears. His attempts to bring her around were in vain.

During the drive back to Brookville, Allan noticed a large flight of Canada geese. He pulled over onto the grass. "Look, Nance. Look at them! What a terrific sight seeing them migrate in perfect V formation. In the spring they'll be back again. You can count on that. And me too," he said, squeezing her hand.

"Daddy," Craig pleaded when they reached the house. "How come you had Nance all to herself? Do me the same as you did her. Same as her." He had just come from a birthday party, his shirt stained with chocolate ice cream and cake.

"Next time, Craig, it'll be just you and me." He was up in Allan's arms in a hug, his face nestled at his father's shoulder. "We could go flying."

Allan looked over at his daughter. "We'll pick up corn at the farm stand on the way to the Parkers'. And have a game of catch on their lawn."

"I don't want to. Not with Craig. He's a brat."

"C'mon, Nance. He worships you and wants to do everything you do."

"Well, tell him not to take my stuff. He doesn't even ask, he—" She raised her fist, trying to hit her brother, who darted behind his father. Allan caught her arm. He took each child by the hand, pulled them together and kissed each on top of their heads. "Change into your dress, Nance. I'll clean Craig up."

The Parker home was an old colonial in Locust Valley built in the 1920s on several acres among tall oaks and maples. In the rear was a screened-in porch, pool, and outdoor grill, plus a small putting green at the edge of the lawn.

♦ ♦ ♦

Pauline Ellsworth Nash was raised in Portland, Maine, the only daughter of an old family whose Nash descendants arrived on the second voyage of ships that brought those plucky tourists from England in the 1600s. Her parents had met in New Haven, when her father was a student at Yale Law School and her mother was a senior at Wellesley.

One could not say Polly would stand out in a crowd. She refused to wear any makeup on her somewhat ordinary face, nothing around her doe-brown eyes. She found most things amusing. Within her there was a place her friends knew was very private. "They get me as I really am," she once told her mother. "If they don't like the way I look, well, their problem." Her face now revealed the toll time had taken but also expressed that her life had been fundamentally good. "Everything you are, Polly," Bob kidded her once, "is obviously due to that fantastic man in your life."

"You mean my father?" she rejoined. "You have to be kidding, Parker. You're lucky I gave you a second chance." She screwed up her face and gave him a sloppy, wet kiss.

Polly had graduated at the top of her high-school class, the captain of her lacrosse team and president of the student body. She was tall, five feet eight, very competitive and highly regarded. After six months of wandering around Europe with a girlfriend, she chose Princeton with a long-term plan to go to medical school. But when she met Bob, she gave up the idea and convinced him they should take her father's sloop for a summer cruise up the coast to Labrador, Canada. He did not need to be asked twice.

When the steaks were ready, Bob brought them over to the table, which Polly had set festively with a multicolored tablecloth and napkins. Allan carried the corn in a steaming pot from the kitchen.

"Well, everyone," Bob said, "real nice to have you with us. After we've eaten, there's Frisbee. Or we can have a putting contest."

"My mother's not here," Nance blurted out, looking at her father, then at the Parkers. When no one responded, she got up and ran out onto the patio. Polly and Allan both followed her.

"You're right about that," Polly acknowledged. "I wish your mother *was* here. She's my friend, too, you know. And *I* don't like your parents not being together, either."

"Maybe you should have a barbeque with her and not my father."

"We might sometime," Polly countered.

"Maybe she'll have a new boyfriend. Maybe he'll be my everyday father." She began to cry. Allan tried to embrace her.

"Leave me alone!" she yelled. "I want to go home."

Allan's entreaties were for naught. He apologized to the Parkers, said good-bye and departed.

As Allan drove into his old driveway, Joyce opened the front door. He waved to her and tried to hug Nance good-bye, but she pulled loose and raced into the house. Craig squeezed his father hard. Tears ran down his cheeks. "Daddy, come tomorrow? Please?"

"Sure. I'll pick you up at school. Remember, son, I love you very, very much. Good night, sweet boy." Craig slid from his father's arms, turned, and ran to the house. He turned and waved. About a block from the house, Allan pulled over, leaned his head on the steering wheel, and began to sob.

32

Look, Allan," his junior partner, Leo Guthart, remarked one morning in Allan's office. "I know you've got a lot on your mind, but you know our practice depends on details. And especially client relations." Guthart was tall, attractive by some standards, in top physical condition, and an "A" tennis player. He had a dry sense of humor but became serious when business required. He grew his hair long in the back to take attention away from his baldness. His beard was short, stubby, and graying. Leo had graduated near the top of his class at MIT and had been with Allan's firm for six years. Allan liked him. Trusted him.

Allan stood next to his board, working on drawings for a two-story office building in Commack. For dramatic effect, the conference room would be located above the entry and would have curved walls made from grain-matched elm plywood. Offices for the top executives would be designed with exterior patios set back from half walls that held planters for hanging ivy and flowering shrubs.

"Damn it, Leo, I'm well aware of that! How the hell do you think I built this practice?" He stepped away from the board. "I'm sorry. I didn't mean to go off that way."

"Mind if I close the door?" Guthart asked. Allan nodded.

"I mean, Allan, since Florida, you've been . . . I don't know . . . terribly distracted. Sort of out of it. The plane crash must have been traumatic, I realize. But, frankly, we need your regular leadership."

Allan moved back to his desk, leaned back, and folded his hands behind his head. "When I made you a junior partner, it was to give me some creative time," he said strongly. "No, I didn't mean for you to take on all the responsibilities, but, shit, if I'm away, you seem to run around in a panic."

"Certain clients only want to deal with you, Allan. *Your* developers."

Allan swung around in his swivel chair, got to his feet, and walked over to the window. He watched cars and trucks wend their way through the heavy traffic on Northern Boulevard. *Going somewhere, going nowhere* . . . "If you want to become more than a junior partner, Leo, then you damn well better demonstrate you can handle situations and solve problems."

"Excuse me," Guthart observed dryly. "I wouldn't have brought this up if it wasn't necessary. Everyone feels it. The office, contractors. Calls have been coming in from Sweeney, Rose, and some of our other developers who are pissed you haven't gotten back to them. Even D'Alessio and Hamer. These people don't want to deal with me. I can deal with a lot, believe me, but certain key clients want to hear it from the boss himself."

"All right, I hear you!" Allan yelled, then caught himself. "I'm sorry, Leo. I'm under a lot of pressure right now. Do me a favor. List the most important things that need my attention. But I'm counting on you to get a lot of the other shit off my back. OK?"

Half an hour later, a call came in from Jerry Sweeney, one of Allan's original clients. "Good God, I've been trying to reach you forever! The sectional details your guys drew are confusing the shit out of the subs, and—damn it—I call you and you're on some goddamn trip out of the state!"

"Look, Jerry, I'm no damn babysitter," Allan shot back. "Leo covers for me when I'm not around. Besides, I couldn't call you. I was stuck in the middle of the fucking Everglades!"

"Yeah, I heard about that. Sorry. But I've got a building to finish. There's a deadline and penalties. Shit, you've never acted like this before. Get your ass over here and straighten things out!"

"I'll be there as soon as I can," Allan said, annoyed. "Around one. I'm bringing Leo. We'll talk over sandwiches, then throw up together."

33

ALLAN SAT QUIETLY IN HIS OFFICE for several minutes with the door closed. Then he suddenly picked up the phone and dialed.

"Sue, it's me, Allan."

"Oh, hi, Allan. Why are you calling me?" she answered.

"Just to see how you are. I wish there was a way for us to . . . you know, talk. First, I just want to apologize for not telling you sooner about Tommy. I should have."

"Yes, you should have." She paused, then said in a lighter tone, "You sure have had an interesting effect on this town." She laughed, then said seriously, "Anything else?"

"I'm going to try to find him."

"I thought you might."

"Sue, I . . ."

"What?"

"I'm coming back down soon. I'd like to see you."

"I'm not sure, Allan, I'm not sure."

"You sound angry."

"I'm not angry, just upset. And saddened. Oh, I have to go. I see the kids coming down the driveway. Bye."

"Good-bye, Sue."

Allan closed his eyes, his head shaking, trying to deny how deep he was sinking. The thought of facing Florida again was excruciating. He wanted something to hold onto, something he could depend upon. His mind flashed back to Lake Dunmore at the base of Moosalamoo Mountain, near the Middlebury campus. Once, in late March, he had taken Joyce out in a canoe. She started clowning around, and the next thing they knew they ended up in the frigid water. Despite their waterlogged clothes, they made their way back to the canoe and together pushed it to shore. She whooped at the top of her lungs. He shook his index finger at her, in mock admonition, then laughed along with her.

He thought about the enormous boulder at the edge of the lake, dropped there during the last glacial age. Water covered its bottom, as if it wanted to have it both ways: sit in the water but also be exposed to light and air. He had caught some nice bass and perch near that boulder. But its greatest attraction was that it symbolized permanence and strength. From time to time, he would return to sit in the temple of green near the shore and reflect on the boulder. Here on the heavily wooded beach were the sounds of blue jays, mockingbirds, an occasional hawk, squirrels and chipmunks chatting or complaining about something or other. Once, in September, he waded out, his arms spread-eagled against the huge granite mass. How strange but how good it made him feel, how it helped settle him down. Permanence and strength. He needed that now, to find purpose and direction, believe more in himself, exorcise some of the self-doubt dragging him down. He felt a little like he was dealing with the ten plagues of Passover.

Allan decided to make time for a few visits to some of the south-shore beaches. Jones or Gilgo, perhaps Smith Point Park. Only a few people went this time of year. Sit alone at the water's edge, inhale, and absorb the endless certainty of waves breaking uniformly on the sand. Contemplate infinity . . .

The phone rang on his private line. It was Joyce.

"Things to go over with you. OK to come over to the office?"

"Sure."

She entered his office an hour later, after his staff had left for the day.

"Visitation, vacation rights, and financial," she began. "We have to settle these. Not later. Now."

He gave her a pained look. "C'mon, too soon for that. Let's take it slowly. For you, me, the kids. I'm hurting," he protested. "I'm —"

"It's amazing," she cut in, "how when it comes to what you want you try to convince me how much you care. You should go into analysis. Therapy. Figure out for once who the hell you are. How you create problems. Ours, for example."

"Damn it, will you let me finish? You know being with our kids is critical for them, for you, for me. Tell your attorney not to be such an asshole. That's what they do, Joyce. Get the couple angry with each other, and drag out the settlement so they can get enormous fees."

"Perhaps," she responded acidly. "But right now, I trust my attorney more than I trust you."

"You shouldn't. Half of them try to get into their women clients' pants. I mean, the guy's a stranger, for Pete's sake."

"Are you quite finished? For your information, Mister Know-It-All, it's Danielle Carr who's handling my case. She's among the best."

"I don't give a good fuck if she's the queen of Sheba," Allan almost shouted. "She's only going to make things worse."

Joyce waited a few seconds and then said in a measured voice, "Allan. There's no point in dragging this out. And don't tell me what I can and can't do!" With that, she got to her feet, strode to the door, and left, slamming the door behind her.

Allan flung a chair across the room, smashing one of its legs. "Shit! Shit, shit, shit!"

When he had calmed down, he finished up some calls and paperwork, picked up some Kentucky Fried Chicken, and drove to his apartment. He fell asleep watching an old flying movie on TV, awoke several hours later, and tumbled into bed. In his dreams that night he was very much alone. And lonely.

◆ ◆ ◆

"Hey, Dad," Allan said in a call from his office next morning. "That lunch you wanted to have? How about Tofu in Roslyn Heights. Twelve-thirty?"

Allan arrived a few minutes before his father and selected a booth in the rear. When Martin came in, the two men hugged. Father and son resembled each other, except Allan's skin was darker and he was taller by a good two inches. Martin Daniels's features were not distinguished. His hair was full but white, his eyes blue-green with bushy eyebrows, which were also turning white. His gait had slowed, and once in a while Allan watched him stand straighter to try to look younger.

After they ordered, Allan asked, "How about taking in the revival of *Long Day's Journey into Night*? Saturday matinee in the city. I do watch television, but I'm not getting much culture these days. Things like we used to do. After the play, a couple of drinks and good porterhouse steaks. Smith and Wollensky. On me."

"That'd be nice, I'd really like that. Except Joyce set something up for us with Nance and Craig. Her parents are coming down." Allan didn't respond, so his father added, "How about the following Saturday. Want me to get tickets?"

"Can't. That's the weekend the kids are staying over."

His father changed the subject. "I'm very worried about you, Allan. Florida. Want to talk about it?"

"Not much to say. Sheriff Haskins called earlier, insists I check in with him every few days. I don't know what the hell's taking him so long. Probably has it in for northerners."

The elder Daniels put his hand gently against his son's face. "I don't like what I see happening to you here, either. You and Joyce—"

"I'll be OK, Dad. Just need to get away for a bit. Bob and I are taking off for the mountains. Like we used to every fall. Clear my head. Also, I can use the exercise."

"C'mon, you'll freeze your butt off this time of year. You're not twenty any more. Maybe just you and me alone on a weekend at Gurney's Inn in Montauk. Father and son trek."

"Sure. We'll do that soon. Bob and I will be fine. He used to be a guide summers in the White Mountains, and I'm no slouch."

"I wish I could be more help to you, son."

"You are. Just your caring."

Outside, they turned to each other and hugged for a long moment. "I love you, Dad," Allan said.

"I love you, too, son."

34

A MESSAGE HAD BEEN LEFT on his desk when he was out to lunch with his father. Allan returned the call.

"Hello." Sue sounded so different from the other day. "Hey Allan, some great news! My agent has set up a couple of meetings in New York Wednesday with publishers. Kind of exciting."

"I didn't think I'd hear from you again."

"I didn't either. It's a little difficult for me to separate my feelings about what happened with that young Indian . . . from our wonderful time together."

"There's nothing I can do to bring him back." he said. He paused, then said, "Anyway, I'm glad you called."

"You've messed up my head more than a little, Allan Daniels."

"I'm sorry if I have. I miss you, our . . . conversations."

"Don't lie to me. It's not our conversations you miss."

"No, you're right. Let's say our conversations and other things."

"I'll be staying at the Hilton on Sixth Avenue."

"Lunch?"

"No. Meetings. But in the afternoon. Say four o'clock? A glass of expensive wine," she said, laughing, "in the lounge. Conversation. Nothing more. Agree?"

"OK."

"I'll be the one with the tan. Speaking Conch. I'll get a translator for you."

"Have a good flight. And good luck with the publishers. Let them fight over you."

Allan parked and was in the Hilton lobby by 3:45. He looked in the lounge first, then sat down opposite the elevators. When she walked out of one, a surge of desire coursed through him. She was stunningly dressed. For him or for the publishers? Probably the latter. From their corner table, the cacophony of the city sounded a little like zoo animals who hadn't had lunch.

"You look splendid, Sue. People were ogling as you came out of the elevator. Very chic," Allan commented. "How'd the meetings go?"

"My agent schooled me not to say too much. She's very sharp. 'Let your manuscript do the talking,' she advised. Told both publishers there was competition. We'll know in a couple of weeks." She shook her head. "The big outfits have layers of bureaucracy. Waiting is frustrating." A waitress came over. Allan ordered Piper-Heidsieck.

Sue smiled. "Hmm . . . very nice." She leaned forward. "I've been thinking a lot about your situation with Haskins and that young man." She studied his face. "Even if the sheriff doesn't prosecute you, you'll have to carry this with you for the rest of your life."

"Think I'm not aware of that?"

She touched him on his arm and said, "The point is, though, you were definitely threatened."

"I've replayed every scenario," Allan replied. "They all stink. I can't eradicate —"

"This champagne," Sue said, changing the subject. "Really special. We Conchs from the Keys don't ever get to drink this hifalutin' wine. Too sophisticated for us hicks."

"Yeah, I figured as much," he said. "Wanted to test your tastebuds."

She reached for the bottle and poured more into their glasses. Exactly even. "It's just nice to be able to sit here and talk. I also wanted to apologize. I was too harsh on you the last time we met. Down in Islamorada. We became close . . . also friends. I'm not sure you know what I mean. I thought more about . . . when I was writing . . . about sex in people's lives." She chuckled, gazed out the window at the hustle and bustle. "It's so complicated. Animals. We're animals. Humans but animals in every way. Instincts. Chemistry. Biology. Good sex, bad sex. Love, commitment, fidelity, people's ages. One part of me believes sex doesn't have anything to do with love. Or marriage. Of course it can, it does. Sounds like I'm really a hussy, doesn't it?"

"You talk about things I think about but don't often verbalize," he said. "You're no hussy, Sue Watts. You have a wonderful capacity to express what you feel."

"Now, this next thing," she offered, "I've *never* discussed it with anyone." She took another sip and closed her eyes. "This will sound a little crazy because I'm basically an up person. I can't seem to talk about it with Ken. I've tried a couple of times and it won't come out. Anyway, Allan, when I'm old, maybe very old — assuming I get there — if my body is rebelling and no longer able to give me an acceptable life, I think I might commit suicide. *Might.* Sounds like I'm a coward, but I may want that choice."

"I hope you never get to that point, Sue. We're obviously on a one-way trip, and the end is never pretty. But suicide? You've got so many good years. Hundreds of things you still have time to be and do." He reached over and held her hand. "Sue, we've only known each other for a very short time, but believe me when I say I feel very deeply about you. If you ever start to feel that way, will you call me? Promise?"

She squeezed, then kissed, his hand. "Yes," she said. "I promise."

As he watched her stride to the elevator, he couldn't help thinking, *Why is she so warm, so caring, and Joyce so cold?*

35

WHEN HE GOT TIRED OF BRINGING FOOD IN, Allan would cook himself a steak or make pasta, even broil half a chicken. He made salad, vegetables, baked potatoes. Once in a while, he'd eat with his parents or with Bob and Polly. A few nights he would go out to a restaurant, very early or very late, when he would be less likely to run into anyone he'd have to talk to.

One night he chose a Korean restaurant in Flushing that he heard served interesting food. "A table over there, please?" he asked the attractive young Asian woman who greeted him. "It looks quieter." While waiting for his food he scanned the room. The restaurant was full. His eyes stopped at a table not too far away: Joyce was sitting with a friend of theirs, Adam Rosenberg. He had never married but always wanted to. He didn't know whether Joyce saw him or not, but when they finished their meal, they would have to walk by his table. Twenty minutes later, they did.

"The food's really unusual here, isn't it?" she offered. Neutral. Inwardly, he was seething.

Allan nodded, stood, and shook Adam's hand. He turned to Joyce. "I'll call you in a couple of hours. We'll compare notes about the evening."

"Not nice, Allan," she said. "Don't forget your manners."

"I won't, Joyce. Don't forget yours." With that, the couple about-faced and left, arm in arm. Allan kicked the chair next to him.

Allan called Haskins. "Sheriff, I was wondering if anything new has turned up."

"I kinda thought I might be hearin' from you, Mister Daniels.

Matter of fact, I asked an old Miccosukee friend of mine to check with the reservation Tommy goes to once in a while. Now, of course, this friend sure wasn't going to tell me *when* Tommy goes, but he was willin' to say that he hadn't been by there in quite a spell.

"My friend hinted that the girl Tommy's been seein' had a dream. Somethin' bad happened. Wouldn't be much of a surprise if they'd gone lookin' for him. Those people, Mister Daniels, can sense and smell things country miles away. Uncanny. Mind you, he didn't say this, but I kinda imagine they could've even found that island you put him on. Incredible trackers, Indians. Way back, they survived those three wars with U.S. troops. The Miccosukees, who split off from the Seminoles, didn't believe the government bullshit. A lot of Seminoles got shipped off to Oklahoma. Geronimo and his Apaches. You've heard about the Trail of Tears, I'm sure. A couple hundred escaped into the Everglades. Mostly Miccosukees. Kinda interestin', don't you think?

"Of course, now with all the drugs comin' in," he continued, "some are runnin' stuff. Another reason I want to find that kid."

"Maybe he goes to a different reservation," Allan offered.

"Not likely. Only one that's Miccosukee — and it'd be too far away. You keep callin' in, Mister Daniels."

Fuck off, Allan thought. "Of course," he answered dryly.

"Oh. One more thing, Mister Daniels. The forensic people are still tryin' to connect the blood from the boat with that shooting up in Everglades City. Might be the same blood. Handley's, possibly. Up in Everglades City, he'd cut himself on some glass. Now the question is — was any of it *his*?" he said. "Know what I'm sayin'? I'm anxious — real anxious — to find these things out. Talk to you soon, Mister Daniels."

"I'm sure you are, Sheriff," Allan responded, "And so am I. So am I."

"Sure you are, Mister Daniels. You make sure as hell you keep callin' me, Mister Daniels. I need to know where you are an' what you're doin'."

"Well, Thursday, Sheriff, I'm going camping with a friend. Need a break, some exercise. Returning Sunday."

"Where exactly?" Haskins asked.

"Either the Greens or the Catskills. Vermont or upstate New York."

"An' what's his name — your buddy?"

"Robert Monroe Parker," Allan replied. *And fuck you, Sheriff,* he thought.

"All right, Mister Daniels, so you call me Monday. First thing. Understand?"

"I sure do."

36

New England's fall presentation in the Green Mountains was on full display, reminding Allan a little of fall hiking when he was a student. He and Bob had made the arduous Long Trail hike from the Lincoln Gap to the Appalachian Gap. The trail snaked along the top ridge, which undulated and traced the contours of the mountains. They camped in lean-tos both nights. Now they were driving south on the Taconic Parkway. Although more than a little sore and achy, they relished hiking and camping together. They always did, especially in late autumn when the leaves had fallen and views across the Champlain Valley to the Adirondacks were exhilarating. Renewed and refreshed, they immersed themselves totally in the magnificence of the mountains.

Few people had been on the Long Trail that weekend. Their favorite shelter on Mt. Abraham was empty. Allan felt invigorated, as he almost always did after having experienced the restorative power of nature, being surrounded by the breathtaking splendor, smells, and sounds. A certain peace, balance, the sureness of continuity. The weight of his backpack pulling hard on his shoulders, his own sweat, a cold stream, the smell of the campfire and grilled food, the Scotch — all of it creating a completeness. At night, tightly zipped up in his sleeping bag. Talking with Bob until one of them fell off into a heavy sleep. All of it so fundamental, so significant.

When they were about halfway home, he said to Bob, "Up there on Abraham, especially when we reached the summit, it all began to come together." He paused and continued reflectively, "I'm going back. There's got to be evidence. What happened to Tommy. Maybe that shaman, Osceola, will help me."

Bob wagged a finger at Allan. "You must really enjoy being down there in the swamps."

Allan frowned, shook his head, and said, "I've got to clean things up. Once and for all. You understand. Do it right this time."

Bob looked carefully at Allan. "I was going to tell you I was wrong to suggest you bag it. Want me to come along?"

"No, have to do this myself," he said. "Maybe at some point, if I need you. But thanks."

"I remember those times when I got real smashed and was wandering around in the girls' dorm," Bob recalled. "You were there to save my ass. Told the housemother I was delirious with flu, had a high temperature or some other bullshit. She believed you. Other times, too."

"You've been my best friend, Bob, from the day we met."

Next morning Allan called Haskins. The sheriff told him the lab had postponed the investigation in favor of a double-murder sex crime in a fancy section of Coconut Grove. There was talk of nothing else in Miami. They'd get back on his case in about ten days to two weeks. "You just keep checkin' in with me," the sheriff said.

Allan decided he needed a good week to organize his office so that returning to Islamorada would not prevent Leo and his staff from serving their clients effectively. He would call in as often as possible, review problems, and when necessary talk to their developers and contractors. He had made plans to take Nance and Craig for the weekend before leaving.

When he brought them home Sunday evening, Joyce looked particularly alluring. Allan wondered if she was having another date with that asshole Rosenberg. Nancy and Craig ran in past her to jump on and be licked by Max von Dog. They ran to the playroom.

"There's a rumor you're off to the Keys again," she said coldly. "Haven't you had enough of that place?" He stood awkwardly at the door. She shook her head. "You look silly standing there in the cold. Come on in."

"You look terrific," he said as he entered the house.

She ignored his remark. "You amaze me. Going back there."

"That mess . . . until I get it squared away . . . you don't understand."

"You're right. I don't think I do," she said.

"It's got to be finalized," he said. "Until it is I can't focus, think straight. I want what's right for the kids. For me. And for you, believe it or not. Especially for you."

She gazed at him and seemed to struggle with her feelings. "I hope you finally get the monkey off your back. I sincerely do. No matter what happens with us." She smiled and showed him to the door.

Special, he thought as he drove west, back to his apartment in Great Neck. *Is and always has been.*

Allan called Bob at home. "Heading back to Florida tomorrow," he told him.

"Listen, Daniels," Bob ordered, "you damn well better keep me informed on what's happening down there. Old Parker here is responsible for keeping you from making any more stupid moves. Remember kiddo, I care about you. Got that?"

"Hey," Allan suggested, "when this is over, how about an expensive king salmon fishing trip in Alaska? Think you can handle that? It'll be on you, of course. You make the big money."

"Like some of your other shit-ass ideas, Daniels, we'll split the cost. I know how hard fresh young architects have to struggle to make a living." He changed gears. "Hey buddy, be careful down there. Stay real alert."

37

At Miami International, Allan rented a car and drove the two hours to Islamorada. This time he found an out-of-the-way hotel, a small, four-cottage colony called Barefoote Pointe. Just right. He registered under the name Robert Monroe Parker and gave a false address in Bristol, Vermont.

He had noticed a small boat operator to the east, on Windley Key. The building stood alone on the north side of the highway. Allan observed three boats tied to a small dock in the rear. He parked and walked in. The proprietor, Calvin Hutchinson, was thin, unshaven, had thinning black hair, and wore dirty, oversized glasses. Gray roots gave away that his hair was dyed. Badly, as if he intended to look comical.

"Say you want my Whaler for two days? Well, mister," the old man said gruffly, "that'd be forty-five bucks for each day, an' a hundred deposit. Gas be extra." He coughed, pulled another drag on his cigarette. "Don't know you, see, an' you're a outta-stater, aren't ya?"

"Sounds fair, Mr. Hutchinson. Here's the money. Better give me an extra tank of gas, OK? No, make it two extra."

"That'll be another twenty bucks." He coughed again and asked, "Know how to handle this kinda boat? I'd show ya, except I gotta stay put much as possible. Been gettin' dizzy spells lately. Where ya goin' with it?"

"Back country. Up around Manatee and Stake Keys."

"Better off over by Crane and Crab. Closer. Fishin's better."

"Yeah, maybe. But I want to photograph flamingos and other exotic birds I heard were around Manatee. You don't have to worry. I've had boats like this one. And I'm allowing plenty of time for daylight."

The owner's face still registered concern, but he softened a little. "Ya sure? Maybe get ya a guide. Don't cost much an' could really show ya the back country."

"No thanks. I came all the way down to do some photography and a little fishing. Alone, peace and quiet in there. It's special for me."

Hutchinson shrugged and pocketed the cash.

Back at the Barefoote Pointe, Allan entered his small but cozy cottage. The complex was located off the main highway on a dirt road, away from the Holiday Inn, the Trade Winds, and Tiki Bar. And away from where he might be seen by Norm or any of the others, away from the Green Turtle, Sue and Ken Watts. And from Haskins. Especially Haskins.

Early that evening, he watched a dull Western on TV. He sipped from a glass of Scotch and ate the fried chicken in front of him. Thoughts of Tommy jumped out from hidden corners in his mind. He turned the TV off, rolled over on his back, and listened to the comforting harmony of small waves slapping the beach.

He decided to chance a call to Sue. If Ken answered, he'd hang up. It was Samantha. "Hello," she said in an adorable voice, "who is this calling, please?"

Allan dropped his voice several levels. "Your mother home? I'm calling from the book store in Coral Gables."

Allan heard Samantha calling her mother. "Mommy, it's a man from a book store, and the man's in . . . in Gables."

"Hi," Allan said rapidly to Sue, "I'm at Barefoote Pointe. Tomorrow, real early, I'm heading out. Expect to be back in the afternoon."

"Oh, Mister Kaplan. Surprised to hear from you. That was my daughter, Samantha. She's standing right here. Yes, I'd like very much to do a reading. You could schedule it after the book is published."

Allan couldn't help laughing. "What day, Missus Watts? We find Sunday afternoons are best for major new writers."

"That sounds fine. Why don't you get back to me after you've checked out your schedule. Yes, Mister Kaplan. You too."

Allan's alarm went off at five the following morning. He had been dozing the past hour or so, waiting for its ring. Everything was planned. He plugged in the small coffee maker, cut a grapefruit into sections, and munched on an apple turnover. He had filled a five-gallon plastic water bag the night before. Compass, binoculars, NOAA maps detailing the Keys' water depths in Florida Bay. Brimmed hat, flashlight, Swiss Army knife, two cans of beans, two of tuna fish, and several granola bars. Mosquito repellent, extra sneakers and socks, a rain slicker, and an extra hat. All of it in his backpack.

He noted on his maps the location where he had probably gone down, roughly where Tommy's camp was in relation to it, and where he had come out of the Everglades. Plus, he had stopped the day before and purchased a map at the ranger station in Key Largo. The key he was planning to look for was not where he told Calvin Hutchinson he was going. Manatee and Stake Keys were about sixty degrees to the northeast. He would travel north-northwest.

Allan had studied the map as he would an airplane navigational chart and concluded the twenty-five or so nautical miles to Windley and Middle Ground Keys should take no more than two hours, depending on the tides. He had charted his course, and the weather was cooperating. At Hutchinson's dock, he started the engine, untied the boat, and headed out through the channel. A ten-knot wind scrambled the water.

He passed Twin and Gopher Keys, Spy and Corinne Keys on the starboard, then Topsey and Whipray Islands on his port side. With so many keys, it became more difficult to follow the course. Five degrees one way or the other made a big difference. The keys were similar in appearance. He had to backtrack once or twice. He wished he had paid closer attention when he was with Haskins. As he proceeded, the water became more and more shallow. *OK, OK,* he thought. *That marker . . . where's that goddamn marker? That has to be Johnson and Man of War Keys over there . . . yeah, Cluett on the right.*

He skirted a sand bar, cut back about ninety degrees. The islands appeared almost mythical: half land, half water, covered with mangroves and mud flats, sometimes with sandy fringes. He glanced at the caution note on the map: "Temporary changes or defects subject to shoaling are the rule, not the exception."

Allan idled the motor, stood up, and located the Number Three marker through his binoculars. Continuous mangled mangrove roots formed the coast of the island, if it could be called one. He came closer, so intent on looking for the small beach he didn't see a puff of wind catch the map. He retrieved it just in time.

The craft glided closer until not enough water separated its bottom from the sand underneath. He jumped out, lifted the propeller, pushed the boat up onto the small shore, drove the anchor into the sand, and tied the bowline to a thick root.

He climbed onto the vines, remembered more accurately where he had placed the body, retraced his steps to the point of the island. The tarp had been taken by Haskins as evidence. But the reason he came was to investigate the entire area for any clues, clothing fragments, anything. There was nothing. Any footprints had been washed away by rain. Allan kept looking around, then sat down on some roots. He felt his heart beating fast.

Maybe the Miccosukees had somehow found Tommy's body and taken it . . . but how, when it was so well hidden?

Another thought lurked, developed, and became larger and more convincing. Haskins had even suggested it. *Maybe Tommy didn't die but somehow made his way back to his camp. Or to the reservation. Where was he now? Where? Is he looking for me?*

Then the mosquitoes stormed in, worse than they had been. Allan pulled his sleeves down over his hands and raced back to the boat. The motor wouldn't start. Maybe he'd flooded it. Maybe a bad plug. Hopefully, someone might see the boat, like last time. Allan began gathering dried roots to make a smudge fire, both to be seen and to keep the mosquitoes at bay. But he changed his mind and decided to check out the motor. One of the electrical wires had become loose. He reconnected it, and the engine started up smartly.

38

ALLAN DIDN'T KNOW THAT SUE had taken the kids for a seaplane ride from the Lorelei marina that Saturday morning, hoping to spot Allan's boat. They were to meet Ken later that evening at a restaurant after his afternoon golf game.

"Mommy, Mommy, Taiga Lily wants to drive," Josh shouted back in the car. "We're teaching her how. Mommy, you're not listening. Mommy . . ."

Sue returned home and strolled down to the boat dock with a mug of coffee, recalling all the details of her exchange on the dock with Allan the evening of her party. She dangled her feet in the water, caught sight of pelicans and cormorants going about their work, then swung around to look at the buoys in the inlet she had viewed so many times. These were dependable fixtures she sometimes used to help stabilize the oscillations in her life.

She dashed back to the house, dropped the kids off with a friend, and drove rapidly to the Lorelei again. As they taxied away from the ramp, she told the pilot, "I want to find my brother. He's out fishing. He knows I might fly in. We'll come back in his boat."

"Sure, miss. Any idea where he is? If you can give me some idea, it'd make it easier."

"He's back country, and . . ." She remembered Allan's statement about leaving the body not far from where he had separated from the Everglades. "Let me see your map. Somewhere . . . about here, I think." She moved her index finger on the map. The pilot nodded.

They flew in a northerly direction, tucking in under the bottoms of the cumulus clouds swelling in the expanding heat of the day. Rain showers were dispersed and looked like miniature curtains over scattered stages.

About twenty minutes later the pilot shouted above the din of the motor, "You sure he's around here? Should have seen him already. I'll swing closer to Flamingo." The pilot flew in wide circles, with the left wing slightly down to observe better. When the glare came on her side, Sue had difficulty seeing much more than sun-blinding water.

The pilot created a typical search pattern, parallel lines about five to ten miles apart. They saw fishing boats, all cabin-type, but none the kind of outboard skiff Allan probably would have rented.

After twenty minutes tracking a large expanse from Flamingo on the north side of the keys, the pilot said, "Sorry, miss. Maybe he went in, decided it was enough." Sue nodded.

39

IN THE TANGLED CONFUSION of the small islands Allan had become a little disoriented, which made the return trip much longer. He was quite surprised when he saw a boat bearing down on him very rapidly. It was Haskins, two people with him. They pulled up alongside his boat.

"Well, there, Mister Daniels, awfully nice to see you again," the sheriff sneered. "I didn't know you liked fishin' so much. Hutchinson wasn't sure about who you were an' gave me a call. I figured you wouldn't give him your actual headin'. Missus Watts here drove over. Said she was concerned. Asked if I'd look for you. Want to tell me exactly what you're doin' out here? Why the goddamn hell you came back without tellin' me?"

Allan smiled and shook his head. "I never believed you'd find me."

Haskins tied the line from the bow of Hutchinson's Whaler to a cleat on the stern of his. He peered at Allan. "I know my business, Mister Daniels. Now, you got somethin' to tell me?" he asked, his fat face reddening.

"Can this wait until we get in, Sheriff? Missus Watts is not involved."

"Well, that's about the first thing you've said that I can agree with. What she's doin' out here is not my concern. But what I'm sayin' is, maybe you know more than you told me so far! Like maybe you never left the Everglades with Handley! That tarp business was just a cover-up you wanted me to fall for." He scrutinized Allan's face, which remained impassive. He turned to his deputy. "OK, now Bobby. You call in, tell Jimmy to say nothin' in case Doc Watts calls. Nothin' about any connection with Daniels." He turned to Sue.

"What you tell your husband or don't is your own business. As far as I'm concerned, it's absolutely nothin' to me."

"You may find it hard to understand," Sue countered, "but Allan Daniels is a very fine person and my friend. I came to help him."

The sheriff looked at her sharply. "Very noble, Missus Watts, but I'm not involved with . . . whatever."

"Just hired to protect us?" she submitted, challenging him. "Never been in a situation where you had to make a difficult decision? When it wasn't so clear?"

He stared at her, caught off guard. He ran his open palm against his grizzled chin. "Pretty clever, Missus Watts. Only right now that's not the question, and I'm not the issue. Your Mister Daniels is. I suspect you have enough problems of your own without takin' on his." He reached for a cigarette, then offered the pack to Sue and Allan, who declined.

"Tide's up," he said, a little calmer. "We'll make it back in less than an hour. I'm not goin' to drop you off at Bud and Mary's or the Lorelei, Missus Watts. Don't need anyone seein' you come in with us."

"I do appreciate that, Sheriff."

Allan and Sue sat in the back of the boat. "I'm sorry you're here, Sue," Allan said. "This is not your problem." He resisted the urge to reach over and hold her hand.

"I know you said you were going to return, but when did you decide?" she asked, but not loud enough for the two law officers to hear.

"Camping up in the Green Mountains with Bob Parker. I told you about him. I thought the sheriff and I might have missed something.

"If Tommy's alive, he's bound to be suffering. But if he's recovered he might come after me. Don't forget, he's already got one shooting on his head. So what's two?"

◆ ◆ ◆

In Haskins's office, Allan told his side immediately. "You asked why I came back. Because I wanted to see for myself any signs of what happened to Tommy. Maybe you and I missed something. What I told you before is exactly what happened. I swear it."

"I know why you came back. You don't think I know how to do my job, Daniels. For shit's sake, I went back there myself. Twice." He took a puff and said, "I'm gettin' the feelin' I can't trust you."

"You can, Sheriff. I just didn't want to involve you. I'm sorry."

"You better be, Mister Daniels. You damn well better be. And obviously, I am involved. Big time. Especially now. You keep stayin' in touch."

That evening, Allan went to the Lorelei and in the restaurant ordered a Red Stripe and fresh grouper for dinner. "Miss, I'm the seaplane pilot who was giving rides this morning. This sweatshirt and towel were left in this bag. Belongs to the Watts kids. Can you call their mother and tell her it's here waiting for her? I put something extra on the tip for your time, all right?"

"Missus Watts? Yes, this is Anastasia over at the Lorelei. Your children must have left some stuff when y'all were flying." She glanced over at Allan, who nodded. "Come right over, because I'm getting ready to leave."

Half an hour later, Sue arrived, took the bag, and walked back to her wagon. None of the items in the bag were Sam's or Josh's. Under the towel was a letter. Allan hid behind a tree and watched her read it:

> Hi:
>
> The man who came out today said the situation is more or less over. I'm heading back north tomorrow but plan to do some searching sometime later. In the Everglades, from the north end.

You are a very special person. I'm so glad we met. I'm not saying this very well. You have a wonderful family. I will always remember Islamorada. I wish you every happiness. I'm sure your book will be published soon and be a huge success.

Your friend

He watched Sue tear the letter into pieces and throw it and the bag into a garbage bin. She got in her car, closed the door, and covered her eyes for a moment with her hands.

Allan watched her leave, then drove east out of Islamorada, past Plantation Key to Tavernier. He parked in a public parking area on the bay, got out, and sat on the hood of the car. He peered out into the darkness. The night was soft and moist, the moonlit clouds swelling, the breeze salty. After a while, he returned to his cottage at Barefoote Point, lay down on the single bed, and closed his eyes, one hand on his forehead. *Still no solution,* he thought.

He remained like that for a long time, dozing. He heard a car pull in, a door open then close quietly, the sound of steps on the gravel. *Someone in the other cottage,* he assumed.

He arose quickly after a gentle knock on his door.

"I guessed correctly this was your cottage. I want to talk to you," Sue said. "You have a funny look on your face. May I come in?" She was wearing a white blouse and tight black slacks. Her hair was tied back.

"I'm . . . I'm just surprised to see you." Allan started toward her.

"No," she said firmly, "sit over there. In that chair." She sat on the bed and pushed her sandals off. "*This* is the way it finishes. With a conversation, *not your damn note!*"

"I've messed up your life enough," he replied. He got up from the chair, walked to the center of the room, and said earnestly,

"Maybe I can work it out with Joyce. You with Ken. There are kids. We have to try."

Sue stared at him for a long time. "Cheating is not what I do. But I did, didn't I?"

Allan walked over and gently laid his hand on her head. "It's not my thing, either, you know."

She put her face in her hands. "But the truth, the hard truth? Mine is a nice, calm, secure relationship. I told you I was on the rebound from a man I loved very deeply. Soon after Ken and I got married, we had Josh. Bought a house, all the rest. Then Samantha. I tucked away the pieces that weren't there."

She walked over to the window, her back to him. "You came along. I wasn't prepared for that. When you went north, I started to acknowledge what was missing. And a growing appreciation of my own mortality." Sue stopped talking, closed her eyes, turned, and said, "Obviously, my marriage is not some storybook romance, but it's OK. But I miss the storms. The storms . . ."

"Let me ask you a question," Allan interrupted. "An important one. When we make love — made love — what did it do to your relationship with your husband?"

She smiled ruefully and sat back down. "Let me put it this way: I used to look down on unfaithfulness as immoral. What you and I, and thousands, millions of other couples want is everything in one relationship. That, I know, is impossible."

"What if you and the other man fall deeply in love, and you want out of your marriages?"

"Yes, that can happen . . . ," she murmured. "But marriages fall apart for other reasons. Often second marriages, too. One partner changes, the other doesn't. Or one wants out. And stepchildren can be a real problem." She stood up and took a bold step toward him.

"You'd better get out of here before we forget what we've promised," Allan said.

She laughed and opened the door. The breeze was singing its customary song through the Australian pines. The distinct sounds of the semitropics permeated the night as if they had been previously recorded.

"I needed to talk. Doubtless we'll never meet again, Allan. But I have to confess you'll always be one of my favorite memories. Send me a poem from time to time."

"And I'll come to one of your book signings," he said.

He opened her car door. She kissed her fingers and pointed them toward him. He waved as she drove away.

Before going to bed, Allan called Delta Airlines and was told he could get a flight out of Ft. Lauderdale. Miami was completely booked.

The next morning at dawn he drove northeast out of the Keys to the airport in Ft. Lauderdale and checked in for his flight to LaGuardia. He called Joyce and told her he had something important to discuss. She replied that after he had spent some quality time with Nance and Craig, they could talk.

"Things have changed for me," Allan added. "Insights. About myself. You. Everything around me."

"There may be hope for you yet. I doubt it, but I'm willing to listen. I am."

40

By November on Long Island, the maples and most of the oak, ash, and specimen trees have shed their leaves. Gardeners and homeowners have raked or blown them into piles to be taken away or to become mulch. The lawns retain some green, but almost all the flowers have died. As he drove home, Allan noticed people smiling. *Getting ready for Thanksgiving,* he thought. He wondered about his.

He rang the doorbell and was immediately greeted by two screeching children, who hugged his legs, plus Max, as excited as they were. Joyce stood back. She looked charming in a plaid skirt and black turtleneck sweater, one of Allan's favorite outfits. Her auburn hair was cut shorter than it had been. As they pulled him into the living room, Nancy and Craig began talking at the same time.

"Daddy, Daddy," Nance cried, "I have so much to tell you!" She grabbed his hand. "We had a wonderful field trip to the Museum of Natural History and—"

"Me too, Daddy, me too," Craig cut in. "Lots of fun with my friends."

"Hold on, you two. One at a time. Take turns." Allan glanced up to see Joyce smiling. "After I put you to bed, Mommy and I are going to have a private talk."

Joyce closed the French doors and sat on the couch across from Allan.

"Things are mostly cleared up down in Islamorada with Sheriff Haskins," he reported, knowing that wasn't the whole truth.

He got up, walked over to a small bronze sculpture of a nude woman, and ran his fingers over it. "I am truly sorry about how I've been behaving, what I've put you and the kids through. I really am." He gazed at her for a moment and added, "Joyce, I want it to work with us. I will do everything I can. We can find again the things we began with. A new start."

No reaction.

"What's left is to try to find Tommy. Haskins originally offered to go back into the Everglades with me. I'm hoping he's still willing. Finalize this whole thing once and for all. I want you to understand."

Joyce got up, turned, and said irately, "I thought you were finished down there. Sounds like more of the same." She shook her head. "Now you're asking me to wait some more? I've waited for too long as it is, Allan."

"Please. There's too much at stake. Please."

That seemed to register with her, slightly. "How long will it take?" she asked, a look of annoyance on her face.

"Not more than a couple of days. I'll go soon, when the damn mosquitoes are gone. The weather'll be cooler. More important, when Haskins can get away."

"I had something planned with the children. But since you're here, we can all go out. They'd like that. Let them decide which restuarant. After we put them in bed though, don't get any ideas; you can't sleep here."

Allan nodded. "I understand. But I'm hoping that one day you will feel differently."

She shrugged. Still, Allan had a fleeting notion that there was a slight thaw in their relations. Or was he just dreaming?

41

IN HIS ARCHITECTURAL PRACTICE, he became more focused, more energetic. He was seeing the children several times a week, had them almost every Sunday.

Being alone was still unfamiliar but not uncomfortable. It gave him more time to think about his life, himself, Joyce, the kids, his family, his heritage. He sought out his mother and learned more about her life growing up. When he had to be in Manhattan, he managed to slip into the Forty-second Street library, dug into the history and culture of the Miccosukees and Seminoles.

What especially piqued his interest were articles about Indians building high-stakes bingo parlors. Maybe the Miccosukees would, too. Then they'd have funds for schools, maybe start up some companies and make some investments. Wisely, he hoped. And also be able to memorialize who and what they were and are, diminished as they had become.

James Osceola. Hope he's had luck convincing the tribal leaders to build a bingo parlor and use the money to capture their vanishing Hitchiti and Miccosukee languages . . . create permanent recorded history . . . reach out more to ones who left, like Mom.

The question of whether or not Indian gambling was beneficial for the tribes was being debated across the nation. Some, like the Mohegans in Connecticut, the Senecas in upstate New York, the Mandans, Hidatsas, and Arikaras up in North Dakota, the Hopis in Arizona, and several tribes in California, were taking in significant sums of money. Inescapably and unfortunately, promoters were involved, and large pieces of the proceeds went to them. But bingo was beginning to provide jobs on the reservations, community projects, schools, scholarships, and other benefits. Some tribes refused to go along, convinced bingo only created problems and changed, or at least denigrated, spiritual values and ethics inherent in their cultures. Either way, historical changes of major import were occurring among the sovereign Indian nations.

Allan did not call Sue, nor she him. He wrote a poem for her but did not send it. Florida was still on his mind.

"Sheriff Haskins, Allan Daniels here. I was hoping your original offer is still good."

"Well, hello, Mister Daniels. What did you have in mind, exactly? And more importantly, when?"

I'll bet he's sitting at his desk, feet propped up, the windows open, looking exactly the same way he did when I last saw him.

"Middle of December now, Sheriff, and with the holidays coming up . . . what about right after the first?"

"Won't work. Florida Sheriffs' conference up in Orlando. Disney World. Maybe the third week, *if* I decide to do it. I'd have to put my deputy in charge." He laughed. "See if I can organize things so nothin' serious takes place while I'm gone. The deputy isn't known for his brilliant thinkin'."

Glad he's in a good mood.

"If we do go, Daniels, plan for about four, maybe five days. Look, you don't know coon shit about the Everglades. Read up on the salt an' freshwater habitats. It'll be January, the dry season, maybe too dry. Those bastards, the developers an' the sugar lobby, are wreckin' our state." Allan heard a huge sigh. "I get real exercised. Too many people movin' down."

"I think I told you I'm Miccosukee on my mother's side."

"Don't you think I remembered that, Mister Daniels?" He laughed. "Oh, another thing. You get yourself in top physical condition. It's no picnic in there. I'm not plannin' to wet nurse you."

"I will, Sheriff. Where do we—"

Haskins cut in. "We'd drive up to Everglades City an' Chokoloskee on the west side of the Tamiami Trail, or go up from Flamingo by boat. But be much better to start from the north end, closer to where the Miccosukees live, turn in to the Chatham River south of there, up by the Watson Place."

"I'll get maps," Allan responded, "and study that whole area. The Everglades look a lot different from a plane."

"I'm a busy man, Mister Daniels. Have to get on to some other things. Read everything you can find about the Everglades. We'll talk again in a couple of weeks. I'll decide then."

"I'll call you after New Year's, Sheriff. I hope you'll say yes. I'll pay all the costs."

"That you certainly will, Mister Daniels. Have a good Christmas. Or whatever you folks do."

42

ALLAN HAD BEEN PUTTING ON a not-so-subtle campaign to get Joyce to let him come home, and had made Nance and Craig his accomplices. "Hey, Butzi, it's time we became a family unit again," he said one Sunday. "Don't you agree? Just ask the kids."

Joyce finally decided that Allan could move back in, but it was a few weeks before she invited him to make love again.

"I did miss you, this way," she acknowledged. "I dated, but there wasn't any sex, regardless of what you may have imagined."

"You didn't have to tell me that, but thank you." He kissed her. "I never take you for granted."

They drove the children into Manhattan to see a performance of *Peter and the Wolf* and, on another day, a ballet Nance and Craig never seemed to get tired of— *The Nutcracker*. They went for a hike on the beach at Robert Moses State Park on Fire Island, and one day they went to Montauk for a cookout, even though the weather was bitterly cold.

"Now, look kids, it's fun not to cook inside all the time," Allan told them. "Like outside, today, here on the beach. Just us, the beach, the boulders, and the ocean. See the lighthouse at the end of the point? Absolutely special and beautiful in its way. Built last century to warn ships not to get so close or they'd crash on the rocks."

"But," Joyce noted as they trudged into a raw east wind, "the beach and the ocean *never* change. Other things do, but not the seagulls, fish, everything you see. Been here for thousands and thousands of years."

"So what *is* different, Mommy?" Nance asked.

"OK. Try to imagine life without cars and telephones. Can you do that? The biggest change is how many people now live on Long

Island. Over two and a half million of us!" She pulled Craig's hat tighter on his head. "Before, very few people — just the Indians — back before white people arrived from all the other countries. Like your great-grandparents from Russia. Of course, Grandma Daniels is a Miccosukee Indian. You know that."

Craig stopped listening and began poking in the sand.

"Only trails, no roads," Allan said. "They had to get their food hunting and fishing. Weren't any stores. Dug clams and oysters. Hunted deer. Farmed corn, beans, and squash. Later, immigrants added strawberries, potatoes, and other vegetables. Now there are vineyards making wine."

Allan zipped his jacket up higher.

"And you know, many of the towns on Long Island have Indian names. For the tribes that lived here. Wantagh, Massapequa, Ronkonkoma, Manhasset, Hauppauge, Nesconset — oh, and Patchogue, Syosset, Quogue, Tuckahoe. A whole bunch more. Most people today don't think of that."

They walked a little farther. "Hey, everyone, I'm going to make us a nice fire from driftwood. Behind that boulder, out of the wind," he said. "After we grill steaks, we can roast —"

"Marshmallows!" Nance and Craig exclaimed together.

"I want to show you something else," Allan proposed, his words inviting. He glanced at Joyce, who smiled, knowing what he was referring to. "Those potatoes we packed? OK, first we soak them in a bucket of salt water, then lay them in the hot coals of the fire." The children's eyes opened wide.

"No, no, they won't be ruined," Joyce promised. "Maybe some of the skins will be burned, but wait 'til you taste the inside. Delicious. We want to show you how much fun it is doing things outdoors."

"Grandma Daniels was raised in a little place way down south. Her whole tribe lived mostly outdoors."

"We know that, Daddy. She told us all about when she was a little girl. She wants to show us."

"I'm going to read you more about them," Joyce said. "Or your father will."

After eating, the children became engrossed in building structures with stones and driftwood they had gathered. The water was too cold to build sandcastles.

Allan turned to Joyce. "Doing this, being here with you and the kids — you can't imagine how great it makes me feel." He stirred the fire, glanced over at her, and said, "Joyce, I'm going back down there in a couple of weeks."

Joyce frowned and shook her head. "The kids won't like it."

"I know that," he said.

"I don't like it either," she added.

"Me neither," he responded, "but I have to. And I hope you'll understand. It's terribly important for me. For us."

43

Allan flew in to Miami International Airport one early afternoon in late January and was met by Sheriff Haskins. He was not wearing his uniform.

"You sure look funny in civilian garb," Allan said, shaking Haskins's hand. "Thanks for coming."

"Well, I do wear other clothes when I'm not on duty." He chuckled. "Pulled a little rank parkin' by the front. Much closer. Costs less. Like — zero."

Allan threw his duffel and bag in the back of Haskins's Ford pickup truck and jumped in. Haskins warned, "But we won't have time to stop at your mother's reservation on Alligator Alley."

"That's OK," Allan responded, "but I still want to visit the reservation, see how they're doing. Maybe someone there might know where James Osceola hangs out."

"I'd be a little careful," Haskins warned. "Been doin' some checkin' with an old friend, Johnny Tigertail. Found out Osceola just might be part of the group that's been runnin' drugs. Maybe yes, maybe no. You an' I are goin' to keep pretty much to ourselves. Over in Everglades City, Ochopee an' Chokoloskee, everybody pretty much knows about everythin', who's doin' what an' why.

"We come around and rent a boat, they get suspicious, especially if they were to find out who *I* am, know what I mean?" He glanced over at Allan. "Sure in hell wouldn't believe we're doin' ecological research." Haskins drew on his cigarette, then crushed it out in his ashtray. "One of these days, I gotta stop these damn weeds."

"How come we aren't going across on Route Forty-one?" Allan asked as he studied the map. "A lot shorter."

"Didn't want to come into Everglades City from the east. Sort of sashay down from Marco. There's another reason, Mister Daniels." He looked over, a big grin on his face. "See, you ain't used to this kind of stuff. We get a lot less noticed if we get a boat out of Marco Island, come down through the Ten Thousand Islands, go right past Chokoloskee. Maybe whoever'd see us would think we were just a couple of dumb campers. So I took a boat out in your name, not mine. Because a few may just know about the case. Wouldn't think I'd be up here."

"Damn clever," Allan agreed. "I didn't know much about the drug thing. My mother told me that back in the twenties and thirties, almost everyone was running booze. She sounded as if they were proud of it."

They turned off State 821, north on Interstate 75. "We'll hit the parkway in about twelve miles," Haskins said, glancing over at Allan. "I'll tell you why your mother feels that way. Back then, things were tough for them. Really poor, livin' in their chickees the old way. Sold baskets an' colorful clothes to tourists along Alligator Alley. Some farmin' an' a lot of huntin', plus doin' whatever else they needed to do. Durin' Prohibition, booze came in from Cuba. Chokoloskee was the perfect place, difficult for the feds to handle, though they sure tried. Too many islands, places to hide stuff. So the Miccosukees found a good way of makin' money. Seminoles were part of it, too. Frankly, I can't blame them. Whites did it, too. Now when you look back, Prohibition was pretty damn stupid," Haskins said.

It was an invigorating January day: fresh, low humidity, a turn-on for activity. The sky was bright, ranging between sapphire and azure, the air clean and crisp, the result of a cold front. A large percentage of cars and trailers displayed out-of-state license plates, northerners and midwesterners escaping winter, some on holiday, some retirees, some with second homes or condos.

"Wish we could put a limit on them movin' here permanently," Haskins mused. "Keep comin' down. Someone said eight hundred to a thousand a day, all needin' services. So much of our land an' water goin' for development. I don't know . . . ain't the right hand of progress, that's for damn sure."

Alligator Alley, also identified as Interstate 75 and State 84, runs almost straight east-west across the state. The two men crossed many dirt roads during the eighty-eight-mile drive to the west coast and Naples. Haskins told Allan they would not actually go that far, but would turn south on 951 into Marco. They passed through Big Cypress Swamp, which seemed to Allan exactly like the Everglades.

With Haskins driving, Allan was able to study the landscape. Cypress trees dominated the strands and open prairies. There were freshwater marshes, pinelands, and hardwood hummocks. He had read that limestone outcrops were just underneath the low ridges, often visible through the thin veneers of saw grass and palmettos. It was obvious that slightly different elevations permitted different species of trees and plants, as well as determined their size.

Endless grass prairies flowing to the horizon, Allan noted. *Dipped in brown and green. Lots of marshes . . . wood storks grabbing small fish — what else did those photos show in those books he had studied? — orchids, ferns, cabbage palms . . . varieties of cypress . . . important they stopped loggers from clearing out all the timber.*

"The terrain," Haskins said after several minutes, "flatter than almost anywhere. Big Cypress is *not* actually a swamp like the Everglades. Sandy islands, and over by the rivers, mangroves, but a bit different. An', of course, the sloughs.

"The thing you have to always keep in mind is water. Sort of controls everythin'. Rainy season — most of the rainfall happens between May an' October, as much as eighty percent. Kind of incredible the way plants an' animals adapt so well. Rainy an' then drought. Have to let it get back to the way it used to be. Otherwise, poof, bang, there goes the bottom half of the Florida peninsula to those sons of bitchin' sugar growers an' developers.

"South of us," Haskins continued, "another special area. Fakahatchee Strand Preserve. Made it a state park. I'll point it out when we go by Miles City. Pretty much the same as Big Cypress except it goes all the way down to the Ten Thousand Islands. Now *that's* one helluva place! The Ten Thousand Islands. We'll go through it on our way down the Gulf Coast. Quite a history. Tell you more when we're in the boat."

"How come you know so much about these parks? I mean, not just your way around, but all kinds of facts about animals and plants?"

"How come?" He glanced over at Allan. "This whole part of Florida has been my life—hell, all of us Conchs down in the Keys—our world, know what I'm sayin'? I told you my father took me in. Gets to be part of you.

"Here's somethin' you didn't know," he went on. "Before my daddy came down to Islamorada, the family lived in Marco, an' before that Everglades City an' Chokoloskee. Grandfather on my mother's side was a Smallwood, an' in there are Browns, an' way back Weeks an' Smiths. Fact is—an' I'll have your head in a basket if you ever talk about this—back durin' the Depression, when times were tough down here, my family ran a still. Whiskey. Bush lightnin' was one of the names, shine another, or corn liquor, but it wasn't, actually. They'd boil beer into buck made from grain, sugar, an' water."

He lit a cigarette. "Those times were big bootleggin' times. Plenty of whiskey around. Rum from the Bahamas and Cuba to the Ten Thousand Islands up to Everglades City. Smuggled the stuff by truck to the Atlantic coast trains that ran north. Smart enough to repack the booze into tomato crates. The guys makin' moonshine hid their stuff out in the mangroves. Impossible to find. They'd get lost sometimes themselves, but any lawman lucky enough to locate 'em rarely made it out. Know what I'm sayin'?" he said as he looked over with a knowing grin. "I kind of think Handley was doing the same thing. Only marijuana. Maybe heroin, too." He yawned. "I dunno. We'll see.

"Real poor, my family. My granddaddy told me that corn came in burlap bags, sugar in cotton bags. They'd make clothin' out of them."

Allan said, "I didn't realize that water, I mean the amounts, was so critical. And something else. What about panthers? Isn't that what they're called in Florida?"

"Yeah. But the big cats have gotten thinned out. They're endangered. Big time. Those idiots in the Fed didn't give a shit when they crossed the state with those big drainage canals. Blockin' the panthers' natural routes. Cut down their habitats. Get hit by cars. Plus mercury contamination. Beautiful animals. Seen a few. We still have black bears, raccoons, possum, fox. An' plenty of deer."

"We may have a few up in Vermont," Allan offered. "People claim to have begun to see catamounts making a small comeback. Same animal. Out west they're called cougars and mountain lions." He turned to Haskins. "Hey, how about some lunch? Haven't eaten since five this morning."

"You city dudes like your comforts, don't you? All right, another half hour to Marco. I'll take you to a place tourists don't go. You like alligator? Maybe fried catfish? Homemade grits? They got it." He laughed. "I'll try to convince them you're a good ol' boy gone astray. Too bad you don't look more Indian," Haskins added. "They might take you for a local." He laughed, amused to see Allan wince a little.

44

AT THE CRACKER ROOST, Haskins commandeered a corner table. "Miss, make sure this dude gets grits, all right? Look," he leaned over, talking quietly after the waitress left, "we are *not* goin' to Marco to rent that boat. Too busy over there, tourists an' all. We go to this little town, Goodland. Small place, doesn't get action like Marco Island. We could leave out of there late this afternoon, but better to get all set up, head out first light."

"You're in charge. Just show me the way."

"Now, Mister Daniels, that's the second smart thing you said. The first was when you asked me to keep Missus Watts out of the situation after I found you footsyin' around out there back country off Cape Sable.

"One helluva woman, if I can say so now I'm off duty. I'm not passin' on the morality of you two an' all, but I can sure understand a . . . an involvement."

"You can, huh? Well, it's very complicated. She's . . . Sue is one of the most interesting women I've ever met," Allan said, looking straight ahead. Then he glanced over at Haskins. "Our friendship is—"

"Hey," Haskins interrupted. "She said that exact same thing about you. That's your business . . . I never knew anythin' about you two, OK?"

"Right," Allan said. "You never did. Or the Indian in me might have to scalp you when you're sleeping."

The alarm rang sharply at 4:30. Haskins was there, on time to the minute.

"You gotta understand about these islands," the sheriff commented as they made their way down the channel that led into the Gulf of Mexico. The water was composed and unruffled, not a ripple. "They're — what do you call it, yeah, a labyrinth — endless. Ten Thousand Islands even worse. Mangrove island after mangrove island. Don't get very far tryin' to get through. Water depth is no more than three feet, an' most much less than that. Even I could get lost and take too much time. We're better off out in the Gulf, go down about oh, twelve or fifteen miles, turn in at Rabbit Key Pass. Pick up the Wilderness Waterway, south of Chokoloskee, so those folks won't see us, get it?"

"OK with me. What about Handley? I mean, how are we ever going to find his camp?" Allan noticed a small pistol strapped around the sheriff's lower leg. *Do I need a gun, too?* he wondered.

"Not really sure. He'd never set up close to the road between Flamingo an' Coe Park on the eastern side by Florida City. Run into the rangers travelin' on it. His camp'd be closer, off Forty Mile Bend on the Tamiami Trail, nearer the tribe. I drew a line from that seaplane base you left from Pahokee to Key West. Guess what? It just about goes over the res. That'd put his camp near the head of Lostman's River, Broad, or the Harney. Perfect place for him, twenty tough miles to the reservation but only a couple to one of the rivers where he could bring his skins an' meet up with Osceola, that shaman you met. Maybe drugs. Someone could be payin' him to hide bundles comin' off boats out in the Gulf. Wherever Tommy's place is, unless you knew exactly where to look, he could hide almost anythin'."

He glanced over at Allan and asked, "Did Handley mention anythin' about drugs? Or did you see anythin'?"

Allan shook his head. He didn't remember noticing anything in Tommy's camp, or any talk or signs when they were with James Osceola.

Allan looked skyward and observed frigate birds drifting

effortlessly above them. Nearby, a school of tarpon plied the shallows, searching for a meal. "You know, there's nothing here," Allan remarked. "Just, well . . . just nothing here."

"That's because you shitass don't know how to look. Or at what. Which is not surprisin' for a sheltered Yankee," Haskins said. "Before we're done, you'll know a helluva lot more than most all the folks who live in South Florida. Say you get stuck or lost. You gotta live off the land, right? I think I can show you how. Farther south, it's more different, but not all that much."

"I'd really like that," Allan said, his voice rising into the breeze as they reached the open water, which was choppy.

"I'll tell you," Haskins continued, "we're lucky it's January. Other times, the insects get you. Black salt-marsh mosquitoes swarm at dawn and dusk. Females feed on you for blood protein to develop their eggs. But not the males. They go for flower nectar an' juices from plants. Also got punkies, sandflies, and no-see-ums."

"You sure know this area." Allan said. "What's that?" he asked, pointing.

"Where?"

"There, at three o'clock. Those spouts."

"Thinkin' they'd be bottle-nosed dolphins. See that island, the other side of the channel? Gettin' close to Chokoloskee Bay."

Allan observed a fish hawk screaming. "Osprey, right?"

Haskins nodded. "Very good."

After another hour of travel, the water became calmer. Haskins turned in from the coast. "Hey," Allan said, "we're in Indian Key Pass. I have it on the map. Thought you said you wanted to steer clear of Chokoloskee."

"Yeah, we will later. Have to chance it an' pull into Everglades City. I need to talk to my friend Johnny Tigertail. Pals when we were kids. His daddy, Charley Tigertail, was a chief. Just about the best-educated Indian in the Everglades. Had a tradin' post down a ways off the head of Lostman's River. Johnny's sort of an in-between guy, a real good politician. Close to the park people, who seek him out for information, but what they don't know is that he's much closer to his own. He might help us if I let him know why we're tryin' to find Handley. It's gotta be handled right."

They edged up the channel, slowing down for better navigation. "You can't actually see freshwater comin' out of Big Cypress Swamp to mix with the salt water from the Gulf," Haskins said, "Fills this place with life. Of course tides make an enormous difference."

Allan nodded. "Fascinating," he said, more to himself than to Haskins.

"Look, sonny boy, the more info I give you, the better you'll be able to make out. You *are* an Indian. At least in part. Your ancestors knew how to exist around here, but you sure as hell don't."

"Great sense of humor, sheriff," Allan said. "But you being a white man . . ."

Haskins fixed him with a hard stare. Then he said, "You know what, Daniels, I might even begin to like you."

45

Before leaving Long Island, Allan had read extensively about the Everglades. The Calusa Indians had inhabited the area around Everglades City for many centuries, before the Weeks and Smith families settled along the Allen River after the Civil War. But it wasn't until Barron G. Collier built a road in the mid-twenties, eventually connecting Miami and Tampa, that enough habitable land could be created from mucking out the river. Collier had also constructed a railroad. By 1929 the town boasted a trolley, a hospital, a couple of hotels. And a jail. Sponge and commercial fishing flourished. It was said that the fish were so thick, fishermen had to hide behind a tree to bait their hooks. Hunting also prospered. Turkey, quail, deer, black bears, and panthers.

President Harry Truman dedicated the Everglades National Park in Everglades City in December 1947. An airfield was completed for the event. In the thirties, the old Sorter home became the well-known Rod and Gun Club. Later, it was opened to the public.

Haskins glided their boat neatly into a slip at a small, out-of-the-way boat yard, tied it up, and stepped out onto the dock. "You hang loose while I try to find Johnny. Stay out of sight, know what I mean? Take a nap down on the bottom. Anybody starts nosin' around, just tell 'em you're here for a little fishin'."

"Yes, Sheriff," Allan said, "I need a little peace and quiet anyway. And just make sure you don't hit any bars on your way."

Haskins shot a hard glance at him. "You got so much to learn, Yankee. I don't know why I ever got mixed up with you. An' a Jewish Indian at that. Nobody'd believe it."

"Yeah, but at least I'm not a wise-ass Conch. And a Cracker."

Haskins pointed his finger at Allan, pulled his hat down over his face, and walked away. About an hour later, a Ford pickup pulled up at the end of the dock. Haskins walked down to the boat.

"All right, sleepin' beauty, Johnny's in his truck waitin' for us. At first he didn't believe me, but he finally said the whole thing is so ridiculous it can't be a bunch of bullshit. I included the part about Tommy tryin' to steal your wallet. Come on, before he changes his mind."

Allan didn't expect Johnny Tigertail to be so tall and handsome. His features were chiseled on a clean, bronzed face that could have been a movie star's. His garb was traditional Miccosukee, a distinctive colorful shirt with trousers made from burlap. His hair was thick and black, moccasins for shoes, and a Bowie-type knife hanging from his belt. He greeted Allan matter-of-factly.

Tigertail drove them to the airfield and turned in on a rut-filled dirt road that followed an old railroad track on the far side of the small operations building. He pulled up behind some cypress trees adjacent to the Barron River.

He reached behind the passenger seat, brought out three Budweisers, and handed one to Haskins, one to Allan. "You sure creamed Handley with that club," he said, looking over at Allan, "but amazingly the boy recovered. Got himself out. Fixed up a beached boat to get all the way from where you left him. Quite a feat. Jimmy Osceola found him close to his camp. Stayed with him a week before he was fit enough to take care of himself."

A hooting and strange-sounding bark was heard from the other side of the river. Tigertail gazed at it. "Barred owl," he said. "Don't usually hear 'em durin' the day." He took a swig of his beer. "Billy, you sure your friend here isn't a fed underneath? DEA or somethin' like that? You wouldn't be after Tommy for somethin' like drugs, because — "

"Hang on, Johnny. I've never shitted you. You know he shot that store owner."

Tigertail turned to them. "Movin' stuff is not that unusual around here. But I'm not telling you anything about what he might be doing. And I do not know where he is. Exactly."

Haskins nodded. "Look, Johnny, you know I'm a lawman. It's not about the drugs he was runnin'. It's more his shootin' that storekeeper an' stealin'. Understand?"

"Well," Tigertail snapped, ignoring what Haskins said, "this is as far as I'm traveling with you two."

There was an awkward silence, a space of time, unexpressed thoughts. Then Allan said, "I guess I've come to realize that my Miccosukee heritage is . . . well, just that. I'm Indian. Look, I have to find Handley. Osceola said he needs to find someone to do what he's doing, because he's about the last shaman. I want to see him again, too."

Tigertail got out of the truck, walked a few paces toward the river, stared across it for several minutes, then returned. "Billy, tell you what. You head down to the Watson place, up the head of Chatham River. You know where that is. Not today. Figure to be there a day or two from now. Jimmy Osceola will find you. If you don't see him there, he'll be at that camp on the other side of Last Hutson Bay. Sweetwater Bay Chickee. You guys watch it in there. It ain't for city types." He poked Haskins. "Even you, Billy."

"Hey, Johnny, do me a favor. Where can I put our boat for now? An' can you run us back to Goodland to my truck? We need more supplies."

"I got a good place for your boat. A real good place."

They checked in to a small motel in Naples, about ten miles north of Marco, a city of winter residents and tourists, a place they would not be noticed. As he had promised, Allan phoned home. He also called his office.

That afternoon Allan rented a Cessna 172 at the Naples airport and flew Haskins over Big Cypress, the Ten Thousand Islands, Chokoloskee, and the northern part of the Everglades National Park.

"One helluva place," Allan shouted over the engine noise. "It's awesome."

"Keep flyin' this direction," Haskins directed. "I want to check out the Wilderness Waterway, the islands and rivers. It'll help later. We'll come up on the Watson place an' Sweetwater Bay Chickee."

"Climbing higher," Allan said. "Damn, I should have brought my camera."

"I'll remember what we see," Haskins said. "You said I was a Cracker. Well, I'm a *local* Cracker. We ain't supposed to be too smart, but we do know our way around. Now just fly this ridiculous rattletrap."

They flew for another half hour, then landed and turned the plane in.

In Haskins's truck, Allan remarked, "You enjoy pretending to be slow and not too bright," he said. "And you know what? You had me convinced at the beginning, but you're as sharp as anyone I've ever met."

"Compliments," Haskins replied with a sly smile, "will get you everywhere. Used to be a man could make a livin' huntin' alligators an' fishin'. Before that, plume feathers for women's hats. By the sixties, just tryin' to survive—you either left this place or you broke the law.

"Some of the men continued alligators, mackerel, an' stone crab. Of course, there were snakes, spiders, an' mosquitoes big time. Others were into smugglin'. My granddaddy used to say he never felt freer than when he was off up some river, huntin' for 'gators. Cookin' snook an' redfish he'd catch. A way of life, a real good life, he told me."

"Hard to imagine those times," Allan said. "Everything changes, doesn't it. Especially for the Miccosukees."

"For them, especially. If they build a bingo hall, it could be very different for the tribe. Big changes. Permanent ones."

"Good or bad?" Allan wondered.

"Not sure," Haskins said. "But we'll sure as hell find out."

46

AT DAYLIGHT THE TWO MEN DEPARTED Everglades City in their boat from the remote dock where Tigertail kept his. The night crew was still on duty at the Coast Guard station. They passed the facility. Carefully Haskins turned off the engine and coasted stealthily against the mangroves on the opposite side of Chokoloskee Bay.

Instead of proceeding on the Wilderness Waterway, which would have brought them past Chokoloskee, they headed southwest through the channel that cut by Sandfly Island, then past Jack Daniels Key and a short distance out into the Gulf of Mexico. "Those knuckleheads are not goin' to know shit about us," Haskins said with a chuckle. "You do what I do, you learn how the other guy thinks."

"You sure as hell did with me," Allan offered.

"Stop talkin' an' keep studyin' that marine map. These waters get real shallow, especially with the tide out. Don't goof up."

Several hours later, farther down the coast, Haskins commented, "If there's nobody usin' the campsite at Pavilion Key, we'll pull in an' stay the night. See it on the map?"

"Yeah, I see it. I do know how to navigate, you know," Allan grumbled.

"We set up camp, show you how to catch some fish. Nothin' like fresh trout or mackerel. Maybe some crab an' oysters off the mangrove roots. Some Red Stripe beer I brought. Before we turn in, bay tea. A real feast to introduce you to proper livin'."

"I'm up for that," Allan responded. "When do we go to the Watson place?"

"Be upriver about eight to ten miles. Get there around midday. If Osceola doesn't show, we mosey up to Sweetwater Chickee. More likely he'll be there. It's remote, more so than Watson. No park people."

They edged into Pavilion Key from a channel that broke through the mud flats and tidal pools. Sanderlings, willets, and plovers poked for small crustaceans, scattering when the boat came too close. "Tie up the front end while I do the rear," Haskins ordered. "Carry the gear into the chickee. I'll work on the rods."

"You sure you weren't an army sergeant, Sheriff? If I didn't have to depend on you, I— "

"Well, my Yankee friend, just do as I tell you, an' we'll make a good Miccosukee out of you yet."

It took a half hour to settle in. Then Haskins motioned to Allan to follow him. "Three kinds of mangroves. Red, black, an' white. The blacks grow tall, whites like higher ground an' mix with buttonwood trees. But here on this key, it's the reds. I'm not goin' into why an' how, just know the mangroves tell you about elevations. Wouldn't be any islands without them. You listenin'?

"OK, now see those crabs? Sand an' mud fiddlers, an' of course horseshoes, pretty big ones. Raccoons find horseshoes trapped under roots or high an' dry when the tides go out. Like the tender parts. Nothin' wrong with eatin' horseshoes. Everythin' feeds on everythin' else. Fill that bucket with oysters. An' don't cut yourself."

The following morning, they decamped and entered the Chatham River at Chatham Bend. The tide was between high and low, providing enough depth to move easily up the river.

"The old Watson place was built by Ed Watson back durin' the early part of the twentieth century," Haskins remarked as they rounded a bend and came upon the house. "More than likely swiped the land. Set a two-story up on an old shell mound the Calusas built above the hurricane water line. Watson was able to farm about forty acres. Absolutely nothin' like it anywhere in the 'glades.

"This guy Watson was real bad. Supposed to have killed the stripper Belle Starr in Oklahoma. He did for sure kill a bunch of men over the years. Eventually the locals had enough. One day he came back to his place. A local told him to give himself up, but he wouldn't. A man named Henry Short put a bullet in him, the others began firin'. He went down."

They docked the boat, set up their tent on flat ground overlooking the river, and spent the afternoon checking out what was left of the house, relaxing, and collecting oysters and periwinkles.

While they were eating, Haskins commented, "Damned if I don't keep gettin' this funny feelin' we're bein' watched. Johnny Tigertail always said a Miccosukee could be right where he would see you an' you couldn't see him for shit. An' when you're with one, they sort of—"

"What?"

"Sort of look right through you. Can't know what they're really thinkin'. Anyway, let's get some sleep. First thing tomorrow, we head farther up the river to Sweetwater."

No one was camping at the chickee when they arrived around ten the next morning. But Haskins told Allan someone had been there.

"How do you know that?"

"I know, that's all."

They were there about an hour when James Osceola appeared, stepping out from some brush. He stood before Allan and Haskins for what seemed like a very long time, his expression flat.

Then, looking at Allan, he said, "I saw you yesterday. I'm not surprised you returned. It is unfinished." He rubbed his hand against his chin, gazed over at Haskins, and said, "I would not have come if Johnny Tigertail didn't vouch for you. He told me you were from here. An old friend." He put out a hand to Haskins, then motioned for them to sit.

He remained quiet but finally looked at Allan and said, "Always a bad thing when someone gets hurt or killed in a fight. Worse when both men from the same tribe. Tommy was in rough shape when I found him. He got to be damn tough, all those years deep in the back."

Allan wanted to ask Osceola where Tommy was, but decided he'd better listen. Osceola stood up, looked around, and then began, "Something has to change, so I'm telling you this. I don't want Tommy hurt. He'd get the stuff they'd leave on shore at night or in storms, hide it. I was putting money away for him. He was two-timing the dealers. Never told me he was cheating them. Stupid. So far he's outfoxed them, but it's only a matter of time."

Haskins said, "You were involved, weren't you?"

Osceola stared at him, his face expressionless. "He's moved his main camp. Must've felt he had to." He looked off at something in the trees. "Always liked him. Underneath all that rough stuff, he's OK. Just mixed up. Felt he could do better and told him. But he is the way he is, and that's the end of it." He paused, then said, "Indians understand better than whites. Tommy was always on the edge, an angry kid. Talked about coming out, doing time for what he did in that store, then maybe getting a life with his girlfriend. Thought he might even work in the bingo parlor."

Allan looked down, then skyward, shaking his head slowly side to side. "What a waste," he finally said.

Then suddenly he began to gasp. He turned in a circle as if he didn't know what to do. "I feel . . . I feel like I'm . . . burning." His own comment startled him.

"With our people," Osceola said carefully as he placed his hand softly on Allan's shoulder, "there is always meaning. For you, Allan Daniels, fire has been raging in your soul. It's supposed to be there. Been long waiting. Means you're changing. That is good, Allan

Daniels. It is important you know that *you* lit the fire, and now you feel it burning. You are finally aware of this. Don't be afraid. You'll be fine. I am sure of this. It was supposed to happen."

The next hour passed quickly. Osceola told Allan how Miccosukees lived in the Everglades so differently from whites. "I want you to learn something about what we know, Daniels. Like *eej-te yo-ga-hé*—fire—whites make *large* ones. Too hot on one side, too cold on the other. Never figured it out. Miccosukees make *small* fires, use less fuel, stay close, get warmth from all sides. We know how to pole through small channels and streams in canoes, or wade rather than use trails. Avoid rattlesnakes that lie on dry ground." Haskins nodded, as if in agreement, but for Allan this was all new. "How to utilize the land and waters for food. How to conserve, waste nothing, make sure we do not abuse what the Great Spirit has provided."

Osceola identified a bird across the channel. "Everglades kite. Feeds on apple snails. We learn to listen to animals as we do people," he said. "Do it without thinking. Instinct. Experience. The animals tell us what's going on."

He sniffed, sensing something, and said, "Daniels, if you ever want to see or talk to me again, get in touch through Johnny Tigertail. It's critical you learn more about your own people. We need you, all Miccosukees like you, wherever they have strayed. As for Tommy . . ." He didn't finish. "I wish good luck to both of you. *Hishuk-ish-ts' awalk.*"

Osceola vanished as quickly and quietly as he had appeared. "He didn't say anything about where Tommy is," Allan said. Haskins smiled and nodded.

Allan walked to the edge of the river, sat down in the Indian manner, arms crossed, closed his eyes, and lowered his head. He remained in that position for a long while.

A whole new life . . . a world I never knew opening before me. I denied my heritage. This can only be positive, helpful. My crash landing . . . I thought I would die. Now I have a sense of rebirth, renewal . . .

Haskins said, "Handley. We haven't found him yet. Could be anywhere. But I've got a feelin' somethin' will turn up."

Allan glanced over at him. "Maybe not."

"Tell you what," Haskins went on, "might as well continue down, end up in Flamingo. Keep our eyes open."

Allan didn't respond, until he remembered something. "Damn. I forgot to ask Osceola about the bingo parlor."

"We get on the Wilderness Waterway," Haskins said, "over to Rodgers River Bay Chickee before it gets dark. Don't have a campin' permit, but I'm an official, ain't I? Catch some largemouth bass, mangrove snapper, an' maybe some blue crab. Terrific boiled."

They packed their gear, placed it in the boat, and proceeded southeast. The wind turned up, the sky became heavy, announcing a change in the weather. No words were spoken, but Allan noticed that Haskins was coughing more and more and that he looked at his watch several times.

It was raining hard when they reached the chickee. Two campers were getting ready to depart, heading north to Chokoloskee. Haskins was coughing even more. "Damn," he said, "Really gotta get rid of the weeds. Won't help the bronchitis."

"Hey, here's some Scotch I brought along," Allan said. "Trade you for the butts."

Haskins handed the cigarettes over to Allan, who disposed of them. He drank from the flask, then passed it to Allan. Allan resmoved his cap and placed it on Haskins' head. It was growing darker, and rain pelted the chickee. Allan rigged a tarp on the front side to prevent water from coming in.

"Now you're catchin' on," Haskins remarked.

The rain soon abated, and a full moon peered out through wispy clouds.

The two men turned in early. Exhausted from their long day, they placed their sleeping bags next to each other but in opposite directions.

"We camped a lot, my family," Allan said. "In Vermont, the Adirondacks, the Catskills. But nothing like this."

"Since the National Park Service came along," Haskins said, "it's pleasure stuff. Like I told you, it was somethin' else for the Indians an' early whites. Still can be rough. Insects, snakes, 'gators, but not like those days."

"Osceola, all the things he said the Miccosukees have figured out. I guess I have a lot to learn."

"You sure do, Mister Daniels, you sure do. Now shut up an' get some sleep," he said. "You Yankees sure do talk a lot."

"No shit?" came Allan's quick retort. "If we were counting, you'd win hands down in the talk department."

"Just shut up, Daniels. You'll wake up the crocodiles."

47

Someone burst through an opening in the shelter, flashed a pistol, and yelled, "OK, you son of a bitch! Now it's your fuckin' turn!" Tommy! Allan glanced at Haskins, who didn't move.

"Just a second!" Allan cried out, thinking fast. "Shoot me and you'll have to shoot him, too."

Tommy looked puzzled, turned to Haskins, then back to Allan, "I don't care shit about him, but if he gets in my fucking way—" As he was talking, Allan and Haskins were gently slipping out of their sleeping bags.

"OK, OK. He won't, he won't," Allan pleaded. "Just *listen* to me for a second." Allan knew he had to come up with something fast. "Look, this whole thing, me coming down in the seaplane, you finding me, meeting Osceola and what he said—"

"So the fuck what!" Tommy interrupted.

Allan noticed Haskins nodding slightly, moving very slowly to his right.

"Then back in your camp. I saw that article on your wall and figured you might try to do me in when you had the chance—so when you took my wallet . . ." Allan kept shifting stealthily to his left, cutting off Tommy's view of the sheriff.

Suddenly, from a crouched position, Haskins sprang up and tackled Tommy before he could turn around. Haskins pinned him down quickly, sat on him, and held his wrists down.

"What the—" Tommy screamed, but Haskins had immobilized him. Allan wrested the pistol free.

"Get some rope!" Haskins yelled. "He ain't gettin' away. There, in my sack. Quick!" Haskins turned Tommy over and put a headlock on him as Allan tied Tommy's wrists tightly behind his back.

"You shits!" Tommy hissed. "All the fucking same."

Allan faced Tommy, Haskins behind him holding his arms in a viselike grip.

"Why don't you shut up!" Allan leveled. "You goddamn listen to what I have to say!"

Tommy sneered, then spat at Allan.

"Look, goddamn it, maybe I can get some sense into that dumb head of yours."

"You're wastin' your time," Haskins said.

"Keep out of this. This is between Tommy and me."

There was a moment of silence before Allan went on. "Whether you want to believe it or not, I never dreamed I'd end up hitting you that terrible night. But that's over. The fact is that you didn't die—"

"Fuck," Tommy mocked him.

"What you're too thick to understand . . . we're both Indians. From the same tribe. That's begun to mean a lot to me." Allan noticed the expression of disgust on Tommy's face. "Yeah, sure, by some accident, I end up north with opportunities. You down here with nothing but trouble. Guess what? You didn't plan it. But neither did I. But here we are and that's the way things are. I'm sorry about that. I really am." Tommy listened, his face a picture of disdain. "So, as you would say, 'what the fuck' now? I'll tell you what the fuck now. I can help you. But you gotta want me to."

"You aren't forgettin', are you?" Haskins reminded. "The law's been after this kid for years." He stared hard at Tommy. "Time to pay up, Tommy-boy!"

"No, I'm not forgetting. He's gotta do time, but maybe it can be shortened. Good behavior and plea bargaining."

"What's plea bargaining?" Tommy asked.

"Less time for confessing to a lesser crime. A deal made with the district attorney. And a good defense lawyer, who I'll pay for."

Tommy shrugged. "You settin' me up?" he said.

"Not at all. Look, you've had a lousy life, I know that. But you're still young. Your life's far from over. And I know Osceola believes in you."

Allan took a long look at Haskins, then back at Tommy. "I'm going to spend time with Jimmy. I plan to do things for our people. Design a tribal building, maybe build another school. Try to improve education. Raise money. When you get out and if you want to take your place in society, we can arrange a job for you."

Tommy listened, doubtless wondering what all this meant.

"Could be," Haskins said, "but I wouldn't count on it. There's not one single positive thing in his record."

"Maybe so," Allan answered, "but I'm going to try to help him change all that. At least try. And, by the way, I'm also doing this for me."

Allan squatted down beside Tommy. "You're going to get a chance, a real chance. You can fuck it up—and you very well might—be in and out of jail for the rest of your life. Or you can get it together. Up to you."

Tommy swung his head around. "You serious, ain't you? There's blood somewhere between us. That means somethin' . . ."

"Very nice an' sentimental, Mister Daniels," Haskins interrupted. "But for now, this boy goes to jail."

How are we going to get him out of here? Boat's too small for three, Allan asked himself.

Haskins provided the answer. "This is what we do," he said with typical Haskins authority. "You take the boat an' head south. Didn't see any rangers so far, so there's a good chance you'll meet up with one pretty quickly. They patrol the waterway."

He motioned for Allan to get going. "First, help me tie his ankles. Indians are real good at gettin' loose. Make it easier for me to keep him calmed down."

After Allan put his gear in the boat, he returned and shook hands with Haskins. "I'll move as fast as I can. See you real soon."

"Yeah, well, it's goin' to be no problem here," Haskins said. "Pay attention when you are in the channels, meanin' stay near the markers. Don't run aground."

Allan walked over to where Tommy was sitting. "I'm sure you hate all this," he said, "but try thinking of it as a step in the right direction. But for now—I mean this—you need to trust me, and also Sheriff Haskins." Allan waited for a reaction but didn't get one. "We're not your friends, Tommy, but we're also not your enemies."

After three hours of fast travel, Allan reached the Shark River Chickee. A ranger was cooking over a small Coleman stove. He looked like a teenager. Allan quickly tied his bowline to a post.

"Sheriff Haskins is holding a prisoner at Rodgers Chickee," Allan blurted out. "He needs a helicopter over there right away."

The ranger's eyes widened and his eyebrows rose when Allan said "Sheriff."

"A prisoner!" he exclaimed.

"Now!" Allan ordered.

"Yes, sir!" The young man dropped his cup, ran to his skiff, and brought back a portable radio. He called in for a police helicopter.

Allan turned to the ranger. "There's a renegade outlaw back there. We've been looking for him."

The ranger's eyes were almost glazed. "You a police officer, too?"

Allan frowned.

"Sir, want me to take you to Flamingo? My boat's fast. I'll check where the helicopter's going to take them. We can get you up there."

"Yes," Allan said. "Need to leave a note on the boat. Wouldn't want anyone taking it."

"I'll call that in. One of our guys will bring it to Flamingo," the ranger offered, then added, "Let's go, sir."

As they skimmed over the calm water, Allan turned to watch the V-groove wake the skiff made behind the boat. He looked up and marveled at the sky's special blend of pastels. Then his thoughts focused on Tommy and Haskins. *What a way this is ending. Lucky the sheriff came. Damn sure Tommy would have shot me.*

He and the ranger continued south on Whitewater Bay, at above twenty miles per hour.

Not enough Indian in me . . . yet, Allan mused.

With a quartering tailwind, they made good time. They entered the narrow passage to Coot Bay and the two miles through Buttonwood Canal. When they exited the Wilderness Waterway into Florida Bay, the water was only a few feet deep. That slowed the final leg to Flamingo. Finally, under the bridge of the main park road from the Coe Park entry in Florida City, some thirty-eight miles northeast. It had been some hours since they had departed from the Shark River Chickee.

48

WHERE THE HELL HAVE YOU BEEN, Daniels?" Haskins asked outside the police station in Homestead. "C'mon, let's get some chow. I'm hungry as hell. There's a good place across the street."

After they sat down, Haskins grinned and said, "I was really hopin' you'd got lost an' were eaten by alligators. Of course, they'd spit you out," he said with a smile. "Don't like Yankee meat very much. But then again, you might have convinced them you're a Miccosukee."

"Your sense of humor remains as atrocious as your accent," Allan countered.

"Yeah, well, I've got somethin' to tell you," Haskins said, turning serious. "All things considered, you were damn good in there. Tougher than I thought you'd be. An' you learn pretty good, too." He hesitated, then added with a smile, "Hate to admit this. I sure as hell can't figure out why, but I've also gotten to like you, believe it or not!"

Allan looked pleased. "It damn well wouldn't have worked out the way it did if you hadn't been there, that's for sure."

"I hope you're right about that boy," Haskins said. "Maybe between you an' Osceola — plus a stint in the hoosegow — Tommy'll make a turnaround."

"What kind of time will he have to do?"

"Can't tell. Maybe ten years, possibly out in three. Depends."

"I plan to write him and see him. Also visit Jimmy Osceola."

Allan put down a ten-dollar bill and got up from the table. "Look, I have to make some calls. Give me a few minutes. I can drive you over in my rental to where your truck is parked, then get a plane out of Naples."

Haskins said, "I'll work out somethin' with the rangers to take the boat back up. Or one of the sheriffs I know."

Allan called home. No answer. He decided to call again later. Then he called his office. Leo briefed him on the situation with the firm's clients.

"Thanks, Leo. I'll be back in the office most likely Wednesday. Sounds like you're doing a great job."

He made a third call. "Sue, Allan. I just wanted to let you know how it came out."

"Oh, Allan. I've been worried. Where are you?"

"Homestead." He took a deep breath. "It's a long story. I'll give you the short version."

"I'm glad it's finally over, that you're all right," Sue said.

"And you?" Allan asked.

"Me? Writing a bushel, playing some tennis. The publisher wants me to do a rewrite."

There was a long silence. Allan looked outside the phone booth. No one was waiting. "Sue, can people like us . . . can we continue as friends?"

"You've shown me about not giving up, and about how a person can change," she responded. "Good-bye, Allan, my dear friend. All good things."

"Sue?"

"Yes?"

"Send me a copy of your book." He hesitated. "No, tell me when it's published, and I'll buy a dozen copies. Better yet, tell me where you'll be reading, and I'll come by and have you sign them."

"Promise?"

"I swear. On my mother's Miccosukee head!"

49

ALLAN AND HASKINS DROVE halfway across the Florida peninsula on Route 41, the Tamiami Trail, pulling over at the Miccosukee village. "I want to look around for a few minutes, use the phone, see what's here," Allan said. "Hey, Sheriff, go buy yourself some Indian medicine. Might make a new man out of you."

Haskins just shook his head.

"If I can get a plane," Allan said on the phone to Joyce, "I'll be home either late today or tomorrow. I can't wait."

"I'm glad you're all right," she said. "What happened?"

Allan told her about the trip with Haskins, meeting Tigertail in Everglades City, their time with Osceola, that Tommy wasn't dead—that he would be going to jail.

"No more albatross around my neck. Tommy and I are both Miccosukee. I'm going to try to get him rehabilitated, come back for visits. You and the kids. Mom and Dad, also. Meet her family. They're mine, too. But before anything or anyone else, Joyce, I want you to know *you* will always come first. There's more between us than I ever realized."

There was silence on the line.

"Joyce?"

"Yes."

"I've been thinking about your suggestion I go into therapy. I've been afraid of what I might find."

"It will make all the difference," she said. "You've become open to change. And I feel good about our chances. You've already changed. I like it. And I can do some changing, too."

♦ ♦ ♦

Allan found a flight that was leaving at eight that evening. Over dinner, Haskins told Allan he needed to have him sign some statements but would send them to Long Island.

"Now, Daniels," Haskins said finally at the airport, "get the hell out of here. I'm damn tired of lookin' at your Yankee face."

"Good-bye, ya big lug. I'm planning to bring my family down. I want them to meet you — so you can scare them. My mother will take us around and show us all her — our — places."

"That'll be fine. The next time you decide to ferry a plane down, call me so I can catch you when you fall."

"Strange the way it's all gone," Allan said pensively. "I never expected it would come out like this. Especially with you. Osceola said nothing is an accident. *Hishuk-ish-ts' awalk.* Everything is one . . ." He looked away for a moment. "I believe that. In any case, I want you to know how much I appreciate everything you've done for me. Norm Seltzer said you're the best man in Islamorada. He's right. They're lucky to have you. So am I."

Haskins reached out his hand, then opened both arms. They hugged, patting each other on the back.

"Thanks again, Sheriff," Allan said, turning for his gate.

Haskins nodded, smiling, and shouted back, "Hey, Allan, you can start callin' me Billy."

The Everglades — in raised memories, a rich garden, a place of secrets, vast and not unlike a universe of its own. Remembered in thought and feeling, trials endured, from which trust and strength developed.

50

ALLAN AND JOYCE WERE LYING ON THEIR BED, his arm behind her head. A quiet moment that comes with intimacy, a moment when sex and love merge, when oneness infuses body and mind, moments when everything else fades away.

"Hmmm," Joyce mumbled. "I could really get used to this. I wish you could see yourself. What a face."

But she also sensed something was missing. And she thought she knew what it was. "Want to talk about it?"

"Talk about what?" He looked over at her. "This was — nothing could — I love you very much."

"Yes, I know you do. I don't mean *this*."

"It's only been weeks since I've been back. There's catching up to do. You, the kids, my practice."

"I didn't mean therapy either. You're doing fine, but something's missing," she said, sitting up.

"I don't know what you're talking about."

"It has something to do with Tommy. His effect on you."

Allan sat up, too, silent for a while. "It shook me up . . . going down in the Everglades, what happened with Tommy, then going back, how it ended." She put her hand on his.

"I will never again deny my heritage," he continued. "It smacked me square in the face. All these years of never letting it be part of me. The Miccosukees in another world."

"Except your mother," Joyce said. "You've become more sensitized, Allan. It makes you more . . . attractive to me. And to others."

"I rejected what she tried to teach me."

"Once she got over her shock about what happened, she was

very pleased. She told me the other day how happy she was about your interest in her people."

"I'm going to take her to lunch, make sure she knows," Allan said, as Joyce kissed him on his cheek. "I want to talk some more . . . I'll get some coffee. The kids are still asleep."

He returned several minutes later, put the coffee carafe and two mugs on the table near the window, and sat on a bergère chair. Joyce sat on another.

"You know, you're gorgeous," he stated.

"Nice to hear that *after.* Men usually tell women things like that to get them to . . . open up."

"OK, from now on, I'll tell you before *and* after!" he said, shaking his head. "And you can tell me how beautiful I am, too."

He sipped his coffee and gazed outside. Rain bathed the lawn, preparing it for spring.

"I need to go see Tommy," he said. "In a couple of weeks."

"Yes, you should. But you shouldn't feel you're doing penance. You should not feel any guilt."

"There's some of that. But it's also accepting who I am."

"I'd say the same thing if you denied being Jewish."

"Which reminds me, what about Hebrew school for the kids? We'll have to join a temple."

"Think we can find a congregation that doesn't mind American Indians?" she asked.

"Yeah," he laughed. "There's bound to be at least one. Otherwise, I'll start one. Maybe get Bob to convert. Unlikely. His family goes back to the *Mayflower* . . . As a matter of fact, he's got a little Cherokee in him. Sister's name is Quana. But there are three Jewish Indians with Nance, Craig, and me. That's a start, white woman. Watch out!"

"Don't forget your mother, wiseass. She converted, but she's still Indian."

Allan grimaced.

The next morning, Allan left for the office earlier than usual, driving into the Roslyn Village park, at the bottom of a small valley. He walked to a familiar bench on the edge of the largest pond and sat, the lone person in the early morning. Daffodils, their yellow taken from the sun, lay in wait. The pond, caressed by the wind, emptied onto an old wooden water wheel that scooped water into a tiny stream feeding into Roslyn Harbor. A swan roosted on her nest, set back against the tall reeds, while the mist lifted off the water.

How best to manage his responsibilities and also see Tommy? He had decided to talk to Jimmy Osceola and meet some of the tribal leaders, discuss how he might help them improve the lives of the tribe members on and off the reservation. Especially the children. One of the centerpieces had to be better education. They also needed to record their stories and write an in-depth history of their culture and languages.

Allan felt a strong pull to become part of the change. He wanted to make a difference, contributing his training as an architect. But it would take time, and right now there wasn't any extra.

I'll visit once a month, he thought. *It'll be a beginning.*

51

THE SECRETARY REFERRED ALLAN to the Inmates' Visitors Department, which took his name and said they would get back. They didn't. He called again. It became an exercise in frustration. Red tape was the official policy. Then he had his attorney call and advise the warden's office of the legalities involved.

On a pleasant April afternoon, he checked in at the front gate of the Loxahatchee Road Prison in Palm Beach County. A series of checkpoints brought him to the bare visitor's room, where he was assigned a seat at a desk. A young guard stood next to him, reeking of body odor.

"Look," Allan said, "I'm not smuggling anything in. Can't we have a little privacy? I've been searched twice."

"The rules, man. I don't make 'em."

Allan shook his head in frustration. Older women sat talking to men, some their age, some much younger. Young women, a few with infants, also huddled closely with prisoners. *Mothers, wives, and girlfriends*, he thought.

Ten minutes later, Tommy came in, handcuffed. He didn't acknowledge Allan as he sat down, his lips tightening, his eyes narrowing.

"Hi," Allan said. No response. "So, how's it going?"

Then Tommy exploded. "Why the fuck are you here? I don't need anyone visitin'. Especially you. When they told me someone was here, I supposed it'd be Jimmy. Shit, *you.* How's it goin'? Shitty. Like last time. Another rat hole."

"Think of this as part of the deal," Allan said. "Start with, you know, you did something wrong . . . Say you capture a baby alligator. The mother comes after you. She wants you to pay the price.

Well, you *did* do something wrong. Now you gotta serve time. But it comes to an end. Good behavior, you're out in three years."

"Five-fuckin'-year sentence," Tommy said, not listening. "Too goddamn long. I'll go fuckin' crazy, locked up. Shit, I'm used to bein' free. In my 'glades."

"I can help you out while you're doing time. How to manage. Make things, get into some books. You'll do better out there. One thing to live like you did when you're young, another when you get older. Think about it. That girl you have on the reservation—or someone like her. Serve your time, get out. Osceola and I will find you something, a job. Raise a family. Be a father. One like you wish you had."

Tommy didn't say anything. Time was up. Allan put out his hand, which Tommy did not take.

"I'll be back soon. Every month, OK? My kids want me to send you some games, books, food. All right?"

"OK," Tommy muttered, shuffling toward the prisoners' door.

It became a pattern. Three or four weeks on Long Island, a few days in Florida. More and more, Allan enjoyed being closer to Tommy, Osceola, and the tribe. But it split him.

Maybe it was an old habit, looking at land ads in the Sunday real-estate section of the *New York Times.* He and Joyce were sitting in their library, perusing the paper as they did most Sunday mornings, especially during inclement weather like today's. The kids were playing hide and seek.

Allan didn't notice it right away, but one of the ads struck him. "Beautiful, .75 acre. Old trees. On lake. Fully developed. Builder's own piece. Must sell. Asking $270,000. Brokers invited."

Call, he thought, *take a look next week. Maybe we . . . You never know . . . hard to move, start anew. . . if she's even willing. . . could always build a spec house.*

♦ ♦ ♦

"Look," the owner said on the phone, "I'll be honest with you. The only reason I'm selling is because I'm going up to North Carolina. Better opportunities up there."

The phrase *I'll be honest with you* usually meant anything but. "It's the best piece in all of Broward County." Allan held his tongue. Let him squirm and see what happens. "Tell you what. You can have it for two-fifty. How's that sound?"

"Not so sure," Allan said evenly. "There are other pieces that I think are better and at a lower price."

"Have you seen this one?"

"Yeah. Walked it last week. It's OK, but your price is too high."

"I might go two-thirty-five. That's the bottom."

"Two-twenty-five. Ten percent refundable on contract, held in escrow by an attorney. Three weeks' due diligence. A survey — topo, if you have one — everything on utilities, a title report, *and* an appraisal."

"I think you should be willing to drop ten thousand if you don't take it after all that."

"No way. And there's no broker."

"All right, but no purchase money mortgage. All cash on title. If you've got decent credit, you can probably get a seventy-percent building loan. You can talk to my bank."

"I'll let you know about that."

The developer promised to have his lawyer draw up a contract.

52

I'VE BEEN THINKING," Allan said after dinner.

"I can tell," Joyce said. "You've got that look in your eye."

"How about . . ." He cleared his throat. "How about a new house, home . . . in Florida. Plenty of neurotics down there who need your help, great schools, and clients for me."

"What have you been smoking?"

"I know. It would mean a whole new life. New friends. A sea change for the kids."

"Absolutely ridiculous," she said, walking into the library, Allan trailing her. "We've finally arrived. Our work—we're established. After all these years. Plus our parents are up here. I don't even want to *consider* moving."

Allan took a deep breath. "You're absolutely right. Long Island's fine. But there's nothing wrong with change. You've always talked about how important change is, how it keeps us vibrant and enterprising."

"Do you even know what you're suggesting? I know you'd like to be closer to the reservation and that jail, but it's out of the question. Forget it."

But Allan didn't. Over the next week, he argued how it could work. Joyce listened and each time shook her head.

"At least take a look. No commitment, just look!"

The Delta airliner from Islip landed on time at the Fort Lauderdale airport. Allan and Joyce drove to Tamarac, through downtown, past the country club, churches, and a small synagogue. The property lay at the end of a small but very attractive development.

A large blue heron had taken a stance at the edge of the lake.

Breezes shuddered first through the live oaks and then across the water. In the west, clouds were forming. Virga rain came down from one of them, and on the horizon the crested umbrella of blue-white lightning opened.

Joyce entwined her fingers around his and shook her head. Then she looked up at him, smiled, and squeezed his hand.

EPILOGUE

FATE, IF THAT'S WHAT YOU CALL IT, represents the inevitable. It is full of surprises and harbingers that are not always recognizable. But its striking confluence of mysterious circumstances can become fact. Devoid of any judgment or compromise or emotion, it simply becomes a new reality.